VAL McDERMID

Val McDermid grew up in a Scottish mining community then read English at Oxford. She was a journalist for sixteen years, spending the last three years as Northern Bureau Chief of a national Sunday tabloid. Now a full-time writer, she lives in Cheshire.

Clean Break is the fourth of six novels featuring Kate Brannigan. The third, *Crack Down*, was shortlisted for the Crime Writers' Association Gold Dagger Award in 1994.

Val is also the author of three tense psychological thrillers featuring criminal profiler Tony Hill. The first of these, *The Mermaids Singing*, was awarded the 1995 Gold Dagger Award for Best Crime Novel of the Year, while the second, *The Wire in the Blood*, lends its name to the acclaimed ITV series featuring Robson Green as Tony Hill. She has also written two stand-alone thrillers, *Killing the Shadows* and *A Place of Execution*, and five novels featuring journalist-sleuth Lindsay Gordon.

By the same author

The Last Temptation
The Wire in the Blood
The Mermaids Singing

The Distant Echo
Killing the Shadows
A Place of Execution

Kate Brannigan Novels

Star Struck
Blue Genes
Crack Down
Kick Back
Dead Beat

Lindsay Gordon Novels

Hostage to Murder
Booked for Murder
Union Jack
Final Edition
Common Murder
Report for Murder

Non-fiction

A Suitable Job for a Woman

VAL McDERMID

Clean Break

HarperCollins*Publishers*

HarperCollins*Publishers*
77–85 Fulham Palace Road
London W6 8JB

The HarperCollins website address is:
www.**fire**and**water**.com

First published in Great Britain by
HarperCollins*Publishers* 1995

This edition 2011

ISBN 978-0-00-789274-7

Typeset in Meridien by Palimpsest Book Production Limited,
Polmont, Stirlingshire

Printed and bound Great Britain by
Clays Ltd, St Ives plc

ACKNOWLEDGEMENTS

The usual gang all let me pick their brains to make this a better and more accurate book than it would otherwise have been – Coop, Uncle Lee, BB, Paula, Jai, Brother Brian, Lisanne and Jane, and Julia. I also scrounged assistance from Frankie Hegarty, Fairy Baillie and Diana Muir. Don't blame them if you spot any mistakes. To anyone who recognizes where we went on our holidays – my heartfelt sympathies.

To Chelsea fans everywhere,
in deepest sympathy;
God knows, you need something to
cheer you up.

1

I don't know much about art, but I know what I don't like. I don't like paintings that go walkabout after I've set up the security system. I especially don't like them when I've packed my business partner off to the Antipodes for two months with the calm assurance that I can handle things while he's gone.

The painting in question was a small Monet. When I say small, I mean in size, not in value. It would barely cover the hole my lover Richard punched in the wall of his living room in a moment of drunken ecstasy when Eric Cantona clinched the double for Manchester United, but it was worth a good dozen times as much as both our adjoining bungalows put together. Which, incidentally, they never will be. The painting depicted an apple tree in blossom and not a lot else. You could tell it was an apple tree; according to our office manager Shelley, that's because it was painted quite early on in Monet's career, before his eyesight

1

began to go and his whole world started to look like an Impressionist painting. Imagine, a whole artistic movement emanating from one bloke's duff eyesight. Amazing what you can learn from the Open University. Shelley started a degree course last year, and what she doesn't know about the history of art I'm certainly not qualified to uncover. It's not one of the course options in Teach Yourself Private Dicking.

The Monet in question, called, imaginatively enough, *Apple Tree in Blossom*, belonged to Henry Naismith, Lord of the Manor of Birchfield with Polver. Henry to his friends, and, thanks to John Major's classless society, to mere tradespeople like me. There were no airs and graces with Henry, but that didn't mean he didn't hide his thoughts and feelings behind his charming façade. That's how I knew it was serious when I picked up the phone to his perfect vowels that September morning. 'Kate? Henry Naismith,' he started. I leaned back in my chair, expecting the usual cheery chat about his recent exploits before we got down to the nuts and bolts. Not today. 'Can you come over to the house?' he asked.

I straightened up. This sounded like the kind of start to a Monday morning that makes me wish I'd stayed in bed. 'When did you have in mind, Henry?'

'As soon as you can. We ah . . . we had a burglary in the night and a chap from the police is popping round for more details. He'll want to know things about the security system that I probably won't be able to answer, and I'd be awfully grateful if you could take a run over.' All this barely pausing for breath, never mind giving me the opportunity to ask questions.

I didn't have to check the diary to know that I had nothing more pressing than routine inquiries into the whereabouts of a company chairman whose directors were rather eager to ask him some questions about the balance sheet. 'No problem,' I said. 'What's missing?' I prayed it was going to be the TV and the video.

No such luck. There was silence on the end of the phone. I thought I could hear Henry drawing in a deep breath. 'The Monet,' he said tersely.

My stomach clenched. Birchfield Place was the first security system I'd designed and watched installed. My partner Bill Mortensen is the security expert, and he'd checked my work, but it was still down to me. 'I'm leaving now,' I said.

I drove out through the southern suburbs to the motorway on automatic pilot. Even the inevitable, ubiquitous roadworks didn't impinge. I was too busy reviewing Mortensen and Brannigan's involvement with Henry Naismith. When I'd seen his original appointment in the office diary, I'd thought Shelley was at the wind-up, especially since I'd been having one of my periodic anti-monarchy rants only the day before, triggered by the heir to the throne asserting that what was wrong with the country was not enough

Shakespeare and smacking of small children. Once I realized the appointment was for real, I'd expected some chinless wonder with the sort of inbred stupidity that's only found among the aristocracy and the population of isolated mountain villages. I couldn't have been more wrong, on both counts.

Henry Naismith was in his late twenties, built like an Australian lifeguard with the blonde hair to match and with more than enough chin to provide a boxer with a target. According to *Who's Who*, his only listed recreations were sailing and ocean yacht racing, something I could have guessed for myself the first time I saw him. He had sailor's eyes, always looking beyond me to some distant horizon only he could see. His face was burnished a ruddy brown by wind and sun, apart from the white creases round those dark blue eyes. He'd been educated at Marlborough and New College, Oxford. Even though I'd grown up there, I didn't think his city of dreaming spires and mine of car factories would give us much in common to reminisce about. He had the same clipped accent as Prince Charles, but in spite of that and everything else, I liked him. I liked anybody who was prepared to get off their backsides and graft. And Henry could graft, no messing. Anyone who tells you yacht racing is a holiday doesn't know an anchor from a wanker.

The newspaper archive database that we use had coloured in the outline. Henry had inherited his title, a black and white Tudor manor house in

Cheshire, a clutch of valuable paintings and not a lot of readies a couple of years before when his parents had been caught in an avalanche in some chic Alpine resort. Henry had been sailing in the Caribbean at the time. Life's a bitch, and then you marry one. Only Henry hadn't. Married, that is. He was right up there in the gossip columnists' lists of eligible bachelors. Maybe not in the top twenty, on account of the lack of dosh, but the good looks and the tasty gaff put him in the running nevertheless.

Henry had come to us precisely because of the serious deficiencies in the cashflow area. Because his father hadn't anticipated dying at the age of forty-seven, he hadn't got round to the sort of arrangements the landed gentry usually make to avoid the Exchequer getting their mitts on the widow's mite. Having done his sums, Henry realized the only way he was going to be able to hang on to the house and the art collection and still spend half the year at the helm of a racing yacht was to bite the bullet and open Birchfield Place to the day-trippers.

The great British public are notoriously sticky-fingered on the stately home circuit. You wouldn't think it to look at the coach-loads of little old ladies that roll up on bank holidays, but they'll walk off with anything that isn't actually nailed down, and one or two things that are. This makes insurance companies even more twitchy than usual when it comes to providing cover, which in turn makes the security business a nice little earner for private investigation agencies like us. These days, security makes up about a quarter of our annual turnover, which is why Bill and I had decided I needed to learn that side of the business.

It's impossible to make any building impregnable, unless you brick up the doors and windows, which makes it hard to get a decent light to do your petit point. The best you can do is make it obvious that you've made it as hard as possible to get in, so the prospective burglar goes away discouraged and turns over the next manor down the road. To make sure I got it right, as well as picking Bill's brains I'd consulted my old friend Dennis, himself a recovering burglar. 'You know the one deterrent, Brannigan?' Dennis had demanded.

'Heat-seeking thermonuclear missiles?' I'd hazarded.

'A dog. You get a big Alsatian, give him the run of the place and your professional thief doesn't want to know. When I was at it, there wasn't an alarm system in the world that I wouldn't have a pop at. But dogs? Forget it.'

Unfortunately, clients aren't too keen on having Rottweilers running around on their priceless Oriental carpets. They're too worried about finding dog hairs – or worse – on the Hepplewhite. So Birchfield Place had relied, like most stately homes, on a state-of-the-art mix of hard-wired detectors on doors and windows, passive infrared detectors at all key points and pressure-activated alert pads in front of any items of significance. Given the fail-safes I'd put in place, I couldn't for the life of me see how anyone could have got through my system undetected without setting off enough bells to drive Quasimodo completely round the twist.

I turned off the motorway and headed into the depths of the leafy Cheshire stockbroker, soap star and football player belt. As usual, I almost missed the gap in the tall hedgerow that marked the end of Birchfield Place's drive. The trippers' entrance was round the back, but I had no intention of parking in a field half a mile from the house. I yanked the wheel round just in time and turned on to a narrow ribbon of road curling between fields where placid sheep didn't even glance up from their chewing as I passed. I always feel slightly edgy out in the country; I don't know the names of anything and very quickly develop anxiety about where my next meal is coming from. Give me an urban landscape where no sensible sheep would think for even a fleeting moment it might safely graze. The field gave way to thick coppices of assorted trees that looked like they'd been on the planet longer than my Granny Brannigan. Then, suddenly, the drive took a sharp right-hand bend and I shot out of the trees to a full frontal view of Birchfield Place.

Built by some distant Naismith who had done some unmentionable service to his monarch, the house looked as if it should be on a postcard or a jigsaw. The passage of time had skewed its black beams and white panels just enough to make sure no self-respecting building society would grant you a mortgage on it. It never looked real to me.

I pulled up beside an anonymous Ford which I assumed belonged to the police on account of the radio. A peacock screamed in the distance, more shattering to my composure than any amount of midnight sirens. I only knew it was a peacock because Henry had told me the first time one had made me jump out of my skin. Before I could reach out for the ancient bell-pull, the door swung open and Henry smiled apologetically at me. 'I really appreciate this, Kate,' he said.

'All part of the service,' I said reassuringly. 'The police here?'

'An Inspector Mellor from the Art Squad,' Henry said as he led the way across the inner courtyard to the Great Hall, where the Impressionist paintings hung incongruously. 'He doesn't say much.'

We passed through the Hall Porch, whose solid oak door looked like it had taken a few blows from a heavy sledge-hammer. At the door of the Great Hall, I put out a hand to delay Henry. 'So what exactly happened?'

Henry rubbed his jaw. 'The alarm woke me. Just before three, according to the clock. I checked the main panel. It said Hall Porch, Great Hall door, Great Hall and pressure pads. I phoned the police to confirm it wasn't a false alarm, and ran downstairs. When I got to the hall, there was nobody in sight and the Monet was gone. They must have been in and out again in less than five minutes.' He sighed. 'They obviously knew what they were looking for.'

'Didn't the beeper on the courtyard security lights waken you?' I asked, puzzled.

Henry looked sheepish. 'I turned the beeper off. We've been having a bit of a problem with foxes, and I got fed up with being wakened up night after night.' I said nothing. I hoped the look on my face said it for me. 'I know, I know,' Henry said. 'I don't think Inspector Mellor's overly impressed either. Shall we?'

I followed him into the hall. It was a surprisingly bright room for the period. It was two storeys high, with a whitewashed vaulted roof and gallery for Blondel unplugged. The wall that gave on to the inner courtyard had a couple of feet of wood panelling above floor level, then it was hundreds of tiny leaded panes of glass to a height of about eight feet. The outer wall's panelling was about four feet high before it gave way to more windows. I didn't envy the window cleaner. At the far end was a raised dais where Henry's distant ancestors had sat and lorded it over the plebs and railed against the iniquities of the window tax. It was around the dais that the paintings hung. A tall, thin man was stooped like a crane over the space where the Monet used to be. As we entered, he turned towards us and fixed me with a glum stare.

Henry performed the introductions while Inspector Mellor and I weighed each other up. He looked more patrician than Henry, with a high forehead over a beaky nose and a small, cupid's bow mouth. At his request, I ran him through the security arrangements. He nodded noncommittally as he listened, then said, 'Not a lot more you could have done, short of having CCTV.'

'Professional job, yeah?' I said.

'No doubt about it. They obviously chose their target, cased the place thoroughly, then did a quick in and out. No identifiable forensic traces, according to my colleagues who turned up after the event.' Mellor looked as depressed as I felt.

'Does it put you in mind of anyone in particular?' I asked.

Mellor shrugged. 'I've seen jobs like this, but we haven't managed an arrest on any of them yet.'

Henry closed his eyes and sighed. 'Is there any chance of getting my Monet back?' he asked wearily.

'If I'm honest, sir, not a lot. Thieves like this only take what they've already got a market for,' Mellor said. 'Sooner or later, we'll get a lucky break and we'll nail them. It could be on this case. What I'd like to do is send a couple of my lads over when your staff are next in. These thieves will have been round the house more than once. It's just possible one of your attendants noticed repeat visitors.'

'They'll be in at half past nine on Thursday,' Henry said. 'The house is closed to the public on Mondays, Tuesdays and Wednesdays, excepting bank holidays.'

Mellor turned away and spent a few minutes

10

studying the Boudin, the Renoir and the two Pissarros that flanked the space where the Monet had been. 'Personally,' he said softly, 'I'd have gone for the Boudin.'

Not me. The Monet would have looked much better with my colour scheme. But maybe Inspector Mellor's living room was blue-based rather than green, cream and peach. While Henry escorted Mellor off the premises, I mooched around the hall, wondering what to do next. Mellor's plan to interrogate the staff had disposed of the only idea I had for pursuing any kind of investigation. I slumped in the attendant's chair by the door and stared down the hall at the wires sticking out of the ancient panelling where the Monet had been attached to the alarm system and the wall. Inspiration failed to strike; but then, nothing does in this country any more.

When Henry came back, I forced myself upright and said brightly, 'Well, Henry, Mellor didn't sound too optimistic about what the forces of law and order can achieve. Looks like it's down to me to get your Monet back.'

Henry tugged at the lobe of his ear and looked uncomfortable. 'Is there much point, Kate?' he asked. 'I mean, if the specialists don't know where to start looking, how can you expect to succeed?'

'People have a tendency to tell me things they don't necessarily want to share with the police. And that includes insurance companies. I also have more unorthodox sources of information.

I'm sure I can develop leads the police will never encounter.' It was all true. Well, all except the last sentence.

'I don't know, Kate. These are professional thieves. Looking at the state of the porch door, they're clearly quite comfortable with a considerable degree of violence. I'm not sure I'm entirely happy about you pursuing them,' he said dubiously.

'Henry, I might only be five foot three, but I can look after myself,' I said, trying not to think about the last occasion where I'd told the men in my life the same damn lie. The scar on my head was just a distant twinge when I brushed my hair now, but the scar inside went a lot deeper. I hadn't exactly lost my bottle; I'd just acquired an overdose of wariness.

'Besides,' I carried on, seeing his look of frank disbelief, 'you're entitled to the first thirty hours of my time for free, according to your contract.'

'Ah. Yes. Of course.' His reserve was nailed firmly in place again, the eyes locked on the middle distance.

'Apart from anything else, me nosing around will convince your insurance company that you're not trying it on,' I added.

His eyes narrowed, like a man who's seen a bloody great wave heading straight for his bows. 'Why should they think that?' he said sharply.

'It wouldn't be the first time somebody's set up their own burglary for the insurance,' I said. 'It happens all the time round where I live.' A frown flickered across Henry's face. 'There's nothing you want to tell me, Henry, is there?' I added apprehensively.

'There's no earthly reason why I should arrange this,' he said stiffly. 'The police and the insurance company are welcome to check the books. We're making a profit here. House admissions are up on last year, the gift shop has increased its turnover by twenty-five per cent and the Great Hall is booked for banquets almost every Saturday between now and February. The only thing I'm concerned about is that I'm due to leave for Australia in three weeks and I'd like the matter resolved by then.'

'I'd better get weaving, in that case,' I said mildly.

I drove back to Manchester with a lot on my mind. I don't like secrets. It's one of the reasons I became a private eye in the first place. I especially don't like them when they're ones my client is keeping from me.

2

The atrium of Fortissimus Insurance told me all I needed to know about where Henry's massive premiums were going. The company had relocated in Manchester from the City, doubtless tempted by the wodges of cash being handed out by various inner city initiative programmes. They'd opted for a site five minutes' walk down Oxford Road from the rather less palatial offices of Mortensen and Brannigan. Handy, we'd thought, if they ever needed any freelance investigating, though if they had done, it hadn't been our door they'd come knocking on. They probably preferred firms with the same steel-and-glass taste in interior decor, and prices to match.

Like a lot of new office complexes in Manchester, Fortissimus had smacked a brand new modern building behind a grandiose Victorian façade. In their case, they'd acquired the front of what had been a rather grand hotel, its marble and granite buffed to a shine more sparkling than its native century had ever seen. The entrance hall retained some of the original character, but the glassed-in atrium beyond the security desk was one hundred per cent *fin de* quite another *siècle*. The pair of receptionists had clearly absorbed their customer care course. Their grooming was immaculate, their smiles would have made a crocodile proud, and the mid-Atlantic twang in their 'Good morning, how may I help you?' stopped short of making my ears bleed. Needless to say, they were as misleading as the building's façade. After I'd given them my card, asked for Michael Haroun and told them his department, I still had to kick my heels for ten minutes while they ran their debriefing on the weekend's romantic encounters, rang Mr Haroun, filled out a visitor's pass and told me Mr Haroun would be waiting for me at the lift.

I emerged on the fifth floor to find they'd been economical with the truth. There was no Mr Haroun, and no one behind the desk marked 'Claims Inquiries' either. Before I could decide which direction to head in, a door down the hallway opened and someone backed out, saying, 'And I want to compare those other cases. Karen, dig out the files, there's a love.'

He swivelled round on the balls of his feet and *déjà vu* swept over me. Confused, I just stood and stared as he walked towards me. When he got closer, he held out his hand and said, 'Ms Brannigan? Michael Haroun.'

For a moment, I was speechless and paralysed.

I must have been gawping like a starving goldfish, for he frowned and said, 'You are Ms Brannigan?' Then, suspicion appeared in his liquid sloe eyes. 'What's the matter? Am I not what you expected? I can assure you, I am head of the claims division.'

Power returned to my muscles and I hurriedly reached out and shook his hand. 'Sorry,' I stammered. 'Yes, I . . . Sorry, you're the spitting image of . . . somebody,' I stumbled on. 'I was just taken aback, that's all.'

He gave me a look that told me he'd already decided I was either a racist pig or I didn't have all my chairs at home. His smile was strained as he said, 'I didn't realize I had a doppelgänger. Shall we go through to my office and talk?'

Wordlessly, I nodded and followed his broad shoulders back down the hall. He moved like a man who played a lot of sport. It wasn't hard to imagine him in the same role as I'd first seen his likeness.

When I was about fourteen, we'd gone on a school trip to the British Museum. I'd been so engrossed in the Rosetta Stone, I'd got separated from the rest of the group and wandered round for ages looking for them. That's how I stumbled on the Assyrian bas-reliefs. As soon as I saw them, I understood for the first time in my life that it wasn't entirely bullshit when critics said that great art speaks directly to us. These enormous carvings of the lion hunt didn't so much speak as resonate inside my chest like the bass note of an organ. I fell in love with the archers and the charioteers, their shoulder-length hair curled as tight as poodle fur, their profiles keen as sparrowhawks. I must have spent an hour there that day. Every time I went to London on shopping trips after that, I always found an excuse to slip away from my mates as they trawled Oxford Street so I could nip to the museum for a quick tryst with King Ashurbanipal. If Aslan had come along and breathed life into the carving of the Assyrian king, he would have walked off the wall looking just like Michael Haroun, his glowing skin the colour of perfect roast potatoes. OK, so he'd swapped the tunic for a Paul Smith shirt, Italian silk tie and chinos, but you don't make much progress up the corporate ladder wearing a mini-skirt unless you're a woman. Just one look at Michael Haroun and I was an adoring adolescent all over again, Richard a distant memory.

I followed Haroun meekly into his office. The opulence of the atrium hadn't quite made it this high. The furniture was functional rather than designed to impress. At least he overlooked the recently renovated Rochdale Canal (European funding), though the view of the Canal Café must have been a depressing reminder of the rest of the world enjoying itself while he was working. We settled down on the L-shaped sofa at right angles to each other, my adolescent urge to jump on him held in check by the low coffee table between us. Haroun dumped the file he'd been carrying on the table. 'I hear good things about your agency, Ms Brannigan,' he said. From his tone, I gathered he couldn't quite square what he'd heard with my moonstruck gaze.

I forced myself to get a grip and remember I was twice the age of that romantic teenager. 'You've obviously been talking to the clients who haven't been burgled,' I said in something approaching my normal voice.

'No security system is burglar-proof,' he said gloomily.

'But some are better than others. And ours are better than most.'

'That's certainly how it looked when we first agreed the premium. It's one of the factors we consider when we set the rate. That and how high-risk the area is.'

'You don't have to tell me. My postcode is M13,' I complained.

He pulled a face and sucked his breath in sharply, the way plumbers are trained to do when they look at your central heating system. 'And I thought you security consultants made a good living.'

'It's not all a hellhole,' I said sharply.

He held his hands up and grinned. I felt the years slide away again and struggled to stay in the present. 'Henry Naismith called to say you'd be coming in. He faxed me a preliminary claim,' he said.

'I'm investigating the theft on Henry's behalf, and he thought it might be helpful if we had a chat,' I said briskly.

'My pleasure,' he said. 'Of course, one of our staff investigators will also be looking into it, but I see no reason why we can't talk to you as well. Can you run it past me?'

I went through everything I'd learned from Henry and Inspector Mellor. Haroun took notes. 'Just as a matter of interest,' I finished up, 'Inspector Mellor mentioned they'd had other burglaries with a similar style. Were any of them insured with you?'

Haroun nodded. 'Yes, unfortunately. Off the top of my head, I'd say three others in the last nine months. And that's where we have a problem.'

'We as in you and me, or we as in Fortissimus?'

'We as in Mr Naismith and Fortissimus.'

'Does that mean you're not going to tell me about it?'

Haroun stared down at the file. 'Client confidentiality. You should understand that.'

'I wouldn't be here if Henry didn't trust me. Why don't you give him a call and confirm that you can tell me anything you would tell him? That way, I get it from the horse's mouth rather than via Chinese whispers.'

His straight brows twitched. 'Even if he agreed, it wouldn't be fair of me to have the conversation with you before I have it with him.'

'So get Henry over. I don't mind waiting.' As long as I can keep looking at you, I added mentally.

Haroun inclined his head, conceding. 'I'll call him,' he said.

He was gone for the best part of ten minutes. Instead of fishing a computer magazine out of my shoulder bag, or dictating a report into my micro-cassette recorder, I daydreamed. What about is nobody's business but mine.

When Haroun came back, he looked serious. 'I've explained the situation to Mr Naismith, and he was quite insistent that I should discuss the ramifications with you.'

I was too well brought up to say, 'I told you so,' but according to Richard I've cornered the market in smug smiles. I hoped I wasn't displaying one of them right then. 'So, tell me about it,' I said, locking eyes.

Haroun held my gaze for a long few seconds before turning back to his file. 'As I said, we've had other incidents very similar to this. These thefts have all been from similar properties – medium-sized period properties that are open to the public. In each case, the thieves have broken in as near to the target as they could get. In a couple of cases, they've smashed through a window, but in a property like Birchfield Place, that obviously wasn't appropriate. They ignore the alarms, go straight to the object they're after, whip it off the wall or out of its case and get out. We estimate the longest they've been inside a property is five minutes. In most cases, that's barely enough time to alert the police or the security guards, never mind get anyone to the site.'

'Very professional,' I commented. 'And?'

'We're very unhappy about it. It's costing us a lot of money. Normally, we'd simply have to bite the bullet and increase premiums accordingly.'

'I hear the sound of a "but" straining at the leash,' I said.

'You have very acute hearing, Ms Brannigan.'

'Kate,' I smiled.

'Well, Kate,' he said, echoing the smile, 'here comes the "but". The first of our clients to be robbed in this way was targeted again three months later. Following that, my bosses took a policy decision that in future, after stately homes had been robbed once, we would refuse to reinsure unless and until their security was increased to an acceptable level.'

He might have looked like an ancient Assyrian, but Michael Haroun sounded exactly like a twentieth-century insurance man. We won't make a drama out of a crisis; we'll make a full-scale tragic grand opera. Pay your spiralling premiums for ten years good as gold, and then when you really need us, we'll be gone like thieves in the night. Nothing like it for killing adolescent fantasies stone dead. 'And what exactly is your definition of "an acceptable level"?' I asked, hoping he was receiving the cold sarcasm I was sending.

'Obviously, it varies from case to case.'

'In Henry's case then?'

Haroun shrugged. 'I'd have to get one of our assessors out there to make an accurate judgement.'

'Go on, stick your neck out. I know that comes as easy to an insurance man as it does to an ostrich, but give it a go.' I kept my voice light with an effort. This was my security system he was damning.

He scowled, obviously needled. 'Based on past

experience, I would suggest a security guard on a 24-hour basis in the rooms where the most valuable items are sited.'

I shook my head in disbelief. 'You really believe in getting shut of clients who have the temerity to get robbed, don't you?'

'On the contrary. We want to ensure that neither we nor our clients are exposed to unacceptable losses,' he said defensively.

'The cost of that kind of security could make the difference between profit and loss to an operation the size of Henry's. You must know that.'

Haroun spread his hands out and shrugged. 'He can always put up the admission charges if it's that crucial to the economics of running the place.'

'So you're saying that as of now Birchfield Place is uninsured?'

'No, no, you misunderstand me. But we will retain a portion of the payout on the stolen property until the security levels are rendered acceptable. Kate, we do care about our clients, but we have a business to run too, you must see that.' His eyes pleaded, and my fury melted. This was bad for my business, so I forced myself to my feet.

'We'll keep in touch,' I said.

'I'd like that,' he said, getting to his feet and nailing me with the sincerity in his voice.

As we walked back to the lift, my brain checked in again. 'One more thing,' I said. 'How come I haven't been reading about these raids in the papers?'

Haroun smiled the thin smile of a lizard. 'We like

to keep things like this as low profile as possible,' he said. 'It does our clients' business no good at all if the public gain the impression that the choicest exhibits in their collections are no longer there. The thefts have been quite widely scattered, and the policy has been only to release the information to local press, and even then to keep it very low key. You know the sort of thing: "Thieves broke in to Bloggs Manor last night, but were disturbed before they could remove the Manor's priceless collection of bottle tops."'

'You just omit to mention that they had it away on their toes with the Constable,' I said cynically.

'Something like that,' he agreed. The lift pinged and I stepped inside as the doors opened. 'Nice talking to you, Kate.'

'We must do it again some time,' I said before the doors cut him off from me. The day was looking up. Not only had I met Michael Haroun, but I knew where to go next.

I'm convinced that the security staff at the *Manchester Evening Chronicle* think I work there. Maybe it's because I know the door combination. Or maybe it's because I'm in and out of the building with a confident wave several times a week. Either way, it's handy to be able to stroll in and out at will. Their canteen is cheap and cheerful, a convenient place to refuel when I'm at the opposite end of town from the office. That day, though, I wasn't after a bacon butty and a mug of tea. My target was Alexis Lee, the

Chronicle's crime correspondent and my best buddy.

I walked briskly down the newsroom, no one paying any attention. I could probably walk off with the entire computer network before anyone would notice or try to stop me. Mind you, if I'd laid a finger on the newsdesk TV, I'd have been lynched before I'd got five yards.

I knew Alexis was at her desk. I couldn't actually see her through the wall of luxuriant foliage that surrounds her corner of the office. But the spiral of smoke climbing towards the air-conditioning vent was a clear indicator that she was there. When they installed the computer terminals at the *Chronicle*, the management tried to make the newsroom a no-smoking zone. The policy lasted about five minutes. Separating journalists from nicotine is about as easy as separating a philandering government minister from his job.

I stuck my head round the screen of variegated green stuff. Alexis was leaning back in her seat, feet propped up on the rim of her wastepaper bin, dabbing her cigarette vaguely at her mouth as she frowned at her terminal. I checked out her anarchic black hair. Its degree of chaos is a fairly accurate barometer of her stress levels. The more uptight she gets, the more she runs her hands through it. Today, it looked like I could risk interrupting her without getting a rich gobful of Scouse abuse.

'I thought they paid you to work,' I said, moving through the gap in the leaves into her jungle cubbyhole.

She swung round and grinned. 'All right, KB?' she rasped in her whisky-and-cigarettes voice.

'I think I'm in love, but apart from that, I'm fine.' I pulled up the other chair.

Alexis snorted and went into Marlene Dietrich growl. *'Falling in love again, never wanted to,'* she groaned. *'Though I'm ninety-two, I can't help it.* I've told you before, it's about time you got shut of the wimp.' She and Richard maintain this pretence of hostility. He's always giving her a bad time for being a siren chaser, and she pretends to despise him for devoting his life to the trivia of rock journalism. But underneath, I know there's a lot of affection and respect.

'Who said anything about Richard?' I asked innocently.

'And there's me thinking you two were getting things sorted out between you,' she sighed. 'So who's the lucky man? I mean, I'm assuming that you haven't seen the light, and it is a fella.'

'His name's Michael Haroun. But don't worry, it's only lust. It'll pass as soon as I have a cold shower.'

'So what does he do, this sex object?'

I pulled a face. 'You're going to laugh,' I said.

'Probably,' Alexis agreed. 'So you might as well get it over with.'

'He's in insurance.'

I'd been right. She did laugh, a deep, throaty guffaw that shook the leaves. I half expected an Amazonian parrot to fly out from among the undergrowth and join in. 'You really know how to pick them, don't you?' Alexis wheezed.

'You don't pick sex objects, they just happen,' I said frostily. 'Anyway, nothing's going to happen, so it's all academic anyway. Things between me and Richard might have seen better days, but it's nothing we can't fix.'

'So you don't want me to call Chris and get her to build a brick wall across the conservatory?'

Alexis's girlfriend Chris is the architect who designed the conservatory that runs along the back of the two houses Richard and I live in, linking them yet allowing us our own space. It had been the perfect solution for two people who want to be together but whose lifestyles are about as compatible as Burton and Taylor. 'Restrain yourself, Alexis. I'm not about to let my hormones club my brain into submission.'

'Is that it, then? You come in here, interrupting the creative process, just to tell me nothing's happening?'

'No, I only gave you the gossip so you wouldn't complain that I was only here to exploit you,' I said.

Alexis blew out a cloud of smoke and a sigh. 'All right, what do you want to know?'

'Is that any way to speak to a valued contact who's brought you a story?' I asked innocently.

Alexis tipped forward in her seat and crushed out her cigarette in an already brimming ashtray. 'Why do I have the feeling that this is the kind of gift that takes more assembling than an Airfix kit?'

3

I left Alexis to hassle the police of six counties in search of the story we both knew was lurking somewhere and headed back to Mortensen and Brannigan. Shelley was busy on the phone, so I went straight through to my office. I stopped in my tracks on the threshold. I heard Shelley finish her call and swung round to glare at her. 'What exactly is that?' I demanded.

She didn't look up from the note she was writing. 'What does it look like? It's a weeping fig.'

'It's fake,' I said through gritted teeth.

'Silk,' she corrected me absently.

'And that makes it OK?'

Shelley finally looked up. 'Every six weeks you buy a healthy, thriving, living plant. Five weeks later, it looks like locust heaven. The weeping fig will have paid for itself within six months, and even you can't kill a silk plant,' she said in matter-of-fact tones that made my fingers itch to get round her throat.

'If I wanted a schneid plant, I'd have bought one,' I said.

'You sound . . .'

'"Like one of my kids",' I finished, mimicking her calm voice. 'You don't understand, do you? It's the challenge. One day, I'm going to find a plant that runs riot for me.'

'By which time the planet will be a desert,' Shelley said, tossing her head so that the beads she had plaited into her hair jangled like a bag of marbles.

I didn't dignify that with a reply. I simply marched into my office, picked up the weeping fig and dropped it next to her desk. 'You like it so much, you live with it,' I said, stomping back to my office. If she was going to treat me like one of her teenage kids, I might as well enjoy the tantrum. I pulled the brownish remains of the asparagus fern out of the bin and defiantly dumped it on the windowsill.

Before I could do anything more, my phone rang. 'What now?' I barked at Shelley.

'Call for you. A gentleman who refuses to give his name.'

'Did you tell him we don't do matrimonials?'

'Of course I did. I'm not the one who's pre-menstrual.'

I bit back a snarl as Shelley put the call through. 'Kate Brannigan,' I said. 'How can I help you?'

'I need your help, Ms Brannigan. It's an extremely confidential matter. Brian Chalmers from PharmAce recommended you.'

'We're noted for our client confidentiality,' I reeled off. 'As you doubtless know if you've spoken to Brian. But I do need to know who I'm talking to.'

There was a moment's hesitation, long enough for me to hear sufficient background noise to realize my caller was speaking from a bar. 'My name's Trevor Kerr. I think the company I run is being blackmailed, and I need to talk to you about it.'

'Fine,' I said. 'Why don't I come round to your office this afternoon and have a chat about it?'

'Christ, no,' Kerr said, clearly alarmed. 'The last thing I want is for the blackmailers to find out I'm talking to a private detective.'

One of the ones that watches too many movies. That was all I needed to make my day. 'No problem. You come to me.'

'I don't think that's a good idea. You see, I think they're watching me.'

Just when you thought it was safe to pick up the phone . . . 'I know how disturbing threats can be when you're not accustomed to being on the receiving end,' I tried. 'Perhaps we could meet on neutral ground. Say in the lounge of the Midland?'

The reassuring tone hadn't worked. 'No,' Kerr said urgently. 'Not in public. It's got to look completely normal. Have you got a boyfriend, Ms Brannigan?'

*　　*　　*

29

I should have put the phone down then and there, I realized four hours later as I tried to explain to Richard that a crumpled cream linen suit might be fine for going on the razz with Mick Hucknall, but there was no way it would help him to pass as a member of the Round Table. 'Bloody hell, Brannigan,' he grumbled. 'I'm old enough to dress myself.'

I ignored him and raked through his wardrobe, coming up with a fairly sober double-breasted Italian suit in dark navy. 'This is more like it,' I said.

Richard scowled. 'I only wear that to funerals.'

I threw it on the bed. 'Not true. You wore it to your cousin's wedding.'

'You forgotten her husband already? Anyway, I don't see why you're making me get dressed up like a tailor's dummy. After the last time I helped you out, you swore you'd never let me near your work again,' he whinged as he shrugged out of the linen jacket.

'Believe me, if Bill wasn't out of the country, I wouldn't be asking you,' I said grimly. 'Besides, not even you can turn a Round Table treasure hunt and potluck supper into a life-threatening situation.'

Richard froze. 'That's a bit below the belt, Brannigan,' he said bitterly.

'Yeah, well, I'm going next door to find something suitably naff in my own wardrobe. Come through when you're ready.'

I walked down Richard's hall and cut through his living room to the conservatory. Back in my own house, I allowed myself a few moments of deep breathing to regain my equilibrium. A few months before, I had enlisted Richard's help in what should have been a straightforward case of car fraud. Only, as they say in all the worst police dramas, it all went pear-shaped. Spectacularly so. Richard ended up behind bars, his life in jeopardy, and I nearly got myself killed tracking down the real villains. As if that hadn't been enough, I'd also been landed with looking after his eight-year-old son Davy. And me with the maternal instincts of a Liquorice Allsort.

The physical scars had healed pretty quickly, but the real damage was to our relationship. You'd think he'd have been grateful that I sorted everything out. Instead, he'd been distant, sarcastic and out a lot. It hadn't been grim all the time, of course. If it had been, I'd have knocked it on the head weeks earlier. We still managed to have fun together, and sometimes for nearly a week things would be just like they used to be; lots of laughs, a few nights out, communal Chinese takeaways and spectacular sex. Then the clouds would descend, usually when I was up to the eyeballs in some demanding job.

This was the first time since our run-in with the drug warlords that I'd asked Richard to do anything connected with work. I'd argued with Trevor Kerr that there must be a less complicated way for us to meet, but Clever Trevor was convinced that he was right to take precautions. I nearly asked him why he was hiring a dog and still barking himself, but I bit my tongue. Business hadn't been so great lately that I could afford to antagonize new clients before they were actually signed up.

With a sigh, I walked into my own bedroom and considered the options. Richard says I don't have a wardrobe, just a collection of disguises. Looking at the array of clothes in front of me, I was tempted to agree with him. I pulled out a simple tailored dress in rough russet silk with a matching bolero jacket. I'd bought it while I'd been bodyguarding a Hollywood actress who was over here for a week to record an episode in a Granada drama series. She'd taken one look at the little black number I'd turned up in on the first evening and silently written me a cheque for five hundred pounds to go and buy 'something a little more chic, hon'. I'm not proud; I took the money and shopped. Alexis and I hadn't had so much fun in years.

I stepped into the dress and reached round to zip it up. Richard got there before me. He leaned forward and kissed me behind the ear. I turned to gooseflesh and shivered. 'Sorry,' he said. 'Bad day. Let's go and see how the other half lives.'

The address Trevor Kerr had given me was in Whitefield, a suburb of mostly semis just beyond the perennial roadworks on the M62. It's an area that's largely a colony of the upwardly mobile but not strictly Orthodox Jews who make up a significant proportion of Manchester's population. Beyond the streets of identical between-the-wars semis lay our destination, one of a handful of architect-designed developments where the serious money has gravitated. My plumber got the contract for one of them, and he told me about a conversation with one of his customers. My plumber thought the architect had made a mistake, because the plans showed plumbing for four dishwashers – two in the kitchen and two in the utility room. When he queried it, the customer looked at him as if he was thick as a yard of four-by-two and said, 'We keep kosher and we entertain a lot.' There's nothing you can say to that.

The house I'd been directed to looked more Frankenstein than Frank Lloyd Wright. It had more turrets and crenellations than Windsor Castle, all in bright red Accrington brick. 'Sometimes it's nice to be potless,' Richard remarked as we parked. It had a triple garage and hard-standing for half a dozen cars, but tonight was clearly party night. Richard's hot pink Volkswagen Beetle convertible looked as out of place as Cinderella at a minute past midnight. When the hostess opened the door, I smiled. 'Good evening,' I said. 'We're with Trevor Kerr,' I added.

The frosting on her immaculate coiffure spilled over on to the hostess's smile. 'Do come in,' she said.

The man who'd been hovering in the hall behind her stepped forward and said, 'I'm Trevor Kerr.' He signalled with his eyebrows towards the stairs and we followed him up into a den that looked like it had been bought clock, stock and panel from a country house. The only incongruity was the computer and fax machine smack in the middle of the desk. 'We won't be disturbed here,' he said. 'It'll be at least half an hour before the host distributes the clues and we move off. Perhaps your friend would like to go downstairs and help himself to the buffet?'

I could hear Richard's hackles rising. 'Mr Barclay is a valued associate of Mortensen and Brannigan. Anything you say is safe with him,' I said stiffly. I dreaded to think how many people Richard could upset at a Round Table potluck buffet.

'That's right,' he drawled. 'I'm not just scenery.'

Kerr looked uncomfortable but he wasn't really in a position to argue. As he settled himself in an armchair, we studied each other. Not even a hand-stitched suit could hide a body gone ruinously to seed. I was tempted to offer some fashion advice, but I didn't think he'd welcome the news that this year bellies are being worn inside the trousers. He couldn't have been much more than forty, but his eyes would have been the envy of any self-respecting bloodhound and his jowls would have set a bulldog a-quiver. The only attractive feature the man possessed was a head of thick, wavy brown hair with a faint silvering at the temples.

'Well, Mr Kerr?' I said.

He cleared his throat and said, 'I run Kerrchem. You probably haven't heard of us, but we're quite a large concern. We've got a big plant out at

Farnworth. We manufacture industrial cleaning materials, and we do one or two domestic products for supermarket own-brands. We pride ourselves on being a family business. Anyway, about a month ago, I got a letter in the post at home. As far as I can remember, it said I could avoid Kerrchem ending up with the same reputation as Tylenol for a very modest sum of money.'

'Product tampering,' Richard said sagely.

Kerr nodded. 'That's what I took it to mean.'

'You said: "as far as I can remember",' I remarked. 'Does that mean you haven't got the note?'

Kerr scowled. 'That's right. I thought it was some crank. It looked ridiculous, all those letters cut out of a newspaper and Sellotaped down. I binned it. You can't blame me for that,' he whined.

'No one's blaming you, Mr Kerr. It's just a pity you didn't keep the note. Has something happened since then to make you think they were serious?'

Kerr looked away and pulled a fat cigar from his inside pocket. As he went through the performance of lighting it, Richard leaned forward in his seat. 'A man has died since then, hasn't he, Mr Kerr?' I was impressed. I didn't know what the hell he was talking about, but I was impressed.

A plume of acrid blue smoke obscured Kerr's eyes as he said, 'Technically, yes. But there's no evidence that there's any connection.'

'A man dies after opening a sealed container of your products, you've had a blackmail note and you don't believe there's a connection?' Richard asked, with only mild incredulity.

I could see mischief dancing behind his glasses, so I thought I'd better head this off at the pass. Any minute now, Richard would decide to start enjoying himself, completely oblivious to the fact that not everyone has the blithe disregard for human life that characterizes journalists. 'Suppose you give me your version of events, Mr Kerr?'

He puffed on the cigar and I tried not to cough. 'Like I said, I thought this note was some crank. Then, last week, we had a phone call from the police. They said a publican had dropped down dead at work. It seemed he'd just opened a fresh container of KerrSter. That's a universal cleanser that we produce. One of our biggest sellers to the trade. Anyway, according to the postmortem, this man had died from breathing in cyanide, which is ridiculous, because cyanide doesn't go anywhere near the KerrSter process. Nobody at our place could work out how him dying could have had anything to do with the KerrSter,' he said defensively. 'We weren't looking forward to the inquest, I'll be honest, but we didn't see how we could be held to blame.'

'And?' I prompted him.

Kerr shifted in his seat, moving his weight from one buttock to the other in a movement I hadn't seen since *Dumbo*. 'I swear I never connected it with the note I'd had. It'd completely slipped my mind. And then this morning, this came.' His pudgy hand slid into his inside pocket again and emerged with a folded sheet of paper. He held it out towards me.

'Has anyone apart from you touched this?' I asked, not reaching for it.

He shook his head. 'No. It came to the house, just like the other one.'

'Put it down on the desk,' I said, raking in my bag for a pen and my Swiss Army knife. I took the eyebrow tweezers out of their compartment on the knife and gingerly unfolded the note. It was a sheet from a glue-top A4 pad, hole-punched, narrow feint and margin. Across it, in straggling newsprint letters Sellotaped down, I read, 'Bet you wish you'd done what you were told. We'll be in touch. No cops. We're watching you.' The letters were a mixture of upper and lower case, and I recognized the familiar fonts of the *Manchester Evening Chronicle*. Well, that narrowed it down to a few million bodies.

I looked up and sighed. 'On the face of it, it looks like your correspondent carried out his threat. Why haven't you taken this to the police, Mr Kerr? Murder and blackmail, that's what they're there for.'

Kerr looked uncomfortable. 'I didn't think they'd believe me,' he said awkwardly. 'Look at it from their point of view. My company's products have been implicated in a major tampering scandal. A man's dead. Can you imagine how much it's going to cost me to get out from under the lawsuits that are going to be flying around? There's nothing to show I didn't cobble this together myself to try and get off the hook. I bet mine are the only fingerprints on that note, and you can bet your bottom dollar that the police aren't going to waste their time hunting for industrial saboteurs they won't even believe exist. Anyway, the note says "No cops".'

'So you want me to find your saboteurs for you?' I asked resignedly.

'Can you?' Kerr asked eagerly.

I shrugged. 'I can try.'

Before we could discuss it further, there was a knock at the door and our hostess's head appeared. 'Sorry to interrupt, Trevor, but we're about to distribute the treasure-hunt clues, and I know you'd hate to start at a disadvantage.' She didn't invite us to join in, I noticed. Clearly my suit didn't come up to scratch.

'Be right with you, Charmian,' Trevor said, hauling himself out of his chair. 'My office, half past eight tomorrow morning?' he asked.

I had a lot more questions for Trevor Kerr, but they could wait. 'I thought you were worried about me coming to the office?' I reminded him.

He barely paused on his way out the door. 'I'll tell my secretary you're from the Health and Safety Executive,' he said. 'Those nosey bastards are always poking around where they're not wanted.'

I shook my head in despair as he departed. Some clients are like that. Before you've agreed to work for them, they're practically on their knees. Soon as you come on board, they treat you like something nasty on their Gucci loafers. 'And I thought heavy metal bands were arseholes,' Richard mused.

'They are,' I said. 'And while we're on the subject, how come you knew about the KerrSter death?'

Richard winked and produced one of those smiles that got me tangled up with him in the first place. 'Not much point in having the *Chronicle* delivered if you don't bother reading it, is there?' he asked sweetly.

'Some of us have more important things to do than laze around smoking joints and reading the papers,' I snarled.

Richard pretended to look huffed. At least, I think he was pretending. 'Oh well, if that's the way things are, you won't be wanting me to take you to dinner, will you?' he said airily.

'Try me,' I said. There are few things in life that don't look better after aromatic crispy duck. How was I to know Trevor Kerr would be one of them?

4

As I waited for the security guard in charge of the barrier at Kerrchem's car park to check that I wasn't some devious industrial spy trying to sneak in to steal their secrets, I stared across at the sprawling factory, its red brick smudged black by years of industrial pollution. Somewhere inside there I'd find the end of the ball of string that would unravel to reveal a killer.

Eventually, he let me in and directed me to the administration offices. Trevor Kerr's secretary was already at her desk when I walked in at twenty-five past eight. Unfortunately, her boss wasn't. I introduced myself. 'Mr Kerr's expecting me,' I added.

She'd clearly been hired for her efficiency rather than her charm. 'Health and Safety Executive,' she said in the same tone of voice I'd have used for the VAT inspector. 'Take a seat. Mr Kerr will be here soon.' She returned to her word processor, attacking the keys with the ferocity of someone playing Mortal Kombat.

I looked around. Neither of the two chairs looked as if it had been chosen for comfort. The only available reading material was some trade journal that I wouldn't have picked up even on a twelve-hour flight with a Sylvester Stallone film as the in-flight movie. 'Maybe I could make a start on the documents I need to see?' I said. 'To save wasting time.'

'Only Mr Kerr can authorize the release of company information to a third party,' she said coldly. 'He knows you're coming. I'm sure he won't keep you waiting for long.'

I wished I shared her conviction. I tried to make myself comfortable and used the time to review the limited information I'd gleaned so far. After Richard and I had stuffed ourselves in a small Chinese restaurant in Whitefield, where we'd both felt seriously overdressed, I'd sat down with the previous weeks' papers and brought myself up to speed. Richard, meanwhile, had changed and gone off to some dive in Longsight to hear a local techno band who'd just landed a record deal. Frankly, I felt I'd got the best end of the bargain.

On my way through the stuttering early rush-hour traffic, I'd stopped by the office to fax my local friendly financial services expert. I needed some background on Trevor Kerr and his company, and if there was dirt to be dug, Josh Gilbert was the man. Josh and I have an arrangement: he supplies me with financial information and I buy him expensive dinners. The fact that Josh wouldn't know a scruple if it took him out to the Savoy is fine by me; I don't have to think about that, just reap the rewards.

The financial data would fill one gap in my knowledge. I hoped it would be more comprehensive than the newspaper accounts. When Joey Morton died, the media responded with ghoulish swiftness. For once, there were no government scandals to divert them, and all the papers had given the Stockport publican's death a good show. At first, I couldn't figure out how I'd missed the hue and cry, till I remembered that on the day in question I'd been out all day tracking down a key defence witness for Ruth Hunter, my favourite criminal solicitor. I'd barely had time for a sandwich on the hoof, never mind a browse through the dailies.

Joey Morton was thirty-eight, a former Third Division footballer turned publican. He and his wife Marina ran the Cob and Pen pub on the banks of the infant Mersey. Joey had gone down to the cellar to clean the beer pipes, taking a new container of KerrSter. Joey was proud of his real ale, and he never let anyone else near the cellarage. When he hadn't reappeared by opening time, Marina had sent one of the bar staff down to fetch him. The barman found his boss in a crumpled heap on the floor, the KerrSter sitting open beside him. The police had revealed that the postmortem indicated Joey had died as a result of inhaling hydrogen cyanide gas.

The pathologist's job had been made easier by the barman, who reported he'd smelt bitter almonds as soon as he'd entered the cramped cellar. Kerrchem had immediately denied that their product could possibly have caused the death, and the police had informed a waiting world that they were treating Joey's death as suspicious. Since then, the story seemed to have died, as always happens when there's a dearth of shocking revelations.

It didn't seem likely that Joey Morton could have died as a result of some ghastly error inside the Kerrchem factory. The obvious conclusion was industrial sabotage. The key questions were when and by whom. Was it an inside job? Was it a disgruntled former employee? Was it an outsider looking for blackmail money? Or was it a rival trying to annex Trevor Kerr's market? Killing people seemed a bit extreme, but as I know from bitter experience, the trouble with hiring outside help to do your dirty work is that things often get dangerously out of hand.

It was ten to nine when Trevor Kerr barged in. His eyes looked like the only treasure he'd found the night before had been in the bottom of a bottle. 'You Miss Brannigan, then?' he greeted me. If he was harbouring dreams of an acting career, I could only hope that Kerrchem wasn't going to fold. I followed him into his office, catching an unappealing whiff of Scotch revisited blended with Polo before we moved into the aroma of stale cigars and lemon furniture polish. Clearly, the Spartan motif didn't extend beyond the outer office. Trevor Kerr had spared no expense to make his office comfortable. That is, if you find gentlemen's clubs comfortable. Leather wing armchairs surrounded a low table buffed to a mirror sheen. Trevor's desk was repro, but what it lacked in class, it made up for in size. All they'd need to stage the world snooker championships on it would be a bit of green baize. That and clear the clutter. The walls were hung with old golfing prints. If his bulk was anything to go by, golf was something Trevor Kerr honoured more in the breach than the observance.

He dumped his briefcase by the desk and settled in behind it. I chose the armchair nearest him. I figured if I waited till I was invited, I'd be past my sell-by date. 'So, what do you need from me?' he demanded.

Before I could reply, the secretary came in with a steaming mug of coffee. The mug said 'World's Greatest Bullshitter'. I wasn't about to disagree. I wouldn't have minded a cup myself, but clearly the hired help around Kerrchem wasn't deemed worthy of that. If I'd really been from the HSE, the lack of courtesy would have had me sharpening my knives for Trevor Kerr's well-cushioned ribs. I waited for the secretary to withdraw, then I said, 'Have you recalled the rest of the batch?'

He nodded impatiently. 'Of course. We got on to all the wholesalers, and we've placed an ad in the national press as well as the trade. We've already had a load of stuff back, and there's more due in today.'

'Good,' I said. 'I'll want to see that, as well as the dispatch paperwork relating to that batch. I take it that won't be a problem?'

'No problem. I'll get Sheila to sort it out for you.' He made a note on a pad on his desk. 'Next?'

'Do you use cyanide in any of your processes?'

'No way,' he said belligerently. 'It has industrial uses, but mainly in the plastics industry and electroplating. There's nothing we produce that we'd need it for.'

'OK. Going back to the original blackmail note. Did it include any instructions about the amount of money they were after, or how you were to contact them?'

He took a cigar out of a humidor the size of a small greenhouse and rolled it between his fingers. 'They didn't put a figure on it, no. There was a phone number, and the note said it was the number of one of the public phones at Piccadilly Station. I was supposed to be there at nine o'clock on the Friday night. I didn't go, of course.'

'Pity you didn't call us then,' I said.

'I told you, I thought it was a crank. Some nutter trying to wind me up. No way was I going to give him the satisfaction.'

'Or her,' I added. 'The thing that bothers me, Mr Kerr, is that killing people is a pretty extreme thing for a blackmailer to do. The usual analysis of blackmailers is that they are on the cowardly side.

45

The crimes they commit are at arm's-length, and usually don't put life at risk. I would have expected the blackmailer in this case to have done something a lot more low key, certainly initially. You know, dumped caustic soda in washing-up liquid, that sort of thing.'

'Maybe they didn't intend to kill anybody, just to give people a nasty turn,' he said. He lit the cigar, exhaling a cloud of smoke that gave me a nasty turn so early in the day.

I shrugged. 'In that case, cyanide's a strange choice. The fatal dose is pretty small. Also, you couldn't just stick it in the drum and wait for someone to open it up. There must have been some kind of device rigged up inside it. To produce the lethal gas, cyanide pellets need to react with something else. So they'd have had to be released into the liquid somehow. That's a lot of trouble to go to when you could achieve an unpleasant warning with dozens of other chemical mixtures. If it was me, I'd have filled a few drums either with something that smelled disgusting, or something that would destroy surfaces rather than clean them, just to persuade you that they were capable of making your life hell. Then, I'd have followed it up with a second note saying something like: "Next time, it'll be cyanide."'

'So maybe we're dealing with a complete nutter,' he said bitterly. 'Great.'

'Or maybe it's someone who wants to destroy you rather than blackmail you,' I said simply.

Kerr took his cigar out of his mouth, which remained in a perfect 'O'. Finally, he said, 'You've got to be kidding.'

'It's something you should consider. In relation to both your professional and your personal life.' He was having a lot of trouble getting his head round the idea, I could see. If he'd been a bit nicer to me, I'd have been gentler. But I figure you shouldn't dish it out unless you can take it. 'What about business rivals? Is anybody snapping at your heels? Is anybody going under because you've brought out new products or developed new sales strategies?'

'You don't murder people in business,' he protested. 'Not in my line of business, you don't.'

'Murder might not have been what was planned,' I told him flatly. 'If they wanted to sabotage you and stay at arm's-length, they might have hired someone to do the dirty. And they in turn might have hired someone else. And somewhere along the line, the Chinese whispers took over. So is there any other firm that might have a particular reason for wanting Kerrchem to go down the tubes?'

He frowned. 'The last few years have been tough, there's no denying that. Firms go bust, so there's not as much industrial cleaning to be done. Businesses cut their cleaners down from five days to three, so the commercial cleaners cut back on their purchases. We've kept our heads above water, but it's been a struggle. We've had a couple of rounds of redundancies, we've been a bit slower bringing in some new processes, and we've had to market ourselves more aggressively, but that's the story across the industry. One of our main competitors went bust about nine months ago, but that wasn't because we were squeezing them. It was more because they were based in Basingstoke and they had higher labour costs than us. I haven't heard that anybody else is on the edge, and it's a small world. To be honest, we're one of the smaller fishes. Most of our rivals are big multinationals. If they wanted to take us out, they'd come to the family and make us an offer we couldn't refuse.'

That disposed of the easy option. Time to move on. 'Has anybody left under a cloud? Any unfair dismissal claims pending?'

He shook his head. 'Not that I know of. As far as I know, and believe me, I would know, the only people who have gone are the ones we cleared out under the redundancy deals. I suppose some of them might have been a bit disgruntled, but if any of them had made any threats, I would have heard about it. Like I said, we pride ourselves on being a family firm, and the department head and production foremen all know not to keep problems to themselves.'

We were going nowhere fast, which only left the sticky bit. 'OK,' I said. 'I don't want you to take this the wrong way, Mr Kerr, but I have to ask these things. You've said that Kerrchem is a family firm. Is there any possibility that another member of the family wants to discredit you? To make it look like the company's not safe in your hands?'

Suddenly I was looking at Trevor Kerr's future. Written all over his scarlet face was the not-so-distant early warning of the heart attack that was lurking in his silted arteries. His mouth opened and closed a couple of times, then he roared, 'Bollocks. Pure, absolute bollocks.'

'Think about it,' I said, smiling sweetly. That'll teach him to deprive me of a caffeine fix. 'The other thing is more personal, I'm afraid. Are you married, Mr Kerr?'

''Course I am. Three children.' He jerked his thumb towards a photograph frame on the desk. I leaned forward and turned it round. Standard studio shot of a woman groomed to within an inch of her life, two sulky-looking boys with their father's features, and a girl who'd had the dental work but still looked disturbingly like a rabbit. 'Been married to the same woman for sixteen years.'

'So there're no ex-wives or ex-girlfriends lurking around with an axe to grind?' I asked.

His eyes drifted away from mine to a point elsewhere on the far wall. 'Don't be ridiculous,' he said abruptly. Then, in an effort to win me round, he gave a bark of laughter and said, 'Bloody hell, Kate, it's me that hired you, not the wife.'

So now I knew he had, or had had, a mistress. That was the long shot I'd have to keep in the back of my mind. Before I could explore this avenue further, the intercom on his desk buzzed.

He pressed a button and said, 'What is it, Sheila?'

'Reg Unsworth is here, Mr Kerr. He says he needs to talk to you.'

'I'm in a meeting, Sheila,' he said irritably.

There were muffled sounds of conversation, then Sheila said, 'He says it's urgent, Mr Kerr. He says you'll want to know immediately. It's to do with the recalled product, he says.'

'Why didn't you say so? Send him in.'

A burly man in a brown warehouseman's coat with a head bald as a boiled egg and approximately the same shape walked in. 'Sorry to bother you, Mr Kerr. It's about the KerrSter recall.'

'Well, Reg, spit it out,' Kerr said impatiently.

Unsworth gave me a worried look. 'It's a bit confidential, like.'

'It's all right. Miss Brannigan here's from the Health and Safety Executive. She's here to help us sort this mess out.'

Unsworth still looked uncertain. 'I checked the records before the returns started coming in. We sent out a total of four hundred and eighty-three gallon containers with the same batch number as the one that there was the problem with. Only . . . so far, we've had six hundred and twenty-seven back.'

5

Kerr looked gobsmacked. 'You must have made a mistake,' he blustered.

'I double-checked,' Unsworth said. His jaw set in a line as obstinate as his boss's. 'Then I went back down to production and checked again. There's no doubt about it. We've had back one hundred and forty-four containers more than we sent out. And that's not even taking into account the one that the dead man opened, or ones that have already been used, or people who haven't even heard about the recall yet.'

'There's got to be some mistake,' Kerr repeated. 'What about the batch coding machine? Has anybody checked that it's working OK?'

'I checked with the line foreman myself,' Unsworth said. 'They've had no problems with it, and I've seen quality control's sheets. There's no two ways about it. We only sent out four hundred and eighty-three. There's a gross of gallon drums of KerrSter that we can't account for sitting in the loading bay. Come and see for yourself if you don't believe me,' he added in an aggrieved tone.

'Let's do just that,' Kerr said, heaving himself to his feet. 'Come on, Miss Brannigan. Come and see how the workers earn a living.'

I followed Kerr out of the room. Unsworth hung back, holding the door open and falling in beside me as we strode down the covered walkway that linked the administration offices with the factory. 'It's a real mystery,' he offered.

I had my own ideas about what was going on, but for the time being I decided to keep them to myself. 'The drums that have been returned,' I said, 'are they all sealed, or have some of them already been opened?'

'Some of them have been started on,' he said. 'The batch went out into the warehouse the Tuesday before last. They'll probably have started taking it out on the Thursday or Friday, going by our normal stockpile levels, so there's been plenty of time for people to use them.'

'And no one else has reported any adverse effect?'

Unsworth looked uncomfortable. 'Not as such,' he said.

Kerr half turned to catch my reply. 'But?' I asked.

Unsworth glanced at Kerr, who nodded impatiently. 'Well, a couple of the wholesalers and one or two of the reps had already had containers from that batch returned,' Unsworth admitted.

'Do you know why that was?' I asked.

'Customers complained the goods weren't up to us usual standard,' he said grudgingly.

'What sort of complaints?' Kerr demanded indignantly. 'Why wasn't I told about this?'

'It's only just come to light, Mr Kerr. They said the KerrSter wasn't right. One of them claimed it had stripped the finish off the flooring in his office toilets.'

Kerr snorted. 'He should tell his bloody workforce to stick with Boddingtons. They'll have been pissing that foreign lager all over the bloody tiles.'

'Have you had the chance to analyse any of the containers that have come back?' I butted in.

Unsworth nodded. 'The lads in the lab worked through the night on samples from some of the drums. There wasn't a trace of cyanide in any of them.'

Kerr shouldered open a pair of double doors. As I caught one on the backswing, the smell hit me. It was a curious amalgam of pine, lemon, and soap suds, but pervaded throughout with sharp chemical smells that bit my nose and throat. It was a bit like driving past the chemical works at Ellesmere Port with one of those ersatz air fresheners in the car. The ones that make you feel that a rotting polecat under the driver's seat would be preferable. Right after the smell came the noise of machinery, overlaid with the bubbling and gurgling of liquid. Kerr climbed a flight of narrow iron stairs, and I followed him along a high-level walkway that travelled the length of the factory floor. It was unpleasantly humid. I felt like a damp wash that's just been dumped in the tumble dryer.

Beneath us, vats seethed, nozzles squirted liquid into plastic containers, and surprisingly few people moved around. 'Not many bodies,' I said loudly over my shoulder to Unsworth.

'Computer controlled,' he said succinctly.

Another avenue to pursue. If the sabotage was internal, perhaps the culprit was simply sending the wrong instructions to the plant. I'd thought this was going to be a straightforward case of industrial sabotage, but my head was beginning to hurt with the permutations it was throwing up.

A couple of hundred yards along the walkway, we descended and cut through a heavy door into a warehouse. Now I know how the Finns feel when they walk into the snow from the sauna. I could feel my pores snapping shut in shock. Here, the air smelled of oil and diesel. The only sound came from fork-lift trucks shunting pallets on and off shelves. 'This is the warehouse,' Kerr said. I'd never have worked that one out all by myself. 'The full containers go through from the factory to packing, where the machines label them, stamp them with batch numbers and seal-wrap them in dozens. Then they come through here on conveyor belts and they're shelved or loaded.' He turned to Unsworth. 'Where have you stacked the recalls?'

Before Unsworth could reply, my mobile started ringing. 'Excuse me,' I said, moving away a few yards and pulling the phone out. 'Kate Brannigan,' I announced.

'Tell me,' an amused voice said. 'Is Alexis Lee a real person, or is it just your pen name?'

I recognized the voice at once. I moved further away from Kerr's curious stare and turned my back so he couldn't see that my ears had gone bright red. 'She's real all right, Mr Haroun,' I said. 'Why do you ask?'

'Oh, I think it had better be Michael. Otherwise I'd start to suspect you were being unfriendly. I've just been handed the early edition of the *Evening Chronicle*.'

'And what does it say?'

'Do you really need me to tell you?' he asked, still sounding amused.

'I forgot to bring my crystal ball with me. If you want to hang on, I'll see if I can find a chicken to disembowel so I can check out the entrails.'

He laughed. It was a sound I could easily get used to. 'It'd be a lot simpler to pop into a newsagent.'

'You're not going to tell me?'

'Oh no, I'd hate to spoil the surprise. Tell me, Kate . . . Do you fancy dinner some evening?'

'Michael, it may not look like it, but I fancy dinner every evening.' I couldn't believe myself – I'd read better lines than that in teenage romances.

Bless him, he laughed again. I like a man who doesn't seize on the first sign of weakness. 'Are you free this evening?'

I pretended to think. Let's face it, I'd have turned down Mel Gibson, Sean Bean, Lynford Christie and Daniel Day-Lewis for dinner with Michael Haroun. I didn't pretend for too long, in case he lost interest. 'I can be. As long as it's after seven.'

'Great. Shall I pick you up?'

That was a harder decision. I didn't want to let myself forget that this was a business dinner. On the other hand, it wouldn't hurt to give Richard something to think about. I gave Michael the address and we agreed on half past seven. Unlike everybody on TV who uses a mobile phone, I hit the 'end' button with a flourish, then turned back to a scowling Trevor Kerr.

'Sorry about that,' I lied. 'Somebody I've been trying to get hold of on another investigation. Now, Mr Unsworth, you were going to show us these recalled containers.'

The next half-hour was one of the more boring ones in my life, made doubly so by the fact that I was itching to get my hands on the *Chronicle*. I finally escaped at half past eleven, leaving Trevor Kerr with the suggestion that his chemists should analyse the contents of a random sample of the containers. Only this time, they wouldn't just be looking for cyanide. They'd be checking to see whether the KerrSter in the drums was the real thing. Or something quite different and a whole lot nastier.

* * *

By the third newsagent's, I'd confirmed what I'd always suspected about Farnworth. It's a depressing little dump that civilization forgot. Nobody had the *Chronicle*. They wouldn't have it till some time in the afternoon. They all looked deeply offended and incredulous when I explained that no, the *Bolton Evening News* just wouldn't be the same. I had to possess my soul in patience till I hit the East Lancs. Road. I sat on a garage forecourt reading the results of Alexis's research. She'd done me proud.

CULTURAL HERITAGE VANISHES

A series of spectacular robberies has been hushed up by police and stately home owners.

Now fears are growing that a gang of professional thieves are stripping Britain of valuable artworks that form a key part of the nation's heritage. Among the stolen pieces are paintings by French Impressionists Monet and Cézanne, and a bronze bust by the Italian Baroque master Bernini. Also missing is a collection of Elizabethan miniature paintings by Nicholas Hilliard. Together, the thieves' haul is estimated at nearly £10 million.

The cover-up campaign was a joint decision made by several police forces and the owners of the stately homes in question. Police did not want publicity because they were following up leads and did not want the thieves to know that they had realized one gang was behind the thefts.

And the owners were reluctant to admit the jewels of their collections had gone missing in case public attendance figures at their homes dropped off as a result.

Some owners have even resorted to hanging replicas of the missing masterpieces in a bid to fool the public.

The latest victim of the audacious robbers is the owner of a Cheshire manor house. Police have refused to reveal his identity, but will only say that a nineteenth-century French painting has been stolen.

The cheeky thieves have adopted the techniques of the pair who caused outrage at the Lillehammer Olympics when they stole Edward Munch's *The Scream*.

They break in through the nearest door or window, go straight to the one item they have selected and make their getaway. Often they are in the house or gallery for no more than a minute.

A police source said last night, 'There's no doubt that we are dealing with professionals who may well steal to order. There are obviously a limited number of outlets for their loot, and we are making inquiries in the art world.'

One of the robbed aristos, who was only prepared to talk anonymously, said, 'It's not just the heritage of this country that is at stake. It's our businesses. We employ a lot of people and if the public stop coming because our most famous exhibits have gone, it will have repercussions.

'We do our best to maintain tight security, but you can never keep the professional out.'

There was some more whingeing in the same vein, but nothing startling. Call me nit-picking, but I've never understood how the art of several European cultures has come to be a key part of our British heritage, unless it symbolizes the brigand spirit that made the Empire great. That aside, I reckoned Alexis's story would achieve what I hoped for. With a bit of luck, the nationals would pick the story up the next morning, and the jungle drums would start beating. Soon it would be time for a chat with my friend Dennis. If he ever decides to go completely straight, he could make a living as a journalist. I've never known anybody absorb or disseminate so much criminal intelligence. I'm just grateful some of it comes my way when I need it.

For the time being, I headed back to the office, stopping to pick up a couple of pizzas on the way. I knew Shelley would be waiting behind the door with a pile of paperwork that would cause more concussion than a rolling pin. At least a pizza offering might reduce the aggro to a minimum.

I was halfway through the painful process of signing cheques when Josh arrived. I pretended astonishment. 'Josh!' I exclaimed. 'It's between the hours of one and three and you're not in a restaurant! What's happened? Has the stock market collapsed?'

His sharp blue eyes crinkled in the smile that he's practised to maximize his resemblance to Robert Redford. Frankly, I'm surprised the light brown hair hasn't been bleached to perfect it, since Josh is a man whose energies are devoted to only two things – making lots of money and women. His track record with the latter is dismal; luckily he's a lot more successful with the former, which is how he's ended up as the senior partner of one of the city's most successful master brokerages. Shelley developed a theory about Josh and women after she did her A level psychology. She reckons that behind the confident façade there lurks a well of low self-esteem. So when it comes to women, his subconscious decides that any woman with half a brain and a shred of personality wouldn't spend more than five minutes with him. The logical extension of that is that any woman who sticks around for more than six weeks must by definition be a boring bimbo, and thus he shouldn't be seen dead with her.

Me, I think he just likes having fun. He swears he plans to retire when he turns forty, and that's early enough to think about settling down. I like him because he's always treated me as an equal, never as a potential conquest. I'm glad about that; I'd hate to lose my fast track into the bowels of the financial world. Believe me, the Nikkei Index doesn't burp without Josh knowing exactly what it had for dinner.

Josh flicked an imaginary speck of dust off one of the clients' chairs and sat down, crossing his elegantly suited legs. 'Things are changing in the big bad world of money, you know,' he said. 'The days of the three-hour lunch are over. Except when it's you that's buying, of course.' He tossed a file on to my desk.

'You've stopped doing lunch?' I waited for the world to stop turning.

'Today, I had a Marks and Spencer prawn sandwich in the office of one of my principal clients. Washed down with a rather piquant sparkling mineral water from the Welsh valleys. An interesting diversification from coal mining, don't you think?'

I picked up the file. 'Kerrchem?'

'The same. Want the gossip since I'm here?'

I gave him my best suspicious frown. 'Is this going to cost me?'

He pouted. 'Maybe an extra glass of XO?'

'It's worth it,' I decided. 'Tell me about it.'

'OK. Kerrchem is a family firm. Started in 1934 by Josiah Kerr, the grandfather of the present chairman, chief executive and managing director Trevor Kerr. They made soap. They were no Lever Brothers, though they've always provided a reasonable living for the family. Trevor's father Hartley was a clever chap, by all accounts, had a chemistry degree, and he made certain they spent enough on R & D to keep ahead of the game. He moved them into the industrial cleaning market.' All this off the top of his head. One of the secrets of Josh's success is a virtually photographic memory for facts and figures. Figures of the balance sheet variety, that is.

'Hartley Kerr was an only child,' he continued. 'He had three kids: Trevor, Margaret and Elizabeth. Trevor, although the youngest, owns forty-nine per cent of the shares, Margaret and Elizabeth own twenty per cent each. The remaining eleven per cent is held by Hartley Kerr's widow, Elaine Kerr. Elaine is in her early seventies, in full possession of her marbles, lives in Bermuda, and takes little part in things except for voting against Trevor at every opportunity. Trevor's sons are still at school, but he has three nephews who work at Kerrchem. John Hardy works in R & D, his brother Paul is in accounts and Margaret's son Will Tomasiuk is in sales. Trevor is by all accounts a complete and utter shit, but against all the odds, he appears to run the company well. Never been a history of industrial problems. Financially and fiscally all seems above board. Frankly, Kate, if Kerrchem were going public, they're exactly the kind of company I'd advise you to put your money in if you wanted to keep it unspectacularly safe. Before people started dying, that is.'

'I suppose that rules out an insurance job, then. Is everybody in the family happy with Trevor's stewardship? No young bucks snapping at his heels?'

Josh shook his head. 'That's not the word on the exchange floor. The old lady only votes against Trevor because she thinks he's not a patch on his old man and she wants to make a point. And the nephews have all learned the business from the bottom up, but they're climbing the greasy pole at an impressive rate. So, no, that kite won't fly, Kate.' He glanced at a watch so slim it looked anorexic and uncrossed his legs.

'You're a star, Josh. I owe you a meal.'

'Fix up a date with Julia, would you? I don't have my diary with me.' He stood up and I came round the desk to swap kisses on both cheeks. I watched five hundred pounds worth of immaculate tailoring walk out the door. Not even that amount of dosh to spend on clothes could make me spend my days talking about pension funds and unit trusts.

On the other hand, all it took to get me salivating at the thought of an evening's conversation about insurance was a profile from an ancient carving. Maybe I wasn't such a smart cookie after all.

6

I'd almost forgotten there are restaurants that don't serve dim sum. For as long as I've known Richard, he's maintained that if you don't use chopsticks on it, it ain't food. And Josh has recently taken to extracting his payment in kind in Manchester's clutch of excellent Thai restaurants. I'm not sure if that's down to the food or the subservient waitresses. Either way, I'd entirely lost touch with anything that didn't come out of a wok. Which made Michael Haroun a refreshing change in more ways than one.

He'd arrived promptly at twenty-nine minutes past seven. I'd grown so used to Richard's flexible idea of time that I was still applying eye pencil when the doorbell rang. I nearly poked my eye out in shock, and had to answer the door with a tissue covering the damage. Eat your heart out, Cindy Crawford. Michael lounged against the door frame, looking drop-dead gorgeous in blue jeans, navy silk blouson and an off-white collarless linen shirt that sure as hell hadn't come from Marks and Spencer. My stomach churned, and I don't think it was hunger. 'Long John Silver, I presume,' he said.

'Watch it, or I'll set the parrot on you,' I replied, stepping back and waving him in.

He shrugged away from the door and followed me down the hall. I gestured towards the living room and said, 'Give me a minute.'

Back in the bathroom, I repaired the damage and surveyed myself in the full-length mirror. Navy linen trousers, russet knitted silk T-shirt, navy silk tweed jacket. I looked like I'd taken a bit of trouble, without actually departing from the businesslike image. Michael wasn't to know this was my newest, smartest outfit. Besides, I'd told Richard my evening engagement was a business meeting, and I wasn't entirely ready for him to get any other ideas if he saw me leave.

I rubbed a smudge of gel over my fingers and thrust them through my hair, which I'd kept fairly short since I was shorn without consultation earlier in the year. My right eye still looked a bit red, but this was as good as it was going to get. A quick squirt of Richard's Eternity by Calvin Klein and I was ready.

I walked down the hall and stood in the doorway. Michael obviously hadn't heard me. He was deep in a computer gaming magazine. Bonus points for the boy. I cleared my throat. 'Ready when you are,' I said.

He looked up and smiled appreciatively. 'I don't want to sound disablist,' he said, 'but I have to admit I prefer the two-eyed look.' He closed the magazine and stood up. 'Shall we go?'

He drove a top-of-the-range Citroën. 'Company car?' I asked, looking forward to the prospect of being driven for a change.

'Yeah, but they let me choose. I've always had a soft spot for Citroën. I think the DS was one of the most beautiful cars ever built,' he said as he did a neat three-point turn to get out of the parking area outside my bungalow. 'My father always used to drive one.'

That told me Michael Haroun hadn't grown up on a council estate with the arse hanging out of his trousers. 'Lucky you,' I said with feeling. 'My dad works for Rover, so my childhood was spent in the back of a Mini. That's how I ended up only five foot three. The British equivalent of binding the feet.'

Michael laughed as he hit a button on the CD player and Bonnie Raitt filled the car. Richard would have giggled helplessly at something so middle of the road. Me, I was just glad of something that didn't feature crashing guitars or that insistent zippy beat that sounds just like a fly hitting an incinerator. We turned out of the small 'single professionals' development where I live and into the council estate. To my surprise, instead of heading down Upper Brook Street towards town, he turned left. As we headed down Stockport Road, my heart sank. I prayed this wasn't going to be one of those twenty-mile drives to some pretentious bistro in the sticks with compulsory spinach pancakes and only one choice of vodka.

'You into computer games, then?' I asked. Time to check out just how much I had in common with this breathtaking profile.

'I have a 486 multi-media system in my spare room. Does that answer the question?'

'It's not what you've got, it's what you do with it that counts,' I replied. As soon as I'd spoken, I wished I was on a five-second delay loop, like radio phone-ins.

He grinned and listed his current favourites. We were still arguing the relative merits of submarine simulations when he pulled up outside a snooker supplies shop in an unpromising part of Stockport Road. A short walk down the pavement brought us to That Café, an unpretentious restaurant done out in Thirties style. I'd heard plenty of good reports about it, but I'd never quite made it across the door before. The locale had put me off for one thing. Call me fussy, but I like to be sure that my car's still going to be waiting for me after I've finished dinner.

The interior looked like flea market meets Irish country pub, but the menu had me salivating. The waitress, dressed in jeans, a Deacon Blue T-shirt, big fuck-off Doc Marten boots and a long white French waiter's apron, showed us to a quiet corner table next to a blazing fire. OK, they only had one vodka, but at least it wasn't some locally distilled garbage with a phoney Russian name.

As our starters arrived, I said ruefully, 'I wish finding Henry Naismith's Monet was as easy as a computer game.'

'Yeah. At least with games, there's always a bulletin board you can access for hints. I suppose you're out on your own with this,' Michael said.

'Not entirely on my own,' I corrected him. 'I do have one or two contacts.'

He swallowed his mouthful of food and looked slightly pained. 'Is that why you agreed to have dinner with me?' he asked.

'Only partly.'

'What was the other part?' he asked, obviously fishing.

'I enjoy a good scoff, and I like interesting conversation with it.' I was back in control of myself, the adolescent firmly stuffed back into the box marked 'not wanted on voyage'.

'And you thought I'd be an interesting conversationalist, did you?'

'Bound to be,' I said sweetly. 'You're an insurance man, and right now insurance claims are one of my principal interests.'

We ate in silence for a few moments, then he said, 'I take it you were behind the story in the *Chronicle*?'

I shrugged. 'I like to stir the pot. That way, the scum rises to the surface.'

'You certainly stirred things around our office,' Michael said drily.

'The people have a right to know,' I said, self-righteously quoting Alexis.

'Cheers,' Michael said, clinking his glass against mine. 'Here's to a profitable relationship.'

'Oh, you mean Fortissimus are going to hire Mortensen and Brannigan?' I asked innocently.

He grinned again. 'I think I'll pass on that one. I simply meant that with luck, you might track down Henry Naismith's Monet.'

'Speaking of which,' I said, 'I spoke to Henry this afternoon. He says your assessor was there this afternoon.'

'That's right,' Michael said cagily.

'Henry says your man put a very interesting suggestion to him. Purely in confidence. Now, would that be the kind of confidence you're already privy to?'

Michael carefully placed his fork and knife together on the plate and mopped his lips with the napkin. 'It might be,' he said cautiously. 'But if it were, I wouldn't be inclined to discuss it with someone who has a hotline to the front page of the *Chronicle*.'

'Not even if I promised it would go no further?'

'You expect me to believe that after today's performance?' he demanded.

I smiled. 'There's a crucial difference. I was acting in my client's best interests by setting the cat among the pigeons with Alexis's story. I didn't breach my client's confidentiality, and I didn't tell Alexis anything that wasn't already in the public domain. She just put the bits together. However, if Henry acted on your colleague's suggestion and I leaked that to the press, it would seriously damage his business. And I don't do that to the people who pay my mortgage. Trust me, Michael. It won't go any further.'

The arrival of the waitress gave him a moment's breathing space. She removed the debris. 'So this would be strictly off the record?'

'Information only,' I agreed.

The waitress returned with a cheerful smile and two huge plates. I stared down at mine, where enough rabbit to account for half the population of Watership Down sat in a pool of creamy sauce. '*Nouvelle cuisine* obviously passed this place by,' I said faintly.

'I suspect we Mancunians are too canny to pay half a week's wages for a sliver of meat surrounded by three baby carrots, two mangetouts, one baby sweetcorn and an artistically carved radish,' he said wryly.

'And is it that Mancunian canniness that underlies your assessor's underhand suggestion?' I asked innocently.

'Nothing regional about it,' Michael said. 'You have to have a degree in bloody-minded caution before you get the job.'

'So you think it's OK to ask your clients to hang fakes on the wall?'

'It's a very effective safety precaution,' he said carefully.

'That's what your assessor told Henry. He said you'd be prepared not to increase his premium by the equivalent of the gross national product of a small African nation if he had copies made of his remaining masterpieces and hung them on the walls instead of the real thing,' I said conversationally.

'That's about the size of it,' Michael admitted. At least he had the decency to look uncomfortable about it.

'And is this a general policy these days?'

Slicing up his vegetables gave Michael an excuse for not meeting my eyes. 'Quite a few of our clients have opted for it as a solution to their security problems,' he said. 'It makes sense, Kate. We agreed this morning that there isn't a security system that can't be breached. If having a guard physically on site twenty-four hours a day isn't practical because of the expense or because the policyholder doesn't want that sort of presence in what is, after all, his home, then it avoids sky-high premiums.'

'It's not just about money, though,' I protested. 'It's like Henry says. He knows those paintings. He's lived with them most of his life. You get a buzz from the real thing that a fake just doesn't provide.'

'Not one member of the public has noticed the substitutions,' Michael said.

'Maybe not so far,' I conceded. 'But according to my understanding, the trouble with fakes is that they don't stand the test of time.' Thanking Shelley silently for my art tutorial that afternoon, I launched myself into my spiel. 'Look at Van Meegeren's fake Vermeers. At the time, all the experts were convinced they were the real thing. But you look at them now, and they wouldn't even fool a philistine like me. The difference between schneid and kosher is that fakes date, but the really great paintings don't. They're timeless.'

He frowned. 'Even if you're right, which I don't concede for a moment, that's not a bridge that our clients will have to cross for a long time yet.'

I wasn't about to give up that easily. 'Even so, don't you think it's a bit of a con to pull on the public? A bit of a swizz to spend your bank holiday Monday in a traffic jam just so you can ogle a Constable that's more phoney than a plastic Rolex? Aren't you in danger of breaching the Trades Descriptions Act?' I asked.

'Our clients may be,' Michael said carelessly. 'We're not.'

The brazen effrontery of it gobsmacked me. 'I can't believe I'm hearing this,' I said. 'You work in a business that must spend hundreds of thousands a year trying to catch its customers out in fraud, and yet you're happily suggesting to another bunch of clients that they go off and commit a fraud?'

'That's not how we see it,' he said stiffly. 'Besides, it works,' he said. 'In at least two cases that I know about personally, customers who have been burgled have only lost copies. Surely that proves it's worthwhile.'

In spite of the blazing fire, I felt a chill on the back of my neck. Only a man with no personal knowledge of the strung-out world of crime could have made that pronouncement with such self-satisfaction. It doesn't take much imagination to picture the scene when an overwrought burglar turns up at his fence's gaff with something he thinks is an old master, only to be told it's Rembrandt by numbers. Scenario number one is that the burglar thinks the fence is trying to have him over so he takes the appropriate steps. Scenario number two is that the fence thinks the burglar is trying to have him over, and takes the appropriate steps. Either way, somebody ends up in casualty. And that's looking on the bright side. Doubtless law-abiding citizens like Michael think they've got what they deserve, but even villains have wives and kids who don't want to spend their spare time visiting hospital beds or graves.

My silence clearly spelled out defeat to Michael, since he leaned over and squeezed my hand. 'Trust me, Kate. Our way, everybody's happy,' he said.

I pretended to push my chair back and look frantically for the door. 'I'm out of here,' I said. 'Soon as an insurance man says "trust me", you know you should be in the next county.'

He grinned. 'I promise I'll never try to sell you insurance.'

'OK. But I won't promise I'll never try to pitch you into using Mortensen and Brannigan.'

'Speaking of which, how did you get into the private eye business?' Michael said.

I couldn't decide whether it was an attempt to change the subject or a deliberate shift away from the professional towards the personal. Either way, I was happy to go along with him. I didn't think I was going to get any more useful information out of him, and I only had to look across the table to remember that when I'd agreed to this dinner, my motives hadn't been entirely selfless. By the time we'd moved on to coffee and Armagnac, he knew all about my aborted law degree, abandoned after two years because the part-time job I'd got doing bread-and-butter process serving for Bill Mortensen was a damn sight more interesting than the finer points of jurisprudence.

'So tell me about your most interesting case,' he coaxed me.

'Maybe later,' I said. 'It's your turn now. How did you get into insurance?'

'It's the family business,' he said, looking faintly embarrassed.

'So you followed in Daddy's footsteps,' I said. I felt disappointed. I couldn't put my finger on why, exactly. Maybe I expected him to live up to that profile with a suitably buccaneering past.

'Eventually,' he said. 'I read Arabic at university, then I worked for the BBC World Service for a while. But the money was dire and there were no prospects. My father had the sense to see that sales had never interested me, but he persuaded me to take a shot at working in claims.' Michael raised his shoulders and held out his hands in an expressive shrug. 'What can I say? I really enjoy it.'

All of a sudden, I remembered one of the key reasons I like being with Richard. He lives an interesting life: music journalist, football fan and Sunday morning player, part-time father. I was sure if I hung around with Michael Haroun, I'd learn a lot of invaluable stuff. But not even the most brilliant raconteur can make insurance interesting for ever. With Richard, no two days are the same. With Michael, I suspected variety might not be the spice of life.

Now I'd established that I didn't want to spend the rest of my life with the man, I felt a sense of release. I could take what I needed from the encounter, and that would be that. My life wasn't about to be turned on its head because I'd fallen in love with a profile when I was fourteen.

With that comforting thought in the front of my mind, I had no hesitation about inviting him back for more coffee. The fact that I'd forgotten to mention Richard to him somehow didn't seem too important at the time.

7

Richard's car wasn't home when we got there. I wasn't sure whether to be pleased or not. On the one hand, I wanted him to see me with Michael Haroun. If it took a bit of the green-eyed monster to make Richard start thinking about where our relationship was headed, so be it. On the other hand, the last thing I wanted was for him to throw a jealous wobbler in front of someone who was potentially a useful source, if not a prospective client.

'You live alone, then?' Michael asked casually as we walked up the path.

'Yes and no,' I said. 'I have a relationship with the man next door, but we don't actually live together.' I unlocked the door, switched off the burglar alarm and led him through the living room into the conservatory that links both houses. 'This is the common ground,' I said. 'We each reserve the right to lock the door into the conservatory.' I wasn't sure why I was telling Michael all this.

Maybe there was still a smidgen of lust running through my hormones.

Michael followed me back into the living room, closing the patio doors behind him. 'Coffee?' I asked. 'Or would you prefer a drink?'

He smiled mischievously. 'That depends.'

'Oh, you'll be driving,' I told him. Even if I'd been young, free and single, he'd have been driving, I told myself firmly.

He pulled a rueful face and said, 'It had better be coffee then.'

I'd just finished grinding the beans when I heard the clattering of Richard's engine. I glanced out of the window and watched the hot pink, customized Volkswagen Beetle convertible nose into the space between Michael's car and my Leo Gemini turbo super coupé, a trophy from the case which had put our relationship on the line in the first place. I kept meaning to trade it in for something more suited to surveillance work, the coupé being about as unobtrusive as Chatsworth on a council estate. But it was such a pleasure to drive, I hadn't got round to it yet.

Back in the living room, Michael clearly wasn't brooding on his rebuff. He was absorbed in the computer games reviews again. 'Coffee won't be long,' I said.

He closed the magazine and replaced it in the rack. Either he had very good manners, or he was as obsessively tidy as I was. Richard calls it anal retentive, but I don't see why you have to live in a tip just to prove you're laid back. Before we could get back into computer games, I heard the patio doors on the far side of the conservatory open. Richard's yell of greeting penetrated even my closed doors. 'Brannigan, I'm home,' he called.

Seconds later, he appeared at my doors, brandishing the unmistakable carrier bag of a Chinese takeaway. He pulled the door back, took in Michael and grinned. 'Hi,' he said expansively. I estimated three joints. 'You two still working?'

'We finished ages ago,' I said. 'Michael came back for coffee.'

'Right,' said Richard, oblivious to the implication I was thrusting under his nose. 'You won't mind if I join you then?'

Without waiting for an answer, he plonked himself down on the sofa opposite Michael and unpacked his takeaway. 'I'm Richard Barclay, by the way,' he said, extending a hand across the table to Michael. 'You wait for Brannigan to remember her manners, you could be dead.'

'Michael Haroun,' he said, shaking Richard's hand. 'Pleased to meet you.' Yes, an insurance man born and bred. Only an estate agent could have lied more convincingly.

Richard jumped to his feet and headed for the door. 'Chopsticks and bowls for three?' he asked. 'Sorry, Mike, I wasn't expecting company, but there's probably enough to go around.'

'We've just had dinner, Richard,' I said. 'I did leave you a message.'

'Yeah, I know,' he grinned. 'But I've never known you refuse a salt and pepper rib, Brannigan.'

'Sorry about that,' I said as he left.

Michael winked. 'Gives me a chance to suss out the competition.'

I didn't like the idea that I was some kind of prize, even if it was gratifying to know that he was interested in more than recovering Henry Naismith's Monet. And he didn't even have the excuse of a previous encounter in the British Museum. 'What makes you think there's a competition?' I asked sweetly.

Michael leaned back against the sofa and stretched his legs out. 'I thought you were the detective? Kate, if you two were as happy as pigs, you'd have left me sitting in the car wondering where exactly I'd made the wrong move.'

Before I could reply, Richard was back. 'I'll get the coffee,' I said, annoyed with myself for my transparency. By the time I got back, Richard and Michael were getting to know each other. And they say women are bitches.

'So, what do you do when you're not chipping a oner off people's car theft claims because your assessor spoke to the next-door neighbour who revealed that the ashtray was full?' Richard asked through a mouthful of shiu mai.

As I sat down next to him, Michael smiled at me and said, 'I play computer games. Like Kate.'

I poured the coffee in silence and let the boys

play. 'All a bit sedentary,' Richard remarked, loading his bowl with fried rice and what looked like a chicken hoi nam.

'Oh, I work out down the gym,' Michael said. I believed him. I could feel the hard muscles in the arm pressed against mine.

Richard nodded, as if confirming a guess. 'Thought as much,' he said. 'Bit too pointless for me, all that humping metal around. I prefer something a bit more social for keeping in shape. But then, I suppose it can't be easy finding people who want to play with you when you're an insurance claims manager,' he added, almost as an afterthought. 'Bit like being a VAT man.'

'I've never had any problems finding people to play with,' Michael drawled. I had no trouble believing that. 'What exactly is it that you do to keep fit, Richard? Squash? Real tennis? Polo? Or do you prefer raves?'

Richard almost choked on his food. Neither of us rushed to perform the Heimlich manoeuvre. Recovering, he swallowed hard and said, 'I'm a footie man myself. Local league. Every Sunday morning, never mind the weather.'

Michael smiled. Remember that poem? 'The Assyrian came down like the wolf on the fold'? 'I've never been much into mud myself,' he said.

'Had a good evening?' I chipped in before things got out of hand.

Richard nodded. 'Been down the Academy listening to East European grunge bands. Some good sounds.' He gave me one of his perfect smiles. 'How's your workload progressing?'

I shrugged. 'Slowly,' I said. 'Michael's been giving me some background on the art front, and I've got Alexis to chuck a few bricks into the pond. It's a question of waiting to see what floats to the surface.'

'And we all know what floats,' Richard said drily, glancing at Michael.

Michael decided enough was enough. He drained his mug and put it down on the coffee table. 'I'd better be on my way,' he said. 'Busy day tomorrow.'

We both stood up. 'I'll see you out,' I said.

'Nice to meet you, Richard,' Michael said politely on his way out the door.

'Feeling's entirely mutual,' Richard said ironically.

On the doorstep, I thanked Michael for dinner. 'It was a pleasant change,' I said.

'I can see that,' Michael said. 'Maybe we could do it again some time.'

I only hesitated for a moment. 'That'd be nice,' I admitted.

'Let me know how your investigation progresses,' he said. 'Stay in touch.' He leaned forward and brushed my cheek with his lips. He smelled of warm, clean animal, the last traces of his aftershave lingering muskily underneath. The hairs on the back of my neck stood on end as my body tingled.

I turned my head and met his lips in a swift,

breathless kiss. Before it could turn into anything more, I stepped back. 'Drive safely,' I said.

I watched him walk to his car, enjoying the light bounce of his step. Then I took a deep breath and walked back indoors.

After Michael had gone, Richard polished off the remains of his Chinese, making no comment on my choice of company for the evening. He asked if I wanted to see a movie the following evening and we bickered companionably about what we'd go to see, me holding out for *Blade Runner: The Director's Cut*, revisiting the Cornerhouse for the umpteenth time. 'No way,' Richard had said emphatically. 'I'm not going to the Cornerhouse. I'm getting too old for art houses. They're full of politically correct wankers trying to pretend they understand the articles in the *Modern Review*. You can't move for people rabbiting about semiotics and Foucault and deconstruction.' He paused, then got to the real reason. 'Besides, they don't sell popcorn or Häagen-Dazs. You can't call that a night out at the movies.'

I gave in gracefully. Satisfied that I'd made the concession, Richard announced he had to write an article about the post-Communist rockers for some American West Coast magazine, and he wanted to get it written and faxed before he went to bed. He swept the remains of his takeaway into the carrier bag and gave me a swift hug. 'I love you, Brannigan,' he muttered gruffly into my ear.

I fell asleep with the words of Dean Friedman's 'Love is not Enough' swirling round my head like a mantra. I woke up alone the next morning, and not particularly surprised by that. I felt strangely deflated, as if something I'd been anticipating hadn't happened. I wasn't sure if that was to do with Michael or Richard. Either way, I didn't like the feeling that my state of mind was dependent on anyone else. I stood in the shower for a long time, letting the water pour down. A friend of mine who's into all that New Age stuff reckons a shower cleanses your aura. I don't know about that, but it always helps me put things into perspective.

By the time I walked through the office door, I was feeling in control of my life again. That might have had something to do with the miracle of finding a parking meter that was nearer the office than my house. Parking in this city gets worse by the day. I've been seriously wondering how much it would cost to bribe the security men at the BBC building across the road to let me park my car inside their compound. Probably more than I earn.

Shelley was on the phone, so I headed straight for the coffee maker, a shiny chrome cappuccino machine that my partner, the gadget king of the Northwest, bought us for a treat after a grateful client gave us a bonus because we'd done the job faster than Speedy Gonzales. Somehow, I couldn't see either of our current employers rewarding my swiftness. I was beginning to feel like I was wading through cement on both cases.

Before I could fill the scoop with coffee, I heard Shelley say, 'Hang on, she's just walked in.'

I turned to see her waving the phone at me. 'Alexis,' Shelley said.

I headed for my office. 'Coffee?' It was a try-on, I admit it. Mortensen and Brannigan adopts a firm 'you want it, you make it' policy on coffee. But every now and again, Shelley takes pity on me.

I guess I didn't look needy enough, for there were no signs of her crossing the office after she'd switched the call through. I sighed and picked up the phone. ''Morning,' I said.

'Don't sound so enthusiastic,' the familiar Liverpudlian voice rasped. 'Here am I, bringing you tidings from the front line and you greet me with all the eager anticipation of a woman expecting bad news from her dentist.'

'It's your own fault. Never come between a woman and her cappuccino,' I retorted crisply.

I heard the sound of smoke being inhaled, then a husky chuckle. 'Some of us don't need coffee this late in the day. Some of us have already done half a day's work, KB.'

'Self-righteousness doesn't become you,' I snarled. 'Did you call for a reason, or did you just want to be told there's something clever about having a job that starts in the middle of the night?'

'There's gratitude for you,' Alexis said cheerfully. 'I call you up to pass on vital information, and what thanks do I get?'

I took a deep breath. 'Thank you, O bountiful

one,' I grovelled. 'So what's this vital piece of information?'

'What have you got to swap for it?'

I thought for a moment. 'You can borrow my leather jacket for a week.'

'Too tight under the armpits. What's the matter, KB? Got no gossip to trade? What's happening with the insurance man?'

If the *Chronicle*'s editor ever decides he needs to pacify the anti-smoking lobby and fire Alexis, she'll never starve. She could set up tomorrow in a booth on Blackpool pier. She wouldn't even have to change her name. Gypsy Alexis Lee sounds just fine to me. 'We had dinner last night,' I said abruptly.

'And?'

'And nothing. Dinner at That Café, he came in for coffee, Richard barged in waving a Chinese, they squabbled like two dogs over a bone, he went home.'

'Alone?'

'Of course alone, what do you take me for? On second thoughts, don't answer that. Trust me, Alexis, nothing's happening with the insurance man. You'll be the first to know if and when there is. Now, cut the crap and tell me what you rang for.'

'OK. The jungle drums have obviously been beating after that piece I did yesterday on the robberies.'

Nothing warms the cockles of the heart like the

smug self-satisfaction of being right. 'So what's the word on the street?'

'I don't know about the street. I'm working the stately home circuit these days,' Alexis replied disdainfully. 'I've just come off the blower with a punter called Lord Ballantrae.'

'Who's he?'

'I'm not entirely sure of all the titles, since I've not looked him up in Debrett yet, but he's some sort of Scotch baron.'

'You mean he's in the whisky trade?'

'No, soft girl, he's a baron and he comes from Scotland, though you'd never know to hear him talk.'

'So has he been burgled too?'

'Yeah, but that's not why he rang. Apparently, after he got turned over, he had a chat with some of his blue-blood buddies and found there was a lot of it about, so they got together in a sort of semi-informal network to pool their info and help other rich bastards to avoid the same happening to them. One of them spotted the story I did and told him about it, so he rang me for a chat. I'm doing a news feature on him and his gang, about how they're banding together to foil the robbers. And get this. They call themselves the Nottingham Group.' She paused, expectantly.

I took the bait. It was a small price to pay to keep the wheels of friendship oiled. 'Go on, tell me. I know you're dying to. Why the Nottingham Group?'

'After the Sheriff of Nottingham. On account of their goal is to stop these robbin' hoods from ripping off their wealth for redistribution to the selected poor.'

'Nice one,' I said. 'You going to give me his number?' I copied down Alexis's information and stuck the Post-it note on my phone. 'Thanks.'

'Is that it? What about "I owe you one"?'

Nobody's ever accused Alexis of being a shrinking violet. 'I don't. You're paying me back for your exclusive last night.'

'OK. You free for lunch?'

'Doubt it, somehow. What about tonight? Richard and I are going to the multi-screen. Do you two want to join us?'

'Sorry, we've already booked for *Blade Runner* at the Cornerhouse.'

Typical. 'Don't forget your Foucault,' I said.

I was halfway out of my chair, destination coffee machine, when the phone rang again. Suppressing a growl, I grabbed it and injected a bit of warmth into my voice. 'Good morning, Kate Brannigan speaking.'

'It's Trevor Kerr here.'

I wished I hadn't bothered with the warmth. 'Hello, Mr Kerr. What news?'

'I could ask you the same thing, since I'm paying you to investigate this business,' he grumbled. 'I'm ringing to let you know that my lab people have come up with some results from the analysis I asked them to carry out.'

Not a man to give credit where it's due, our Mr Kerr. I stifled a sigh and said, 'What did they discover?'

'A bloody nightmare, that's what. About half the samples they tested aren't bloody KerrSter.'

'Cyanide?' I asked, suddenly anxious.

'No, nothing like that. Just a mixture of chemicals that wouldn't clean anything. Not only would they not clean things, there are certain surfaces they'd ruin. Anything with a sealed finish like floor tiles or worktops. Bastards!' Kerr spat.

'Are these common chemicals, or what?'

'Ever heard of caustic soda? That's how bloody common we're talking here.'

'So cheap as well as common?' I asked.

'A lot bloody cheaper than what we put in KerrSter, let me tell you. So what are you going to do about it?' he demanded pugnaciously.

'Your killer's a counterfeiter,' I said, ignoring his belligerence. 'Either they're trying to wreck your business or else they're simply after a quick buck.'

'Even I'd got that far,' he said sarcastically. 'What I want you to do is find these buggers while I've still got a business left. You hear what I'm saying, Miss Brannigan? Find these bastards, or there won't be a pot left to pay you out of.'

8

Sometimes I wonder how clients managed to go to the bathroom before they hired us. Trevor Kerr was clearly one of those who think once they've hired you, you're responsible for everything up to and including emptying the wastepaper bins at night. He was adamant that it was down to me to go and see the detectives investigating the death of Joey Morton, the Stockport publican, to inform them that the person who was sabotaging Kerrchem's products was probably the one they should be beating up with rubber hoses. Incidentally, never believe the politicians and top coppers who tell you that sort of thing can't happen now all interviews are tape recorded. There are no tape recorders in police cars or vans, and I've heard of cases where it's taken three hours for a police car to travel two inner city miles.

I wasn't relishing telling some overworked and overstressed police officer how to run an inquiry. If there's one thing your average cop hates more than becoming the middle man in a domestic, it's being put on the right track by a private eye. I was even less thrilled when Kerr told me who the investigating officer was. Detective Inspector Cliff Jackson and I were old sparring partners. The first time one of my cases ended in murder, he was running the show. He hadn't exactly covered himself in glory, twice arresting the wrong person before the real killer had eventually ended up behind bars, largely as a result of some judicious tampering by Mortensen and Brannigan. You'd think he'd have been grateful. Think again.

I drove out to the incident room in Stockport. The one time I'd have welcomed being stuck in traffic, I cruised down Stockport Road without encountering a single red light. My luck was still out to lunch when I arrived at the police station. Jackson was in. I didn't even have to kick my heels while he pretended to be too busy to slot me in right away.

He didn't get up when I was shown into his office. He hadn't changed much; still slim, hair still dark and barbered to within an inch of its life, eyes still hidden behind a pair of tinted prescription lenses. His dress sense hadn't improved any. He wore a white shirt with a heavy emerald green stripe, the sleeves rolled up over his bony elbows. His tie was shiny polyester, in a shade of green that screamed for mercy against the shirt. 'I wasn't expecting to see you again,' he greeted me ungraciously.

'Nice to see you too, inspector,' I said pleasantly. 'But let's not waste our time on pleasantries. I wanted to talk to you about Joey Morton's death.'

'I see,' he said. 'Go on, then, talk.'

I told him all he needed to know. 'So you see,' I concluded, 'it looks like someone had got it in for Kerrchem, and Joey Morton just got in the way.'

He rubbed the bridge of his nose in a familiar gesture. It didn't erase the frown he'd had since I first walked through the door. 'Very interesting, Miss Brannigan,' he said. 'I take it you're planning to pursue your own inquiries along these lines?'

'It's what I'm paid to do,' I said.

'This is a possible murder inquiry,' he said sententiously. 'There's no place for you poking around in it.'

'Inspector, in case you've forgotten, it was me that came to you. I'm trying to be helpful,' I said, forcing my jaw to unclench.

'And your "help" is duly noted,' he said. 'It's our job now. If you interfere with this investigation like you did the last time, I'll have no hesitation in arresting you. Is that clear?'

I stood up. I know five foot three isn't exactly intimidating, but it made me feel better. 'I'll do my job, Inspector. And when I've done it, I'll tell you where you can find your killer.'

I tried to slam the door behind me, but it had one of those hydraulic arms. Instead of a satisfying crash, I ended up with a twisted wrist. I was still fizzing when I got back to the car, so I decided to kill two birds with one stone. Down the Thai boxing gym I could work out my rage and frustration and, with a bit of luck, acquire some information too.

I like the gym. It's a no-frills establishment, which means I tend not to run into clients there. As well as the boxing gym, it's got a weights room and basic changing facilities. The only drawback is that there are never enough showers at busy times. Judging by the number of open lockers, that wasn't going to be a problem today. I emerged from the women's changing room in the breeze-block drill hall to find my mate Dennis O'Brien lounging in a director's chair in his sweats. He was reading the *Chronicle*, his mobile phone, cigarettes and a mug of tea strategically placed on the floor by his feet. Dennis used to be a serious burglar, the kind who turn over the vulgar suburban houses of the nouveau riche. But it all came on top for him when a young lad he'd brought in to help him with a big job managed to drop the safe on Dennis's leg as they were making their getaway. He left Dennis lying on the drive with a broken ankle. By the time the cops arrived, he'd crawled half a mile. When he got out of prison three years later, he swore he was never going to do anything that would get him taken away from his kids again. As far as I know, he's kept his word, with one exception. The lad who abandoned him still walks with a limp.

It was Dennis who got me into Thai boxing. He believes all women should have self-defence skills, and when he discovered I'd been relying on nothing more than charm and a reasonable turn of speed, he'd dragged me down to the gym. His daughter's been a finalist in the national championships for the last three years running, and he lets her beat me up on a regular basis, just to remind me that there are people out there who could cause me serious damage. As if I need reminding after some of the crap I've been through in recent years.

Now he's out of major league villainy and into 'a bit of this, a bit of that, a bit of ducking and diving', Dennis has taken to using the gym as his corporate headquarters. I don't suppose the management mind. All the locals know Dennis's Draconian views on drugs so his presence keeps the gym clear of steroid abuse. And there are never any fights outside the ring. He's not known in South Manchester as Dennis the Menace for nothing.

I checked out a couple of black lads working the heavy bags at the far end of the room. They were too far away to overhear. 'Your backside will start looking like Richard's car if you carry on like that,' I said, smiling over the top of his paper.

'At last, someone worth sparring with,' Dennis said, bouncing to his feet. 'How's it hanging, kid?'

'By a fingernail,' I said, bending over to start my warm-up exercises. 'What do you know?' I glanced over at Dennis, who was mirroring my movements.

He looked glum. 'Tell you the truth, Kate, I'm in the shit,' he said.

'Want to tell me about it?'

'Remember that nice little earner I told you about a while back? My crime prevention scheme?'

How could I forget? Dennis's latest scam involved parting villains from large wads of money by persuading them they were buying a truckload of stolen merchandise from him. Dennis would show them a sample of the goods (bought or shoplifted from one of the dozens of wholesalers down Strangeways) and arrange a handover the following day in a motorway service area. Only, once the punters had swapped their stash for the keys to the alleged wagonload and Dennis's car was a distant puff of exhaust, the crooks would discover that the keys he'd handed them didn't open a single truck on the lorry park. Crime prevention? Well, if Dennis was taking their money off them, they wouldn't be inciting anyone else to steal something for them to buy, now would they?

'Somebody catch up with you?' I gasped between sit-ups.

'Worse than that,' he said gloomily. 'I set up a meet at Anderton Services on the 61. Ten grand for a wagon of Levis. Everything's going sweet as a Sunday morning shag when it all comes on top. All of a sudden, there's more bizzies than you get on crowd control at a United/City match. I legged it over the footbridge and dived into the ladies' toilet. Sat there for two hours. I went back over just in time to see the dibble loading my Audi on to a tow truck. I couldn't fucking believe it, could

I?' Dennis grunted as he did a handful of squat thrusts.

'Somebody tip them off about you?' I asked, fastening a body protector over my front.

'You kidding me? This wasn't regular Old Bill, this was the Drugs Squad. They'd only been staking the place out because they'd had a tip a big crack deal was going down. They see somebody handing over a wad of cash, and they jump to the wrong conclusion.'

'So what's happening?' I asked, pulling the ropes apart and climbing into the ring.

Dennis followed me and we began to circle each other cautiously. 'They lifted my punter and accused him of being a drug baron.' He snorted. 'That pillock couldn't deal a hand of poker, never mind a key of crack. Any road, he's so desperate to get out of the shit he's drowning in that he coughs the lot. Next morning, they're round my house mob-handed. The wife was mortified.'

'They charging you?' I asked, swinging a swift kick in towards Dennis's knee.

He sidestepped and twisted round, catching me over the right hip. 'Got to, haven't they? Otherwise they come away from their big stakeout empty-handed. Theft, and obtaining by deception.'

I didn't say anything. I didn't need to. Dennis might have been clean as far as the law is concerned for half a dozen years now, but with his record, he was looking at doing time. I feinted left and pivoted on the ball of my foot to bring my right leg up in a fast arc that caught Dennis in the ribs.

'Nice one, Kate,' he wheezed as he bounced back off the ropes.

'Bit of luck, your punters might decide it would be bad for their reputations if they weigh in as witnesses when it comes to court.' It wasn't much consolation but it was all I could think of.

'Never mind their reputation, it wouldn't be too good for their health,' he said darkly. 'Anyway, I've got one or two things on the boil. Just a bit of insurance in case I do go down. Make sure Debbie and the kids don't go without if I'm away.'

I didn't ask what kind of insurance. I knew better. We worked out in silence for a while. I was upset at the thought of only seeing Dennis with a visiting order for the next couple of years, but there was nothing I could do to help him out, and he knew that as well as I did. Even though we have more attitudes in common than seems likely on the surface, there are areas of each other's lives we take care to avoid. Mostly they're to do with knowledge that either of us would feel uncomfortable about keeping to ourselves. I don't tell him when I'm about to drop people in it who he knows, and he doesn't tell me things I'd feel impelled to pass on to the cops.

After fifteen minutes of dodging each other round the ring, we were both sweating. I lost concentration for a moment, which was all it took.

Next thing I knew, I was on my back staring at the strip lights.

'Sloppy,' Dennis remarked.

I scrambled up to find him leaning on the ropes. I could have knocked the wind out of him with one kick. Or maybe not. I've come into contact with that rock-hard diaphragm before. 'Got a lot on my mind,' I said.

'Anything I can help with?' he asked. Typical Dennis. Didn't matter how much crap of his own he had to sort out, he was still determined to stay in the buddy role.

'Maybe,' I said, slipping between the ropes and heading for the neat stack of scruffy towels on a shelf.

Dennis followed me, and we sat companionably on a bench while we talked. I gave him a brief outline of the Kerrchem case. 'You know anybody who's doing schneid cleaning fluid?' I ended up.

He shook his head. 'I don't know anybody that stupid,' he said scornfully. 'There's not nearly enough margin in it, is there? And it's bulky. Costs you a lot to shift it around, and you can't exactly set up a street-corner pitch with it, can you? There was a team from Liverpool tried schneid washing powder a couple of years back. They'd done a raid on a chemical firm, nicked one of their vans to do the getaway. There were a couple of drums of chemicals in the back, and they decided not to waste it so they printed up some boxes and flogged it on the markets. Nasty stuff. Took the skin off your fingers if you tried hand-washing. Mind you, there weren't any of them "difficult" stains left. That's because there wasn't a lot of clothes left.'

'So you don't reckon it's any of the usual faces?'

Dennis shook his head. 'Like I said, you'd have to be stupid to go for that when there's plenty of hooky gear around with bigger profits and a lot less risk. I reckon you're looking closer to home on this one. This is a grudge match.'

'An ex-employee? A competitor?' Even though it's a long way removed from his world, it's always worth bouncing ideas off Dennis.

Dennis shrugged. 'You're the corporate expert. Is this the kind of stunt big business pulls these days? I'd heard things were getting a bit tough out there, but bumping people off is a bit heavy for a takeover bid.'

'So an ex-employee, you reckon?'

'That's where I'd put my money. Stands to reason, they're the ones with a real grudge, and there's no comeback. And what about them thingumabobs . . . what do they call it? When they give you the bullet and make you sign a bit of paper saying you can't go off and sell their secrets to the opposition?'

'Golden handcuffs,' I said ruefully. I was slipping. That should have been one of the first half-dozen questions I asked Trevor Kerr.

'Yeah well, nobody likes being stuck in a pair of handcuffs, don't matter whether they're gold or steel,' Dennis said with feeling. 'It was me, I'd feel pretty cheesed. Specially if I was one of them boffins whose expertise goes out of date faster than a Marks and Spencer ready meal.'

I stretched an arm round his muscular shoulders and hugged him. 'You're a pal, Dennis.'

'I haven't done anything,' he said. 'That it? You consulted the oracle?'

'That's it. Unless you know an international gang of art thieves.'

'Art thieves?' he asked, sounding interested.

'They've been working all over the country, turning over stately homes. They go for one item and crash in through the nearest door or window. No finesse, just sledgehammers. Straight in and out. Obviously very professional. Sound like anybody you know?'

Dennis pulled a face. 'I'm well out of touch with that scene,' he said, getting to his feet. 'I'm off for a shower. Will you still be here when I'm done?'

I glanced at my watch. 'No, got to run.' Whatever else happened today, I couldn't leave Richard standing around at the multi-screen.

'See you around, kid,' Dennis said, walking off.

'Yeah. And Dennis . . .'

He looked over his shoulder, the changing room door half open.

'If there's anything I can do . . .'

Dennis's smile was as crooked as his business. 'You'll know,' he said.

Back at the car, I hit the phone. Sheila the Dragon Queen tried to tell me Trevor Kerr was in a meeting, but she was no match for my civil servant impersonation. I had good teachers; I once devoted most of my spare time for six months to screwing housing benefit out of a succession of bloody-minded officials.

'Trevor Kerr,' the phone barked at me.

'Kate Brannigan here. I've spoken to the police, who were very interested in what I had to tell them about the fake KerrSter,' I said. 'They said they would investigate that angle.'

'You pulled me out of a production meeting to tell me that?' he demanded.

'Not only that,' I said mildly. It was an effort. If he carried on like this, I reckoned there was going to be a five per cent surliness surcharge on Trevor Kerr's bill.

'What, then?'

'You mentioned you'd had a round of redundancies,' I said.

'So?'

'I wondered if anyone who'd gone out the door had been subject to a golden handcuffs deal.'

There was a moment's silence. 'There must have been a few,' he admitted grudgingly. 'It's standard practice for anybody working in research or in key production jobs.'

'I'll need a list.'

'You'll have one,' he said.

'Have it faxed to my office,' I replied. 'The number's on the card.' I cut the connection. That's the great thing with mobile phones. There are so many black holes around that nobody dares accuse you of hanging up on them any more.

I took out my notebook and rang the number Alexis had given me earlier. The voice that answered the phone didn't sound like Lord Ballantrae. Not unless he'd had an unfortunate accident. 'I'm looking for Lord Ballantrae,' I said.

'This is his wife,' she said. 'Who's calling?'

'My name is Kate Brannigan. I'm a private investigator in Manchester. I understand Lord Ballantrae is the coordinator of a group of stately home owners who have been burgled recently. One of my clients has had a Monet stolen, and I wondered if Lord Ballantrae could spare me some time to discuss it.'

'I'm sure he'd be happy to do so. Bear with me a moment, I'll check the diary.' I hung on for an expensive minute. Then she was back. 'How does tomorrow at ten sound?'

'No problem,' I said.

'Now, if you're coming from Manchester, the easiest way is to come straight up the M6, then take the A7 at Carlisle as far as Hawick, then the A698 through Kelso. About six miles past Kelso, you'll see a couple of stone gateposts on the left with pineapples on top of them. You can't miss them. That's us. Castle Dumdivie. Did you get all that?'

'Yes, thank you,' I said weakly. I'd got it, all right. A good three to four hours' driving.

'We'll look forward to seeing you then,' Lady Ballantrae said. She sounded remarkably cheerful. It was nice to know one of us was.

9

Richard didn't even stir when the alarm cut through my dreams at ten to six like a hot wire through cheese. I staggered to the shower, feeling like my eyes had closed only ten minutes before. Until I started this job, I didn't even know there were two six o'clocks in the same day. Richard still doesn't. I suppose that's why he suggested a club after the latest Steven Spielberg, enough popcorn to feed Bosnia and burgers and beer at Starvin' Marvin's authentic American diner. We'd been having fun together, and I didn't want it to end on a sour note, so I'd agreed with the proviso that I could be a party pooper at one. It goes without saying that we were still dancing at two.

Even a ten-minute power shower couldn't convince my body and my brain that I'd had more than three hours' sleep. Sometimes I wish I hadn't jacked in the law degree after two years, so I could have become a nine-to-five crown prosecutor. I put a pot of strong coffee on to brew while I dressed.

Just what do you wear for a Scottish baron that won't look like a limp dishrag after four hours behind the wheel? I ended up with navy leggings, a cream cotton Aran jumper and a military-style navy wool blouson that I inherited from Alexis. I'd told her in the shop that it made her look too heavy in the hips, but would she listen?

By the third cup of coffee, I felt like I could be trusted to drive without causing a major pile-up. Not that there was a lot of traffic around to test my conviction. For once, it was sheer pleasure to motor down the East Lancs. Road. No boy racers wanting to get into a traffic-lights Grand Prix with my coupé, no little old men with porkpie hats and pipes dithering between lanes, no macho reps waving their mobile phones like battle honours. Just blissful open road spread out before me and Deacon Blue's greatest hits. Since I was going to Scotland, I thought I'd better opt for the native sound. When I left the motorway at Carlisle, it was just after eight. I promised myself breakfast at the first greasy spoon I passed, forgetting what roads in the Scottish borders are like. There was nothing for the best part of an hour, and then it was Hawick. I ended up with a bacon and egg roll from a bakery washed down with a carton of milky industrial effluent that they claimed was coffee.

At a quarter to ten, I spotted the gateposts. When Lady Ballantrae had said pineapples, I was expecting some discreet little stone ornaments.

What I got were two squat pillars topped with carved monstrosities the size of telephone kiosks. She'd been right when she said I couldn't miss them. I turned into a narrow corridor between two beech hedges taller than my house. The road curved round in a gentle arc. Abruptly the trees stopped and I found myself in a grassy clearing dominated by Lord Ballantrae's house. I use the term 'house' loosely. At one end of the sprawling building was a massive square stone tower with a sharply pitched roof. Extending out from it, built in the same forbidding grey stone, was the main house. The basic shape was rectangular, but it was dotted with so many turrets, buttresses and assorted excrescences that it was hard to grasp at first. The whole thing was surmounted by an incongruous white belvedere with a green roof. One of Ballantrae's ancestors either had a hell of a sense of humour or a few bricks short of a wall.

I pulled up on the gravel between a Range Rover and a top-of-the-range BMW. What they call in Manchester a 'Break My Windows'. Like Henry, Lord Ballantrae clearly kept the trippers' coaches well away from the house. By the time I'd got out of the car, I had a spectator. At the top of a short flight of steps like a giant's mounting block a tall man stood staring at me, a hand shielding his eyes from the sun. I walked towards him, taking in the tweed jacket with leather shooting patches, cavalry twills, mustard waistcoat and tattersall check shirt. He was even wearing a tweed cap that matched the jacket. As soon as I was in hailing distance, he called, 'Miss Brannigan, is it?'

'The same. Lord Ballantrae?'

The man dropped his hand and looked amused. 'No, ma'am, I'm his lordship's estate manager. Barry Adamson. Come away in, he's expecting you.'

I followed Adamson's burly back into a comfortable dining kitchen. Judging by the microwave and food processor on the pine worktops, this wasn't part of the castle's historical tour. Beyond the kitchen, we entered a narrow passage that turned into a splendid baronial hall. I don't know much about weapons, but judging by the amount of military hardware in the room, I'd stumbled upon Bonnie Prince Charlie's secret armoury. 'Through here,' Adamson said, opening a heavy oak door. I followed him through the arched doorway into an office that looked nearly as high tech as Bill's.

A dark-haired man in his early forties was frowning into a PC screen. Without looking up, he said, 'With you in two shakes.' He hit a couple of keys and the frown cleared. Then he pushed his chair back and jumped to his feet. 'You must be Kate Brannigan,' he said, coming round the desk and thrusting his hand towards me. 'James Ballantrae.' The handshake was cool and dry, but surprisingly limp. 'Pull up a seat,' he said, waving at a couple of typist's chairs that sat in front of a desk top that ran the length of one wall. 'Barry, Ellen's in the tack room. Can you give her a shout and ask her to bring us some coffee?' he added as he dragged his own chair round the desk. 'How was your journey?' he asked. 'Bitch of a drive, isn't it? I sometimes wish I could ship this place stone by stone to somewhere approximating civilization, but they'd never let me get away with it. It's Grade Two listed, which means we couldn't even have satellite TV installed without some bod from the Department of the Environment making a meal out of it.'

Whatever I'd been expecting, it wasn't this. Lord Ballantrae was wearing faded jeans and a Scottish rugby shirt that matched sparkling navy blue eyes. His wavy hair fell over his collar at the back, its coal black a startling contrast to his milky skin. There was an air of suppressed energy about him. He looked more like a computer-game writer than a major land owner. He sat down, stretching long legs in front of him, and lit a cigarette. 'So, Henry Naismith tells me you're looking for his Monet?' he said.

I tried to hide my surprise. 'You know Henry?' I asked. Let's face it, they both spoke the same language. Their voices were virtually indistinguishable. How in God's name do Sloanes know who's calling when they pick up the phone?

He grinned. 'We met once on a friend's boat. When my wife told me about your call yesterday, I put two and two together. I'd already spoken to a reporter on the Manchester evening paper about these art robberies and when she mentioned a

106

Monet going missing in Cheshire, I could only think of the Naismith collection. So I gave Henry a ring.'

'The reporter you spoke to is a friend of mine,' I said. 'She passed your number on to me.'

'Old girls' network. I like it,' he exclaimed with delight. 'She did the right thing. God, listen to me. My wife tells me that arrogance runs in the family. All I mean is that I'm probably the only person who has an overview of the situation. The downside of having locally accountable police forces is that crime gets compartmentalized. Sussex don't talk to Strathclyde, Derbyshire don't talk to Devon. It was us who brought to the police's attention the fact that there had been something of a spate of these robberies, all with the same pattern of forced entry, complete disregard for the alarm system and single targets.'

'How did you find out about the connections?' I asked.

'A group of us who open our places to the public get together informally . . .' I heard the door open behind me and turned to see a thirty-something redhead with matching freckles stick her head through the gap.

'Coffee all round?' she said.

'My wife, Ellen,' Ballantrae said. 'Ellen, this is Kate Brannigan, the private eye from Manchester.'

The redhead grinned. 'Pleased to meet you. Be right back,' she said, disappearing from sight, leaving the door ajar.

'Where was I? Oh yes, we get together a couple of times a year for a few sherbets, swap ideas and tips, that sort of thing. Last time we met was a couple of weeks after I'd had a Raeburn portrait lifted, so of course it was uppermost in my mind. Three others immediately chipped in with identical tales – a Gainsborough, a Canaletto and a Ruisdael. In every case, it was one of the two or three best pieces they had,' he added ruefully.

'And that's when you realized there was something organized going on?' I asked.

'Correct.'

'I'm amazed you managed to keep these thefts out of the papers,' I said.

'It's not the sort of thing you boast about,' he said drily. 'We've all become dependent on the income that comes through the doors from the heritage junkies. The police were happy to go along with that, since they never like high-profile cases where they don't catch anyone.'

'What did you do then?'

'Well, I offered to act as coordinator, and I spoke to all the police forces concerned. I also wrote to as many other stately home owners as I could track down and asked if they'd had similar experiences.'

'How many?' I asked.

'Including Henry Naismith's Monet, thirteen in the last nine months.'

I took a deep breath. At this rate, the stately homes of Britain would soon have nothing left but the seven hundred and thirty-six beds Good Queen Bess slept in. 'That's a lot of art,' I said. 'Has anything been recovered?'

'Coffee,' Ellen Ballantrae announced, walking in with a tray. She was wearing baggy khaki cords and a shapeless bottle green chenille sweater. When she moved, it was obvious she was hiding a slim figure underneath, but on first sight I'd have taken her for the cleaner.

I fell on the mug like a deprived waif. 'You've probably saved my life,' I told her. 'My system's still recovering from what they call coffee in Hawick.'

Both Ballantraes grinned. 'Don't tell me,' Ellen said. 'Warm milk, globules floating on top and all the flavour of rainwater.'

'It wasn't that good,' I said with feeling.

'Don't let me interrupt you,' she said, giving her husband's hair an affectionate tousle as she perched on the table. 'He was about to tell you about the Canaletto they got back.'

Ballantrae reached out absently and laid his hand on her thigh. 'Absolutely right. Nothing to do with the diligence of the police, however. There was a multiple pile-up on a German autobahn about a fortnight after Gerald Brockleston-Camber lost his Canaletto. One of the dead was an antique dealer from Leyden in Holland, Kees van der Rohe. His car was shunted at both ends, the boot flew open, throwing a suitcase clear of the wreckage. The case burst open, revealing the Canaletto behind a false lid. Luckily the painting was undamaged.'

'Not so lucky for Mr van der Rohe,' I remarked. 'What leads did they come up with?'

'Not a one,' Ballantrae said. 'They couldn't find anything about the Canaletto in his records. He conducted his business from home, and the neighbours said there were sometimes cars there with foreign plates, but no one had bothered to take a note of registrations.' He shrugged. 'Why should they? There was no indication as to his destination, apart from the fact that he had a couple of hundred pounds' worth of lire in the front pocket of the suitcase. Unfortunately, van der Rohe's body was badly burned, along with his diary and his wallet. Frustrating, but at least Gerald got his painting back.'

Frustrating was right. This was turning into one of those cases where I was sucking up information like a demented Hoover, but none of it was taking me anywhere. The only thing I could think of doing now was getting in touch with a Dutch private eye and asking him or her to check out Kees van der Rohe, to see if he could come up with something the police had missed. 'Any indication of a foreign connection in the other cases?' I asked.

'Not really,' Ballantrae said. 'We suspect that individual pieces are being stolen to order. If anything, I'd hazard a guess that if they're for a private collector, we're looking at someone English. A lot of the items that have been stolen have quite a narrow appeal – the Hilliard miniatures, for example. And my Raeburn too, I suppose. They wouldn't exactly set the international art world ablaze.'

'Maybe that's part of the plan,' I mused.

'How do you mean?' Ellen Ballantrae leaned forward, frowning.

'If they went for really big stuff like the thieves who stole the Munch painting in Norway, there would be a huge hue and cry, Interpol alerted, round up the usual suspects, that sort of thing. But by going for less valuable pieces, maybe they're relying on there being less of a fuss, especially if they're moving their loot across international borders,' I explained.

Ballantrae nodded appreciatively. 'Good thinking, that woman. You could have something there. The only thefts that fall outside that are the Bernini bust and Henry's Monet, but even those two aren't the absolutely prime examples of their creators' works.'

'Can you think of any collectors whose particular interests are covered by the thefts?' I asked.

'Do you know, I hadn't thought about that. I don't know personally, but I have a couple of chums in the gallery business. I could ask them to ask around and see what they come up with. That's a really constructive idea,' Ballantrae enthused.

I basked in the glow of his praise. It made a refreshing change from Trevor Kerr's charmlessness. 'What's the geographical spread like?' I asked.

'We were the most northerly victims. But there doesn't seem to be any real pattern. They go from

Northumberland to Cornwall north to south, and from Lincolnshire to Anglesey east to west. I can let you have a print-out,' he added, jumping to his feet and walking behind his computer. He hit a few keys, and the printer behind me cranked itself into life.

I twirled the chair round and took the sheet of paper out of the machine. Reading down it, I saw the glimmer of an idea. 'Have you got a map of the UK I can look at?' I asked.

Ballantrae nodded. 'I've got a data disk with various maps on it. Want a look?'

I came round behind his desk and waited for him to load the disk. He called up a map of the UK with major cities and the road network. 'Can you import this map and manipulate it in a graphics file?' I asked.

'Sure,' he said. And promptly did it. He gave me a quick tutorial on how to use his software, and I started fiddling with it. First, I marked the approximate locations of the burglaries, with a little help from Ballantrae in identifying locations. I looked at the array.

'I wish we had one of those programs that crime pattern analysts use,' I muttered. I'd recently spent a day at a seminar run by the Association of British Investigators where an academic had shown us how sophisticated computer programs were helping police to predict where repeat offenders might strike next. It had been impressive, though not a lot of use to the likes of me.

'I never imagined I'd have any use for one of those,' Ballantrae said drily.

Ellen laughed. 'No doubt the software king will have one by next week,' she said.

Using the mouse, I drew a line connecting the outermost burglaries. There were eight in that group, scattered round the fringes of England and Wales. Then I repeated the exercise with the remainder. The outer line was a rough oval, with a kink over Cornwall. It looked like a cartoon speech balloon, containing the immortal words of the Scilly Isles. The inner line was more jagged. I disconnected Henry Naismith's robbery and another outside Burnley. Now, the inner line was more like a trapezium, narrower at the top, spreading at the bottom. Finally, I linked Henry and the Burnley job with a pair of semi-circles. 'See anything?' I asked.

'Greater Manchester,' Ballantrae breathed. 'How fascinating. Well, Ms Brannigan, you're clearly the right woman for the job.'

I was glad somebody thought so. 'Have there been any clues at all in any of the cases?' I asked.

Ballantrae walked over to a shelf that held his computer software boxes and manuals. 'I don't know if you'd call it a clue, exactly. But one of the properties that was burgled had just installed closed-circuit TV and they have a video of the robbery. But it's not actually a lot of help, since the thieves were very sensibly wearing ski masks.' He took a video down from the shelf. 'Would you like to see it?'

'Why not?' I'd schlepped all the way up here. I wasn't going home before I'd extracted every last drop of info out of Lord Ballantrae.

'We'll have to go through to the den,' he said.

As I followed him back across the hall, Ellen said affectionately, 'Some days I think he's auditioning for *Crimewatch*.'

We retraced my steps back towards the kitchen, turning into a room only twice the size of my living room. The view was spectacular, if you like that sort of thing, looking out across a swathe of grass, a river and not very distant hills. Me, I'm happy with my garden fence. As Ballantrae crossed to the video, I gave the room the once-over. It wasn't a bit like a stately home. The mismatched collection of sofas and armchairs was modern, looking comfortable if a bit dog-haired and dog-eared. Shelves along one wall held a selection of board games, jigsaws, console games and video tapes. A coffee table was strewn with comics and magazines. In one corner there was a huge Nicam stereo TV and video with a Nintendo console lying in front of it. The only picture on the walls was a framed photograph of James and Ellen with a young boy and girl, sitting round a picnic table in skiing clothes. They all looked as if the world was their oyster. Come to think of it, it probably was.

'Sorry about the mess,' Ellen said in the offhand tone that told me she didn't give a shit about tidiness. 'The children make it and I can't be bothered unmaking it. Have a seat.'

She walked over to the windows and pulled one of the curtains across, cutting down the brightness so we could see the video more clearly. I sat down opposite the TV, where daytime TV's best actors played out their roles as a happily married couple telling the rest of us how to beat cellulite. Ballantrae slumped down beside me and hit the play button. 'This is Morton Grange in Humberside,' he said. 'Home of Lord Andrew Cumberbatch. His was the Ruisdael.'

The screen showed an empty room lined with paintings. Suddenly, from the bottom left-hand corner, the burglars appeared. The staccato movements of the time-lapse photography made them look like puppets in an amateur performance. Both men were wearing ski masks with holes for eyes and mouth only, and the kind of overalls you can pick up for next to nothing in any army surplus store. One of them ran across to the painting, pulled out a power screwdriver and unscrewed the clips that held the frame to the wall. The other, holding a sledgehammer, hung back. Then he turned towards the camera and took a couple of steps forward.

Recognition hit me like a punch to the stomach.

10

One of the mysteries of the universe is how I got out of Castle Dumdivie without confessing that I knew exactly who had had it away on his toes with Lord Andrew Cumberbatch's nice little Ruisdael. I was only grateful that James Ballantrae was sitting next to me and couldn't see my face.

After the first seconds of shock, I tried to tell myself I was imagining things. But the longer I watched, the more convinced I was that I was right. I knew those shoulders, those light, bouncing steps. God knows I'd watched that footwork often enough, trying to gauge where the next kick was coming from. I forced myself to sit motionless to the bitter end. Then I said, 'I see what you mean. Even their own mothers wouldn't recognize them from that.'

'Their lovers might,' Ellen said shrewdly. 'Don't they say a person's walk is the one thing they can never disguise?'

She was bang on the button, of course. 'The

video makes it look too jerky for that, I'd have thought,' I said.

'I don't know.' Ballantrae lit another cigarette and inhaled deeply. 'Body language and gesture are pretty individual. Look at the number of crimimals who get caught by the videos they show on *Crimewatch*.'

'Told you,' Ellen said fondly. 'He's dying to go on and talk about his art robberies. The only thing that's holding him back is that all his cronies are terrified about what the publicity might do to their admissions.'

'Yes, but now the cat's out of the bag with that newspaper story in Manchester, there's no point in holding back,' Ballantrae said. 'Maybe I should give them a ring . . .'

'Any chance you could let me have a copy of the tape?' I asked. 'I'd like to show it to Henry Naismith's staff while everything's still fresh in their memories. Perhaps, as Ellen suggests, there might be something in the way these men move that triggers something off. The police reckon they will have gone round the house a couple of times as regular punters, sussing it out, so we might just get lucky if one of Henry's staff has a photographic memory.'

Ballantrae got up and took the video out of the machine. 'Take this one,' he said. 'I can easily get Andrew to run me off another copy.'

I took the tape and stood up. 'I really appreciate your help on this,' I said. 'If anything else should come to mind that might be useful, please give me a ring.' I fished a business card out of my bag.

'What will you do now?' Ballantrae asked.

'Like I said, show the vid to Henry's staff. I'm also hopeful that the story in the *Chronicle* might stir the pot a bit. The chances are that it's not just the robbers themselves who know who they are. Maybe you should think about getting together with your insurance companies and offering a reward. It would make a good follow-up story for the paper and it might just be what we need to lever the lid off things.' I was starting to gabble, I noticed. Time for a sharp exit. I ostentatiously looked at my watch. 'I'd better be heading back to the wicked city,' I said.

'You're sure you've got to go?' Ballantrae asked with the pathetic eagerness of a small boy who sees his legitimate diversion from homework disappearing over a distant horizon. 'I could show you round the house. You could see for yourself where they broke in.'

Amused, Ellen said, 'I'm sure Ms Brannigan's seen one or two windows in her time.' Turning to me, she added, 'You're very welcome to stay for lunch, but if you have to get back, don't feel the need to apologize for turning down the guided tour of Dumdivie's loot.'

'Thanks for the offer, but I need to hit the road,' I said. 'This isn't the only case we've got on right now, and my partner's out of the country.' I really was wittering now. I took a step towards the door. 'I'll keep you posted.'

I drove back to Manchester on automatic pilot, my thoughts whirling. Shelley phoned at one point, but I'm damned if I know what we talked about. When I hit the city, I didn't go to the office. I didn't want any witnesses to the conversation I was planning. I drove straight home, glad for once to find Richard was out.

My stomach was churning, so I brewed some coffee and made myself a sandwich of ciabatta, tuna, olives and plum tomatoes. It was only when I tried to eat it and found I had no appetite that I realized it was anxiety rather than hunger that was responsible for the awesome rumblings. Sighing, I wrapped the sandwich in clingfilm and tossed it in the fridge. I picked up the phone. Some money-grabbing computer took ten pence off me for the privilege of telling me Dennis's mobile was switched off.

Next, I rang the gym. Don, the manager, told me Dennis had been in earlier, but had gone off a couple of hours ago suited up. 'If he comes back, tell him I've been visiting the gentry and he needs to see me, double urgent. I'll be at home,' I said grimly.

That left his home. His wife Debbie answered on the third ring. She's got a heart of gold, but she could have provided the model for the dumb blonde stereotype. I'd always reckoned that if a brain tumour were to find its way inside her skull it would bounce around for days looking for a place to settle. However, I wasn't planning on challenging her intellect. I just asked if Dennis was there, and she said she hadn't seen him since breakfast. 'Do you know where he is?' I asked.

She snorted incredulously. 'I gave up asking him stuff like that fifteen years ago,' she said. Maybe she wasn't as thick as I'd always thought. 'To be honest, I'd rather not know what he's up to most of the time. Long as he gives me money for the kids and the house and he stays out of jail, I ask no questions. That way, when the Old Bill comes knocking, there's nothing I can tell them. He knows I'm a crap liar,' she giggled.

'When are you expecting him back?'

'When I see him, love. Have you tried his mobile?'

'Switched off.'

'He won't have it turned off for long,' Debbie reassured me. 'If he comes home before you catch him, do you want me to get him to give you a bell?'

'No. I want him to come round the house. Tell him it's urgent, would you?'

'You're not in any trouble, are you, Kate?' Debbie asked anxiously. 'Only, if you need somebody in a hurry, I could get one of the lads to come round.'

Like I said, heart of gold. 'Don't worry, Debbie, I'm fine. I've got something I need to show Dennis, that's all. Just ask him to come round soon as.'

We chatted for a bit about the kids, then I rang off. I knew I should go into the office and pick up Trevor Kerr's list of former employees, but I knew

I wouldn't be able to concentrate on it. I switched on the computer and loaded up Epic Pinball. I thrashed the ball round the bumpers and ramps a few times, but I couldn't get into it. My scores would have shamed an arthritic octogenarian. I decided I needed something more violent, so I started playing Doom, the ultimate shoot-'em-up, at maximum danger level. After I got killed for the tenth time, I gave up and switched the machine off. I know it's as bad as it can get when I can't lose myself in a computer game.

I ended up cleaning the house. The trouble with modern bungalows is that it doesn't take nearly long enough to bottom them when you want a really good angst-letting. By the time the doorbell rang, I'd moved on to purging my wardrobe of all those garments I hadn't worn for two years but had cost too much for me to dump in my normal frame of mind. A disastrous pair of leggings that looked like stretch chintz curtains were saved by the bell.

Dennis stood on the doorstep, grinning cheerily. I wanted to smack him, but good sense prevailed over desire. It seemed to have been doing that a lot lately. 'Hiya. Debbie says you've got something for me,' he greeted me, leaning forward to kiss my cheek.

I backed off, letting him teeter. 'Something to show you,' I corrected him, marching through into my living room. Without waiting for him to sit down, I smacked the tape into the video, turned on the TV and pressed play. I kept my back to him while the robbery replayed itself before our eyes. As the two burglars disappeared from sight, I switched off the TV and turned to face him.

Dennis's expression revealed nothing. I might as well have shown him a blank screen for all the reaction I was getting. 'Nice one, Dennis,' I said bitterly. 'Thanks for marking my card.'

He thrust his hands into the trouser pockets of his immaculate, pearl grey, double-breasted suit. 'What did you expect me to do? Put my hands up when you told me what you was looking into?' he said quietly.

'Never mind what I expected,' I said. 'What you did do has dropped me right in it.'

Dennis frowned. 'What is this?' he demanded angrily. 'You know the kind of thing I do for a living. I'm not some snow-white straight man. I'm a thief, Kate, a fucking criminal. I steal things, I have people over, I pull scams. How else do you think I put food in my kids' mouths and clothes on their backs? It's not like I've been keeping it a big fucking secret, is it?'

'No, but . . .'

'What's wrong? You're quick enough to come to me for help because I can go places and get people to talk that you can't. You think I could do that if I wasn't as bent as the bastards you chase? What is it, Kate? You can't handle the fact that one of your mates is a crook now you're faced with the evidence?'

I found myself subsiding on to a sofa. He was

right, of course. I've always known in the abstract that Dennis was a villain, but I'd never had to confront it directly. 'I thought you weren't doing this kind of thing any more,' I said weakly. 'You always said you wouldn't do stuff that would get you a long stretch again.'

Dennis threw himself on to the sofa opposite me. A grim smile flashed across his face. 'That was the plan. Then everything came on top, like I told you. Kate, I could get five for that. My kids shouldn't have to suffer because I'm a villain, should they? I don't want my kids not being able to go to university because their old man's inside and there's no money. I don't want my family living in some bed-and-breakfast dosshouse because the mortgage hasn't been paid and the house has been repo'ed. Now, the only way I know to make sure that doesn't happen is to salt away some insurance money. And the only way I know to get money is robbing.'

'So you've been doing these art robberies,' I said.

'That's right. Listen, if I'd known that you'd done the security on Birchfield Place, I wouldn't have gone near the gaff. You're my mate, I don't want to embarrass you.'

I shook my head. 'If I recognized you, Dennis, chances are someone else might, especially if they put the tape on the box.'

He sighed. 'So do what you have to do, Kate.' He met my eyes, not in a challenge, but in a kind of agreement.

'You don't think I'm going to shop you, do you?' I blurted out indignantly.

'It's your job,' he said simply.

I shook my head. 'No, it's not. My job is to get my clients' property back. It's the police that arrest villains, not me.'

'You've turned people over to the dibble before,' Dennis pointed out. 'You got principles, you should stick to them. It's OK, Kate, I won't hold it against you. It's an occupational hazard. You work with asbestos, sometimes you get lung cancer. You go robbing for a living, sometimes you get a nicking. There's nothing personal in it.'

'Will you get it into your thick head that I am not going to grass you up?' I said belligerently. 'The only thing I'm interested in is getting Henry Naismith's Monet back. Anyway, you're only a small fish. If I want anybody, I want the whale.'

Dennis's lips tightened to a thin line. 'OK, I hear you,' he said grimly. I didn't expect him to fall to his knees in gratitude. Nobody likes being placed under the kind of obligation I'd just laid on him.

'So cough,' I said.

He cleared his throat. 'It's not that simple,' he said, taking his time over pulling out his cigarettes and lighting up. 'I haven't got it any more.'

'That was quick,' I said, disappointed. From what Dennis had told me about his previous exploits in the field of executive burglary, it often takes some time to shift the proceeds, fences being notoriously

124

twitchy about taking responsibility for stolen goods that are still so hot they risk meltdown.

Dennis leaned back in his seat, unbuttoning his jacket. 'A ready market. That's one of the reasons I got into this in the first place. See, what happened was when I realized this court case wasn't going to go away, I put the word out that I was looking for a nice little earner. A couple of weeks later, I get a call from this bloke I know in Leeds. I fenced a couple of choice antique items with him in the old days when I was pursuing my former career. Anyway, he says he's heard about my bit of bother, and he's got a contact for me. He gives me this mobile phone number, and tells me to ring this bloke.

'So I ring the number and mention my contact's name and this bloke says to me he's in the market for serious art. He says he has a client for top-flight gear, flat fee of ten grand a pop for pieces agreed in advance. I go, "How do I know I can trust you?" And he goes, "You don't part with the gear till you see the colour of my money." I go, "How does it work?" And he goes, "You decide on something you think you can get away with, and you ring me and ask me if I want it. I ring you back the next day with a yes or a no."'

'So you embark on your new career as an art robber,' I said. 'Simple, really.'

'You wouldn't be so sarcastic if you knew what a nause it is shifting stuff like that on the open market,' Dennis said with feeling.

'How did you know what to go for? And where to

go for it?' I demanded. I'd never had Dennis pegged as a paid up member of the National Trust.

'My mate Frankie came out a while back,' he said. I didn't think he meant that Frankie had revealed he was a raging queen. 'He's been doing an eight stretch for armed robbery, and he did an Open University degree while he was inside. He did a couple of courses in history of art. He reckoned it would come in useful on the outside,' he added drily.

'I don't think that's quite what the government had in mind when they set up the OU,' I said.

Dennis grinned. 'Get an education, get on in life. Anyway, we spent a couple of months schlepping round these country houses, sussing out what was where, what was worth nicking and what the security was like. Pathetic, most of it.'

I had a sudden thought. 'Dennis, these robberies have been going on for nine months now. You only got nicked a few weeks ago. You didn't start doing this for insurance money, you started doing this out of sheer badness,' I accused him.

He shrugged, looking slightly shamefaced. 'So I lied. I'm sorry, Kate, I can't change the habit of a lifetime. This was just too good to miss. And watertight. We don't touch places with security guards so nobody gets hurt or upset. We're in and out so fast there's no way we're going to get caught.'

'I caught you,' I pointed out.

'Yeah, but you're a special case,' Dennis said.

'Besides, the CCTV wasn't there when we cased the place. They must have only just put it in.'

'So who is this guy who's giving you peanuts for these masterpieces?'

Dennis smiled wryly. 'It's not peanuts, Kate. It's good money and no hassle.'

'It's a tiny fraction of what they're worth,' I said.

'Define worth. What an insurance company pays out? What you could get at auction? Worth is what somebody's prepared to pay. I reckon ten grand for a night's work is not bad going.'

'A grand for every year if they catch you. You'd get a better rate of pay working in a sweatshop making schneid T-shirts. So who's the buyer? Some private collector or what?'

'I don't know,' Dennis said. 'I don't even know who the fence is.'

I snorted incredulously. 'Come on, Dennis, you've done more than a dozen deals with this guy, you must know who he is.'

'I've never met him before this run of jobs,' Dennis said. 'All I've got is the number for his mobile.'

'You're kidding,' I said. 'You've done over a hundred grand's worth of work for some punter whose name you don't even know?'

''S right,' he said easily. 'My business isn't like yours, Kate, I don't take out credit references on the people I do business with. Look, what happens is, every few weeks I ring the guy up with one of

Frankie's suggestions. He gives me the nod, we go out and do the job, and I give him a bell. We meet on the motorway services, we show him the goods, he counts the dosh in front of us, and we all go home happy boys.'

'What about the fakes?'

There was a deathly silence. He ground out his cigarette viciously in the ashtray. 'How did you find out about them?' Dennis asked warily. 'There's been nothing in the papers or anything about that.'

'What happens when it turns out you've nicked a copy?' I asked, ignoring him.

Dennis shifted in his seat, leaning forward with his elbows on his knees. 'You setting me up, or what?' he asked. 'You saying that Monet wasn't kosher?'

'It was kosher,' I said. 'But they haven't all been, have they?'

Dennis lit his cigarette like an actor in a Pinter play filling one of the gaps with a complicated bit of business. 'Three of them were bent as a nine-bob note,' he said. 'First I knew about it was about a week after we'd done the handover when the geezer bells me and tells me. I said I never knew anything about it, and he goes, "I'm sure you were acting in good faith, but the problem is that so was my client. He reckons you owe him ten grand. And he has very efficient debt collectors. But he's a fair man. He'll cancel the debt if you provide another painting for free." So we to and fro a bit, and eventually he agrees that he'll pay us a grand for expenses for the next kosher one we bring him, and we're all square. So we go and do another one, and bugger me if it isn't bent as well.' He shook his head in wonderment.

'Talk about a scam,' he said. 'These bastards with their country houses really know how to pull a con job on the punters. Anyway, we end up having to do a third job, this time for fuck all, just to get ourselves square. I mean, he's obviously dealing with the kind of money that can buy a lot of very vicious muscle. You don't mess with that.'

'But everything's hunky-dory now, is it?'

He nodded, eating smoke. 'Sweet.'

'Great,' I said. 'Then you won't mind putting the two of us together, will you, Dennis?'

11

Once upon a time I had a fling with a Telecom engineer. It didn't end happily ever after, but he taught me more than I'll ever need to know about crossed lines. Along the way, before I accepted that great sex wasn't a long-term compensation for the conversational skills of Bonzo the chimpanzee, I met some very useful people. I met some bloody boring ones too, and unfortunately the crossover between the two groups was disturbingly large. Even more unfortunately, I was going to have to talk to one of them.

After I'd finally convinced Dennis that I wasn't going to back off and that the price of his liberty was putting me together with his fence, it hadn't taken me long to squeeze out of him the phone number of the contact. He'd left, grumbling that I was getting in over my head and I needn't come running to him when the roof fell in. Naturally, we both knew that in the event of such an architectural disaster, the combined emergency services of six counties wouldn't keep him away.

I watched his car drive away, not entirely certain I was doing the right thing. But I knew I couldn't turn Dennis over to the cops. It wasn't just about friendship, though that had been the key factor in my decision, no doubt about it. But I hadn't been lying when I said I wanted the people behind the whole shooting match. Without them, the robberies wouldn't end. They'd just find another Dennis to do the dirty work and carry the can. Besides, I wanted Henry's Monet back, and Dennis didn't have it any more.

After Dennis had gone, I rediscovered my appetite and wolfed the sandwich from the fridge before settling down to the thankless task of calling Gizmo. Gizmo works for Telecom as a systems engineer, which suits him down to the ground since he's the ultimate computer nerd. The first time I met him, he was even wearing an anorak. In a nightclub. I later discovered it was rare as hen's teeth to catch Gizmo out on the town. Normally the only thing that will prize him away from his computer screen is the promise of a secret password that will allow him to penetrate to the heart of some company's as yet virgin network. He's only ever happy when his modem's skittering round the world's bulletin boards. Gizmo would much rather be wandering round the Internet than the streets of Manchester. I thought Bill and I were pretty nifty movers round the intangible world of computer communications till I met Gizmo. Then I realized our joint hacking skills were the equivalent of comparing a ten-year-old's 'What I did on my holidays' essay with Jan Morris on just about anywhere.

I looked Gizmo up in my Filofax. There were several points of contact listed there. I tried his phone, but it was engaged. What a surprise. I booted up my computer, loaded up my comms software and logged on to the electronic mail network that Mortensen and Brannigan subscribe to. I typed a message asking Gizmo to call me urgently and sent it to his mailbox.

The phone rang five minutes later. I'd specifically asked him to call me person to person. The last thing I wanted was to relay my request to him over the Net. You never know who's looking in, no matter how secure you think you are. That's one of the first things Gizmo taught me. 'Kate?' he said suspiciously. Gizmo doesn't like talking; he prefers people to know only the constructed personality he releases over the computer network.

'Hi, Gizmo. How's life?' Silly question, really. Gizmo and life are barely on speaking terms.

'Just got myself a state-of-the-art rig,' he said. 'She's so fast, it's beautiful. So, what's going down with you?'

'Busy, busy. You know how it is. Gizmo, I need some help. Usual terms.' Fifty quid in used notes in a brown envelope through his letter box. He comes so cheap because he loves poking around other people's computers in the same way that some men like blondes with long legs.

'Speak, it's your dime,' he said. I took that for agreement.

'I've got a mobile number here that I need a name and address for.'

'Is that all?' He sounded disappointed. I gave him the number. 'Fine,' he said. 'I should be back to you later today.'

'You're a star, Giz. If I'm not here, leave a message on the machine. The answering machine. OK?'

'OK.'

The next call was to Lord Ballantrae. 'I think I've got a lead,' I told him. 'To the fence, not the principal behind the robberies. But I need some help.'

'That's quick work,' he said. 'Fire away. If I can do, I will do.'

'I need something to sell him. Not a painting, something fairly small but very valuable. Not small as in brooch, but maybe a small statuette, a gold goblet, that kind of thing. Now, I know that some of your associates have taken to displaying copies rather than the real thing. One of those dummies would be ideal, provided that it would pass muster on reasonably close scrutiny. You think you can come up with something like that?' I asked.

'Hmm,' he mused. 'Leave it with me. I'll get back to you.'

Two down, one to go. I dialled a number from memory and said, 'Mr Abercrombie, please. It's Kate Brannigan.' The electronic chirrup of the

Cuckoo Waltz assaulted my eardrums as I waited for whatever length of time Clive Abercrombie deemed necessary to put me firmly in my place. Clive is a partner in one of the city's prestige jewellers. He would say *the* prestige jewellers. That's the kind of pretentious wally he is. We pulled Clive's nuts out of the fire on a major counterfeiting scam a couple of years back, and I know that deep down he's eternally grateful, though he'd die before he'd reveal it to a mere tradesperson like me. His gratitude had turned into a mixed blessing, however. It was thanks to Clive's recommendation that we'd got the case that had put Richard behind bars and me at risk of parting company with my life. By my reckoning, that meant he still owed me.

We were on the third chorus when he deigned to come on the line. 'Kate,' he said cautiously. Obviously I wasn't important enough to merit solicitous inquiries about my health. Not a stupid man, Clive. He's clearly sussed out that Richard and I are not in the market for a diamond solitaire.

'Good afternoon, Clive,' I said sweetly. 'I find myself in need of a good jeweller, and I can't think of anyone who fits the bill better than you.'

'You flatter me,' he said, flattered.

'I'm like you, Clive. When I need a job doing, I come to the experts.'

'A job?' he echoed.

'A little bit of tinkering,' I said soothingly. 'Tomorrow, probably. Will one of your master craftspeople have a little time to spare for me then?'

'That depends on what we're talking about,' he said warily. 'I hope you're not suggesting something illegal, Kate.'

'Would I?' I said, trying to sound outraged.

'Quite possibly,' he said drily. 'What exactly did you have in mind?'

'I don't have all the details yet, but it would involve . . . a slight addition to an existing piece.'

He sighed. 'Come round tomorrow morning after eleven. I'll discuss it with you then.'

'Thank you, Clive,' I said to dead air.

I checked my watch. Half past four. Just time to nip round to the office and collect Trevor Kerr's list of former staff. I swapped the smart clothes for a pair of leggings and a sweatshirt and took my bike. It would be quicker than the car this time of day, and besides, I wanted the exercise. I found Shelley in the throes of preparing the quarterly VAT return. 'Kate,' she said grimly. 'Just the person I wanted to see.' She waved a small bundle of crumpled receipts at me. 'I know it's really unreasonable of me, but do you suppose you could enlighten me as to what precisely these bills are for? Only, by my calculations, we're due a VAT inspection some time within the next six months, and I don't think they're going to be thrilled by your idea of keeping records. "Miscellaneous petty cash" isn't good enough, you know.'

I groaned. 'Can't you just make it up?' I wheedled,

picking up the top receipt. 'This is from the electrical wholesalers; just call it batteries or light bulbs or cassette tapes. Use your imagination. We don't often let you do that,' I added with a smile.

Shelley curled her lip. 'I don't have an imagination. I've never found it necessary. You're not leaving here till you've told me what's what. And if *you* make it up, I can blame you when the VAT inspector doesn't believe me.'

It didn't take me as long as I feared. Imagination is not something I've ever lacked. What I couldn't remember, I invented. There wasn't a VAT person in the land who'd dare question what I needed thirty-five metres of speaker wire for. Having mollified the real boss at Mortensen and Brannigan, I grabbed my fax and headed out the door before she could think of something else that would keep me from my work.

In the short interval that I'd been out, both Gizmo and Ballantrae had been back to me. The name and address attached to the phone didn't fill me with confidence. Cradaco International, 679A Otley Road, Leeds. On an impulse, I grabbed the phone and rang Josh's office. The man himself was in a meeting, but Julia, his personal assistant, was free. I pitched her into hitting the database right away and finding out whatever details Cradaco International had filed at Companies House. I hung on while she looked. Now that everything's on-line, information it used to take days to dig out of dusty files is available at the touch of a finger-tip.

She didn't keep me waiting long. 'Kate? As you thought, it's an off-the-shelf company. Share capital of one pound. Managing director James Connery. Company Secretary Sean Bond. Uh-oh. Does something smell a bit fishy to you, Kate?'

I groaned. 'Any other directors?'

'Have a guess?'

'Miss Moneypenny? M?' I said, resignedly.

'Nearly. Miss Penny Cash.'

I sighed. 'You'd better give me the addresses, just in case.' I copied down three addresses in Leeds. At least they were all in the same city. One trip would check out the directors and the company. 'You're a pal, Julia,' I said.

'Don't mention it. You could do me a small favour in return,' she said.

'Try me.'

'Could you ask Richard if there's any chance he could get me a bootleg tape of the Streisand Wembley concert?' she asked.

I'd never have put cut-glass, upper-middle-class Julia down as a Streisand fan, but there's no accounting for taste. 'It's a bit off his beat, but I'll see what I can do,' I promised.

Time to get back to Ballantrae. He answered on the first ring. 'I think I've got the very thing for you,' he said. 'How does an Anglo-Saxon belt buckle sound?'

'Useful if you've got an Anglo-Saxon belt,' I said.

He chuckled. 'It's a ceremonial buckle, worn by chieftains and buried with them. It's about five inches by two inches. The original is made of solid gold, chased with Celtic designs and studded with semi-precious stones. There are only two known to be in existence. One's in the British Museum, the other's in a private collection in High Hammerton Hall near Whitby.'

'Sounds perfect,' I said. 'Have you spoken to the owner?'

'I have. He's been displaying a replica for the last five months, but I've managed to persuade him to lend it to you. We were at school together,' he added in explanation.

'What's it made of?' I asked.

'The replica's made of lead and plastic, with a thin coating of gold leaf. He says it would fool someone who wasn't an expert, even close up. He says if you sit the two of them side by side, it's almost impossible to tell them apart.'

'Sounds perfect,' I said. 'When can I get it?'

'He's sending it to you by overnight courier. It will be at your office by ten tomorrow morning.'

'Lord Ballantrae, you are a star,' I said, meaning it. So much for the inbred stupidity of the aristocracy. This guy was more on the ball than ninety-five per cent of the people I have to deal with.

'No problem. I want to get these people as badly as you do. Probably more so. Then we can all get back to the business of doing what we do best.'

Speaking of which, I finally got down to doing

something about Trevor Kerr's case. I felt guilty for ignoring the material he'd sent me, but the art-theft case was far more absorbing. I felt it was something I could get to the bottom of single-handed, unlike the Kerrchem case. I found myself inclined to agree with Jackson. This was a case for the cops, if only because they had the staffing resources to cover all the bases that it would take me weeks to get round. Then the little voice in my head kicked in with the real reason. 'You can't stand Trevor Kerr so you don't want to put yourself out for him. And you're desperate to impress that Michael Haroun.'

'Bollocks,' I muttered out loud, seizing the sheets of fax paper with fresh energy. Someone – the indomitable Sheila, I suspected – had conveniently included the job titles as well as the names and addresses of those made redundant. I reckoned I could exclude anyone who worked on the factory floor or in the warehouse. They would have neither the chemical know-how nor the access to sales and distribution information that would allow them to pull a sabotage scheme as complex as this. That left thirty-seven people in clerical, managerial and scientific posts who had all been given what looked like a tin handshake to quit their jobs at Kerrchem.

By nine, I felt like the phone was welded to my ear. I was using a labour-market research pitch, which seemed to be working reasonably well. I claimed to be working for the EC Regional Fund, doing research to see what sort of skills were not being catered for by current job vacancies. I told my victims that I was calling people who had been made redundant over the previous year to discover whether they had found alternative employment. A depressingly low number of Kerrchem's junked staff fell into that category, and they were mostly low-grade clerical staff. Not one of the ten middle managers had found new jobs, and to a man they were bitter as hell about it. Of the chemists, two out of the three lab technicians were working in less skilled but better paid jobs. The four research lab staff who had been laid off were bound by their contracts and the terms of their redundancies not to work for direct competitors. One had taken a job as an analyst on a North Sea oil rig, two of the other three were kicking their heels and hating it, and one was no longer at the address the company had for him. It looked like I had no shortage of suspects.

I stood up and stretched. Richard still hadn't come home, so there was nothing to divert me from work. I couldn't move on with the Kerrchem stuff tonight, but I wasn't quite stalled on the other investigation. The sensible part of me knew I should go to bed and catch up on last night's missed sleep, but I'd had enough of being sensible for one week. I went through to the kitchen, cut open the other half of the ciabatta and loaded it with mozzarella, taramasalata and some sun dried tomatoes. I wrapped it in clingfilm, and took a small bottle of mineral water out of the fridge.

Fifteen minutes later, I was cruising down the M62, singing along cheerfully to a new compilation of Dusty Springfield's greatest hits that I'd found lying around in Richard's half of the conservatory. Never mind the mascara, check out that voice.

I was in Leeds before ten, nervously navigating my way through the subterranean tunnels of the inner ring road, emerging somewhere near the white monolith of the university. The roads were quiet out through Headingley, but every now and again, a beam of light split the night from on high as the police helicopter quartered the skies, trying to protect the homes of the more prosperous residents from the attentions of the burglars. Burglary has reached epidemic proportions in Leeds these days; I know someone whose house was turned over seven times in six months. Every time they came home with a new stereo, so did the burglars. Now, their house is more secure than Armley jail and their insurance premiums are nearly as much as the mortgage.

I slowed as I approached the Weetwood round-about, scanning houses for their numbers. 679A looked like it might be one of an arcade of shops, so I parked up and stretched my legs. I can't say I was surprised to find there was no 679A. There was a 679, though, a small newsagent's squeezed between a bakery and a hairdresser. I walked round the back of the shops, checking to see if the flats above had entrances at the rear. A couple did, but 679 wasn't one of them. I walked back to the car, with plenty to think about. Whoever Dennis's fence was, he was determined to cover his tracks. Using an accommodation address for his phone bills was about as careful as you could get without actually being sectioned for paranoia.

I decided to check out the directors' addresses while I was in the city, but I held out little hope of finding any of them at home. James Connery's alleged residence was nearest, back in Headingley proper. It was number thirty-nine in a street of ten houses. On to Chapel Allerton, where Sean Bond apparently lived in a hostel for the visually handicapped. Penny Cash was even worse off. According to Companies House, she was living on a piece of waste ground in Burmantofts. I doubled back through the city centre, passing the new Health Ministry building up on Quarry Hill, spotlit to look like a set from Fritz Lang's *Metropolis*. Apparently, the place contains a full-size swimming pool, Jacuzzi and multi-gym. Nice to know our hard-earned taxes are being spent on the health of the nation, isn't it?

It was nearly midnight when I got home. Richard's car was parked outside, though I didn't need that clue to know he was home as soon as I touched the front door. It was vibrating with the pulse of the bass coming through the bricks from next door. As I shoved my key in the lock, I could feel exhaustion flow through me, settling in a painful knot at the base of my skull.

I walked through the house to the conservatory.

Richard's patio doors were open, revealing half a dozen bodies in varying states of consciousness draped over the furniture. Techno dance music drilled through my head like a tribe of termites who have just discovered a log cabin. The man himself was nowhere to be seen. I picked a path to the kitchen, where I found him taking a tray of spring rolls out of the oven. 'Hi,' he said. His eyes were as stoned as the woman taken in adultery.

'Any chance of the volume coming down? I need some sleep,' I said.

'That's cool,' he said, a lazy smile spreading across his face. 'Want some company?'

'You've already got some.'

'They can be out of here in ten minutes,' he said. 'Then I'm all yours.'

He was as good as his word. Eleven minutes later, he crawled into my blissfully silent bed. Unfortunately, I'm not into necrophilia.

12

The buckle got to the office before I did, which gave Shelley something to puzzle over. I arrived to find her using it as a paperweight. 'OK,' she said. 'I give in.'

I don't often find myself one up on Shelley, so I decided to drag it out a bit. 'If you can guess, I'll buy lunch,' I said.

'What makes you think you're going to have time for lunch?' she asked sweetly. 'Besides, I told you yesterday, I don't do imagination. You want me to learn how, you're going to have to pay me a lot more.'

I should know better. The woman is the mother of two teenagers. What chance do I have? 'It's a replica of an Anglo-Saxon ceremonial belt buckle,' I said. 'Also known as a honey pot.' Mustering what was left of my dignity, I scooped up the buckle and marched through to my office.

This time Dennis's mobile was switched on. 'I want you to set up a meet for me with your man,'

I said. 'Tell him you vouch for me, and that I've got something really special for him.'

'I'm not sure if he'll go for it,' Dennis tried. 'Like I told you, we have to wait for a yes or a no before we lift stuff. He's very picky, and he likes to be in control.'

'Tell him there's only two in the world. I've got one and the British Museum's got the other one. Tell him it's from the collection at High Hammerton Hall. And it's gold. He should be able to work it out himself from that. Believe me, Dennis, he'll want this.'

'All right,' he said grudgingly. 'But I'm coming with you on the meet.'

'No, you're not,' I told him firmly. 'You're in enough trouble as it is. This is not going to be heavy, Dennis. I can handle one man in a car park. You should know, you train me.'

'I still think you're crazy, chasing this,' he said. 'Your client's going to be better off with the insurance company's readies in his bank account than he is with a poxy picture on the wall.'

'Call it professional pride.'

'Call it pig-headedness,' he said. 'I'll get back to you.'

I went through to Bill's office and opened the cupboard where we keep our stock of technological wizardry. I found what I was looking for in a cardboard box at the back of the top shelf. It's not something we use very often, reeking as it does of *The Man from U.N.C.L.E.*, but given that Dennis's fence seemed to be an aficionado of James Bond, it seemed entirely appropriate to use a directional bug. If that conjures up images of chunky metal boxes stuck to the bottom of cars, forget it. Thanks to modern miniaturization technology, the bugs we've got are about the size of an indigestion tablet. The transmission batteries last about a week, and allow the bug to send a signal to a base unit. The range is about fifteen kilometres, provided large mountains don't get in the way, and the screen gives a read-out of direction and distance. Perfect for tracking the buckle back to source, so long as the fence was going to get rid of it sharpish.

Next stop, Clive Abercrombie, with a brief detour via the terraced streets of Whalley Range to stuff Gizmo's used tenners through his letter box. When I got to the shop, Clive was hovering behind a counter, ostentatiously leaving the waiting-on to the lesser mortals he employs to be polite to the rich. When I walked in, he shot forward and had me through the door to the back of the shop so fast my feet didn't even leave tracks in the shag pile. Obviously, he doesn't want proles like me hanging around making the place look like Ratners. 'In a hurry, Clive?' I asked innocently.

'I thought *you* would be. You usually are,' he replied acidly. 'Now, what was it you wanted?'

I took the buckle out of my handbag. In spite of himself, Clive drew his breath in sharply. 'Where did you get that?' he demanded, extending one finger to point dramatically at the twinkling gold lump.

'Don't worry, my life of crime runs to solving it, not committing it,' I soothed. 'It's not the real thing. It's a copy.'

If anything, he looked even more disturbed. 'Why are you walking around with it in your *handbag?*' he demanded, giving Lady Bracknell a run for her money.

Knowing Clive's weakness for anything reeking of snobbery, I said, 'I'm doing a job for the Nottingham Group.'

'Should I know the name?' he asked snottily.

'Probably not, Clive. It's a consortium of the landed gentry, headed by Lord Ballantrae of Dumdivie. Art thefts. Very hush-hush. I'm very close to Mr Big, and this is a ploy to smoke him out.' I pulled the bug out of my pocket. 'What I need is for one of your craftsmen to incorporate this in the piece. Preferably on the outside. I'd thought under one of the stones.' I handed the bug and the buckle to Clive, who already had his loupe out.

He took a few minutes to scrutinize the buckle which was heavy enough to make a useful weapon, especially if it was attached to a belt. 'Nice piece of work,' he commented. 'If you hadn't told me it was a fake, I'd have had my work cut out to spot it.' Praise indeed, coming from Clive. He unscrewed the loupe from his eye socket and said, 'It'll take a few hours. And it will cost.'

'Now there's a surprise,' I said. 'Just send us an

invoice. Give me a bell when it's ready.' I turned to go back through the shop, but Clive gripped my elbow and steered me further into the nether regions.

'Easier if you pop out the back door,' he said. Half a minute later, I was in the street. I reckoned I deserved a cappuccino made by someone other than me, so I decided to take the scenic route back to the office. For a brief moment, I toyed with the idea of ringing Michael Haroun and suggesting he play truant for half an hour, but I told myself severely that it wouldn't help my pursuit of the art thieves to involve the insurers at this stage. They'd only start muttering about doing things by the book and informing the police. I smacked my hormones firmly on the wrist and drove the length of Deansgate to the Atlas Café, where they claim to make the best coffee outside Italy. I wasn't going to argue. I dumped the car on a yellow line down by the canal basin and walked back up to the chic glass-and-wood interior. I sat by the window, sipping the kind of cappuccino that acts like intravenous caffeine and pulled the Kerrchem papers out of my bag. Time for a file review.

I didn't know exactly what I was looking for. All I knew was that I wanted to find something, anything that would legitimately allow me to postpone or short-circuit the tedious process of doing background checks into all of the redundant staff that I hadn't been able to eliminate on the phone.

On the second read-through, I found exactly what I was looking for.

Joey Morton's supply of KerrSter came from the local branch of a national chain of trade whole-salers, Filbert Brown. His wife couldn't remember which of them had actually made the trip to the cash-and-carry when the fatal drum of KerrSter had been bought, but there was no doubt that that was the original source of the tainted cleanser.

It wasn't much to go on, but it was a place to start. One of the dozens of pieces of normally useless information cluttering up my dustbin brain was the fact that Filbert Brown were a Manchester-based company. I knew this because I passed their head office and flagship cash-and-carry every time I drove from my house to North Manchester. Suddenly energized, I abandoned the hedonism of the Atlas and trotted down the steps to the car.

It didn't take long to skirt the city centre. It took longer to get through to the customers' car park at Filbert Brown. They occupied an old factory building just off Ancoats Street. The area was in the middle of that chaotic upheaval known as urban renewal. East Manchester is supposedly coming up in the world; home of the new Commonwealth Games stadium, spiffy new housing developments and sports facilities. Oh, and roads, of course. Lots of them. Virgin territory for the traffic cones and temporary traffic lights that have become an epidemic on the roads of the Northwest. My political friends reckon it's the government's revenge because most of us up here didn't vote for them.

Considering it was the middle of the morning when all of us small business people are supposed to have our noses firmly to the grindstone, Filbert Brown was surprisingly busy. I walked in without challenge and found myself in a glorified warehouse. It reminded me of those cheap and cheerless back-to-basics supermarkets that we've imported from Europe in recent years. Anyone who did their shopping in Netto or Aldi would have been right at home in Filbert Brown. Me, I always find it incredibly cheap to shop there – they never stock anything I'd want to buy. The same went for Filbert Brown. I know Richard thinks I have an unhealthy obsession with cleanliness, but even I couldn't get turned on by cases of dishwasher powder, drums of worktop bactericide and cartons of paper towels. I was clearly in a minority, judging by the number of people who were happily filling up their trolleys.

I wandered up and down the aisles for a few minutes, getting a feel for the place. One of the things that struck me was how prominent KerrSter was among the cleansers. It occupied the whole width of a shelf at eye level, the key position in shifting merchandise. Compared with the other Kerrchem products, which seemed to be doing just about OK compared with their competitors, KerrSter was king of the castle.

What I needed now was a pretext. Thoughtfully, I wandered back to the car. I always keep a fold-over clipboard in the boot for those occasions when I need to pretend to be a market researcher. You'd be amazed at what people will tell you if you've got a clipboard. I gave my clothes the once-over. I was wearing tan jodhpur-style leggings, a cream linen collarless shirt and a chocolate brown jacket with a mandarin collar. The jacket was too smart for the pitch, so I folded it up and left it in the boot. In the shirt and leggings, I could just about pass. Freeze, maybe, but pass.

I walked briskly into Filbert Brown and strode up to the customer service counter. I say counter, but it was more of a hole in the wall. Customers here clearly weren't encouraged to complain. The woman behind the counter looked as if she'd been hired because of her resemblance to a bulldog. 'Yes?' she demanded, teeth snapping.

'I'm sorry to trouble you,' I said brightly. 'I'm doing an MBA at Manchester Business School and I'm doing some research into sales and marketing. I wonder if I could perhaps have a word with your stock controller?'

'You got an appointment?'

'I'm afraid not.'

She looked triumphant. 'You'd need an appointment.'

I looked disappointed. 'It's a bit of an emergency. I had arranged to see someone at one of the big DIY stores, but she's come down with a bug and she had to cancel and I really need to get the initial research done this week. It won't take more than half an hour. Can't you just ring through and see if it would be possible for me to see someone?'

'We're a bit busy just now,' she said. 'We' was inaccurate; 'they' would have been nearer the mark, judging by the queues at the tills.

'Please?' I tried for the about-to-burst-into-tears look.

She cast her eyes heavenwards. 'It's a waste of time, you know.'

'If they're busy, I could make an appointment for later,' I said firmly.

With a deep sigh, she picked up the phone, consulted a list taped to the wall of her booth and dialled a number. 'Sandra? It's Maureen at customer services. There's a student here says she wants to talk to you . . . Some project or other . . .' She looked me up and down disaparagingly. Then her eyebrows shot up. 'You will?' she said incredulously. 'All right, I'll tell her.' She dropped the phone as if it had bitten her and said, 'Miss Bates will be with you in a moment.'

I leaned against the wall and waited. A couple of minutes passed, then a woman approached through the checkouts. Her outfit was in the same colours as the rest of the staff, but where they wore red and cream overalls, she wore a red skirt and a blouse in the red and cream material. She smiled as she approached, which explained why she'd never get the job in customer services. 'I'm Sandra Bates,' she greeted me. 'How can I help you?'

I gave her the same spiel. 'What I need is a few minutes of your time so you can run through your shelf-allocation principles,' I finished.

She nodded. 'No problem. Come along to my office; I'll take you through it.'

I fell into step beside her. 'I really appreciate this,' I said. 'I know how busy you must be.'

'You're not kidding,' she said. 'But this business needs more women who can give the boys a run for their money. When I was doing my business studies degree at the poly, it was almost impossible to get any of them to spare any of their precious time,' she added grimly. Thank God for the sisterhood.

She ushered me into an office that was marginally bigger than the room off my office that doubles as a darkroom and the ladies' loo. Most of the floor space was taken up by a desk dominated by a PC. The desk surface and the floor around it were stacked with files and papers. Sandra Bates picked her way through the piles and sat in her chair. 'Give me a second,' she said, staring at the monitor.

I used the time to check her out. She looked to be in her late twenties, about my height, her jaw-length light brown hair expertly highlighted with blonde streaks. She was attractive in a china doll sort of way, pink and white complexion, unexceptional blue eyes and a slightly uptilted nose. Her determined mouth was the only contrasting feature, indicating an inner strength that might just give the boys a run for their money in the promotion stakes.

'Right,' she said, looking up and grinning at me. 'What do you want to know?'

'How you decide what goes where on the shelves?' I said. I don't know why I wanted to know that, but it seemed a good place to start if I wanted to get round to KerrSter.

'The general order of the products in the aisles is ordained from above, based on market research and psychological analysis, would you believe,' she said. 'It's the same way that supermarkets decide you get the fruit and veg first and the booze last. I mean, those of us who actually do the shopping know that your grapes get crushed by the six packs of lager, but I suppose they work on the principle that by the time you've cruised the aisles, you feel like you need a drink.'

My turn to grin. 'So what decisions do you actually make on the shop floor?'

'What we decide is what goes where within each section. The received wisdom is that items placed at eye level sell better than those you have to reach up for or bend down to. Now, all the checkouts are computerized, and I can access all the product figures from this terminal here. That way, I can see what stock is moving fast, and make sure we reorder at the right time so that we neither run out nor end up with huge stockpiles. When a particular line starts to outstrip rival products, it automatically goes into the best shelf position so that those sales are maintained or increased. With me so far?'

I nodded. It was all terribly logical. 'Are there any exceptions?'

Sandra nodded approvingly. 'Oh, yes. Lots. For example, when a company brings out a new product, they will often arrange to pay us a premium in return for our displaying it in the most advantageous shelf position. Or if a company's product has been ousted from its top selling position by a rival, they'll offer us a loss-leader price on the product for a limited period in exchange for them getting their old shelf site back so they can try to re-establish their old supremacy.'

'Is that what Kerrchem have done with KerrSter?' I asked.

Sandra blinked. 'I'm sorry?' she asked, sounding startled.

'I was having a browse round before I asked to see you, and I couldn't help noticing how prominent the KerrSter was. And with that guy dying after he opened it, I'd have thought sales would have gone through the floor,' I said innocently.

'Yes, well, it's always been a popular seller, KerrSter,' Sandra gabbled. 'I suppose our customers haven't seen the stories.'

'I'd have thought Kerrchem would have recalled it,' I went on. For some reason, talk of KerrSter was making Sandra Bates twitchy. Rule number one of interrogation: when you've got them on the run, keep chasing.

'They recalled one batch,' she said, regaining her composure.

'Still, I wouldn't buy it,' I said. 'I'm surprised one of their competitors hasn't tried to exploit the situation. In fact, I'm surprised a small company like them outsells the opposition so comprehensively.'

'Yes, well, there's no accounting for customer preferences. Now, if there's nothing more you'd like to know about the shelf-stacking, I have got a lot on my plate,' Sandra said, getting to her feet and waving vaguely at the paperwork on her desk.

I was back on the street inside a minute. Being hustled twice in one morning was bad for the ego. Clive Abercrombie I could understand. But the mere mention of KerrSter had shifted Sandra Bates from cooperative sisterhood to the verge of hostility. Something was going on that I didn't understand. And if there's one thing I hate, it's things I don't understand.

13

I'm no cyberpunk, but I'm knowledgeable enough about hacking to know that I couldn't have penetrated Filbert Brown's computer network on my own. I was sure they had to have a central computer that dealt with all their individual branches. Via that it should be possible to crawl back inside Sandra Bates's data. Way back in the mists of time – say, around 1991 – I could probably have reached first base. Bill has a program that dials consecutive phone numbers till his modem connects with another computer. I could have set that to run through all the numbers on the same exchange as Filbert Brown's head office. It would probably have taken all night to run, but it would have got me there in the end.

However, the powers that be have decided that darkside hackers like us need to be cracked down on, so now they've got their own sophisticated equipment that picks up on sequential dialling like that and traces it. Then the dibble comes and knocks on your door in a very user-unfriendly way. Besides, getting the computer's number was only the start. I'd need a login to get through the front door, and a password to get any further. Ideally, I needed the password of the sysman – the system manager. Most people who are authorized users of a network system have logins which allow them only limited access to the part of the system they need to work with. The sysman is what computerspeak calls a superuser, which means he or she can wander unimpeded throughout the system, checking out each and every little nook and cranny. With Bill's help, I might just have managed to achieve sysman status on the Filbert Brown network. But Bill was on the other side of the world.

That only left Gizmo. I tried his number, and got lucky. 'Wozzat?' a voice grunted.

'Gizmo?'

'Yeah?'

'Kate. Did I wake you?'

He cleared his throat noisily. 'Yeah. Been up all night. What d'you want?'

I told him. He whistled. 'Can't do that one for the usual,' he said.

'But can you do it?'

'Sure, I can *do* it,' he said confidently. 'Getting in shouldn't be a problem. But if you want sysman status, that'll cost you.'

'How much?' I sighed.

'One and a half.'

Trevor Kerr could stand another hundred and fifty quid, I decided. 'Done deal,' I told Gizmo. 'How soon?'

He sniffed. Probably on account of the whizz he'd have snorted to keep him awake all night. 'Few hours,' he said.

'Sooner the better.'

Back in the office, routine awaited. A stack of background information had arrived in the post that morning. I'd been waiting for it so that I could complete a report for a client on the three candidates they'd short-listed for the head of their international marketing division. One of them looked like he'd have a promising career writing fiction. The candidate's degree from Oxford turned out to have been a two-year vocational course at the former poly. His credit rating was worse than the average Third World country's. And one of his previous employers seemed to think that his financial skills were focused more in the direction of his bank account than theirs. All of which would make the selection panel's job a bit easier.

It was just after four when Clive Abercrombie rang to tell me the buckle was ready and waiting. I worked for another hour, then collected it on the way home. Clive's jeweller had done a good job. I was looking for the bug, and I couldn't see it. No way would the fence spot it in the middle of a motorway service station. Back in the car, I checked the receiver was picking it up. Loud and clear.

When I got in, there was a message from Gizmo on my machine. 'Hi. I've got your order ready. I think you should collect it in person. I'll expect you.' I sighed and got back in the car. Just because you're paranoid doesn't mean they're not out to get you. In Gizmo's case, I thought it was a small miracle the hacker crackers hadn't already kicked his door in. In his shoes, I wouldn't trust the phone lines either.

I hit the cash machine on the way, taking myself up to my daily limit. I parked round the corner from his house, just in case he really was under surveillance, and wishing I'd remembered to do the same on my earlier drop. I rang the bell and waited. Nearly a minute passed before the door cracked open on the chain. 'It's me, Giz,' I said patiently. 'Alone.'

He handed me a piece of paper. I handed him the cash. 'See you around,' he said and closed the door.

Back in the car, I unfolded the paper. There was a telephone number, FB7792JS (the login), and CONAN (the sysman's password). I'd bet it was Conan the Barbarian the sysman had in mind, not the creator of the world's first PI. Yet another wimpy computer nerd with delusions of grandeur. I drove home via Rusholme, where I picked up a selection of samosas, onion bhajis, chicken pakora and aloo saag bhajis. I had the feeling it was going to be a long night, and I didn't know if I could rely on Richard to come home with a Chinese.

I brought the coffee machine through to my study and sat down at the computer with the Indian snacks and the coffee to hand. I booted up and loaded my comms program. Dialling the number on the paper brought me a short pause, then the monitor said, 'Welcome to FB. Login?' I typed the digits Gizmo had given me. 'Password?' the monitor asked. 'Conan' I typed. 'As in Doyle,' I said firmly.

The screen cleared and offered me a set of options. The first thing I had to do was to familiarize myself with the system. I needed to know how the different areas were arranged, how the directory trees were laid out, and how to move around to remote terminals. Somehow, I didn't think I'd be having an early night.

By nine, I'd got the basic layout clear in my mind. My mind and a sheaf of scribbled maps and diagrams that strewed my desk top. Now all I had to do was find Sandra Bates's terminal and start sifting her data. Doesn't sound much, does it? Imagine trying to find a single street in Manchester with only the motorway map as a guide. I took a screen break in the shower, brewed another pot of coffee and settled down to do battle with Filbert Brown's computer.

When the phone rang, I jumped a clear inch off my chair. I grabbed it and barked, 'Hello?'

'It's me,' Dennis's voice announced. 'Sorted.' Dennis is another one who doesn't like confiding in the phone system.

'Great. When?'

'Tomorrow. Half past three, eastbound at Hartshead Services.'

'How will I know him?'

'He drives a metallic green Mercedes. He's about forty, five ten, bald on top. Anyway, I told him to look for a tarty-looking little blonde.' Dennis couldn't keep the triumph out of his voice.

'You did what?'

'I didn't think you'd want to go looking like yourself,' he said defensively. 'Kate, these are not people you want coming after you with a clear picture. Wear a blonde wig, stick on the stilettos and the short skirt. And don't drive that poncy coupé. It sticks out like a prick in a brothel.'

'Thank you very much, Dennis,' I said.

Impervious to my sarcasm, he said, 'My pleasure. Be careful out there now, you hear? Let me know how you go on.'

'OK.'

'Be lucky.'

If only it was as simple as that. With a groan, I turned back to the computer. Just after eleven, I made it into Sandra Bates's data. Interestingly, it looked like Sandra had overall supervisory responsibility for about half of the Filbert Brown warehouses in the Northwest, as well as her day-to-day charge of the Ancoats cash-and-carry. She hadn't mentioned that in our brief encounter. I decided to concentrate on Manchester for the time being. The first thing I went for was the purchase orders

162

for Kerrchem. When I reached those files, I printed the lot out. Analysis could wait until a time when I wasn't wandering round someone else's system like an illegal alien. After a bit of searching, I found the till data, sorted product by product. I scrolled through till I found KerrSter and printed that lot out too. Finally, I made myself at home in the invoices section of Sandra's files. That was the first indication I had that there was something going on. As a matter of course, I'd been checking for hidden files as I went along. When I added up the sizes of the individual files in the invoices subdirectory, it came to less than the amount of space the terminal told me the subdirectory occupied. The difference was about the size of one biggish file.

What Sandra Bates had done was clever. She could have made the file a password file, but anyone from head office trying to get into it would have become immediately suspicious. With a hidden file, there was no way of knowing it was there unless you were looking for precisely that, and nothing to trigger off suspicions in a routine trawl. I copied the hidden file on to my own hard disk, not wanting to interfere with it in Sandra's environment, and also copied the visible Kerrchem invoice file. I couldn't think of anything else I needed right then, so I made my way out of the system. If what I already had suggested fresh avenues of inquiry, I could always go back in. I didn't think I'd left any footprints obvious enough for the sysman to notice and do anything panicky like change his password.

The last thing I did was to open up the hidden file and print out the contents of it and the other invoice file. Then, clutching my pile of papers, I staggered off to bed. Richard hadn't appeared, which meant he was probably out on the razz with a bunch of musicians. When he finally came home, he'd collapse into his own bed rather than waken me. Just one of the advantages of our semi-detached lifestyle.

I woke up just before eight, the light still on, the papers strewn all over the duvet and the floor. I hadn't got past page one before sleep had overwhelmed me. I picked up the papers and shuffled them together. I showered, sliced a banana into a bowl of muesli and took breakfast and coffee out into the conservatory. As I ate, I started to read the paperwork. The purchase order for KerrSter showed a sudden hike about two months previously, virtually tripling overnight. Interestingly, they weren't big orders. According to this print-out, Sandra hadn't increased the amount of KerrSter on each order. It was the number of orders that had shot up. That seemed a pretty inefficient way of doing business to me.

I checked back with the till receipts to see when the sudden surge in sales of KerrSter had started. I knew then that I was on to something. If what Sandra Bates had told me was the truth, the increased orders should have been sales-led. But what I was seeing was something very different. The till receipts for KerrSter didn't start to pick up until a few days after the orders increased dramatically. It looked as if the product had been given its starry position before the sales justified it. I was sure Trevor Kerr hadn't been paying them a premium to improve the profile of his product; I couldn't imagine him parting with his company's cash in a deal like that. Trevor struck me as a man who liked his profits, and wouldn't cede them to anyone.

By now, I was gripped by the paper trail. Time for the invoices. First, I went through the accessible KerrSter invoice file. That was when the alarm bells started ringing. The product orders might have tripled, but the invoices hadn't. I double-checked, but there was no mistake. Filbert Brown were still paying Kerrchem for the same amount of cleaning fluid as they had been before the order hike.

That left the contents of the hidden file. It contained the invoices for the remaining two thirds of the KerrSter. There was one crucial difference. The bank account where the electronic fund transfer was sending the money for the extra KerrSter wasn't the same as the bank account on the other, upfront invoices. Whoever Sandra Bates was paying for the KerrSter, it wasn't Kerrchem.

That left me two possibilities. Either somebody at Kerrchem was creaming off a tidy back-door profit for themselves. Or Sandra Bates was dealing with the chemical merchants who were peddling phoney KerrSter with such disastrous results. I knew which theory looked most likely to me.

I checked the clock. Ten to nine. Chances were that management staff at Filbert Brown didn't start work until nine. If I was quick, I could be in and out of their computer before their sysman logged in to find someone else using his ID. To be on the safe side, I should have waited until the evening, but I was behind the door when they were handing out patience.

Two minutes later, I was in the system again. This time, I wasn't looking for Sandra Bates's terminal. I wanted her personnel file. I got into personnel at three minutes to nine. A minute took me to staff personnel files. Once I was there, I downloaded Sandra Bates's file to my own hard disk. I was back out of Filbert Brown by one minute past nine. A couple of minutes later, I was looking at Sandra Bates's CV.

She'd been to school in Ashton-under-Lyne, a once separate town now attached to East Manchester by a string of down-at-heel suburbs. She'd done a degree in business studies at what was then Manchester Poly and is now Manchester Metropolitan University. You'd think when they got their university status that someone would have noticed their new initials translate only too readily to Mickey Mouse University, endorsing the snooty opinions of those who attended 'real' universities. After her degree, Sandra had gone to work for one of the big chains of DIY stores, havens for suburbanites on Sundays and bank holidays. She'd stayed there for a couple of years before joining

Filbert Brown three years previously. She'd had one promotion since then and was pulling down just over twenty grand. The item that really interested me was her address: 37 Alder Way, Burnage. I needed to check out her house at some point today while she was at work. I would probably have to stake her out or do a little bit of illegal bugging to discover who her phoney KerrSter supplier was, and to do that, I needed to get a picture of the set-up in Alder Way.

Before I could do any of that, I had to get dressed and stop by the office. I had plenty of time before the meet with Dennis's fence, so I could at least put off the tart's disguise till later. I grabbed a clean pair of jeans, my Reeboks and denim-look cotton sweater. If I was going to spend the afternoon teetering on stilettos, I could at least spend the morning in comfort.

Shelley was catching up on the filing when I walked in, a clear sign that she was bored. 'Going part-time now, are we?' she asked acidly.

'I've been doing some work on the computer at home,' I said defensively. Shelley has the unerring knack of making me feel fifteen and guilty again.

'A report would be nice now and then,' she said. 'I know I'm only the office manager, but it does help when clients phone if I know where we're up to.'

'Sorry,' I said contritely. 'It's just that most of the things I've been doing for the last couple of days are the kind of things I don't want the clients to know I'm up to. I'll get something down on tape for you by the end of today, promise.' I smiled ingratiatingly. 'Would you like a cappuccino?'

'How much is it going to cost me?' Shelley asked suspiciously. Abe Lincoln wouldn't have said you can fool all the people some of the time if he'd ever met Shelley.

'Can I borrow you and your car this afternoon?' I asked. 'I've got a meet with the fence who's been handling these stolen art works, and I'm going to need to tail him afterwards. He's going to have clocked the coupé, and it's too obvious a car to follow him in. I want you to come out there with me and after the meet, we can swap cars. I go off in your motor, you come back in the coupé.'

'You saying my Rover's common?' Shelley asked.

'Only in a numerical sense. Please?'

'How do I know you'll bring it back in one piece?'

She had a point. In the past eighteen months I'd written off one car and done serious damage to the Little Rascal, the van we've got fitted out with full surveillance gear. Neither incident had been my fault, but it still made me the butt of all office jokes about drivers. 'I'll bring it back in one piece,' I said through gritted teeth.

'What about the Little Rascal?' Shelley demanded. 'You could tail him in that. All you have to do is make sure he doesn't see you getting out of it. Just be there early, out of the car, waiting for him.'

I pulled a face. 'The guy drives a Merc. I suspect

I'd lose him on the motorway. Besides, he's no dummy. He's probably going to wait till he sees me drive off before he takes off himself.'

'So if you drive off, how are we going to swap cars?'

'Trust me. I'll show you when we get there.'

'I get the coupé overnight?' she bargained.

'But of course. I might as well take your car now, since I've got to look unobtrusive in Burnage.'

We swapped keys and I headed off in her four-year-old Rover to Burnage. My first stop was the local library, where I checked the electoral roll. Sandra Bates was the only resident listed at 37. Alder Way was a quiet street of 1930s semis, each with a small garden. I marched boldly up the path of 37 and knocked on the door. There was no reply. There was an empty carport at the side of the house, and I walked cautiously through it and opened the wrought iron gate leading into the back garden. Sandra was obviously as efficient at home as she was at work. There was a line of washing pegged out, drying in the watery sunlight. Whatever the electoral roll said, Sandra didn't live alone. Hanging beside her underwear were boxer shorts and socks. Flapping in the breeze like a phantom among the shirts and blouses were two pairs of overalls. Maybe I wouldn't have to look so far for the mystery chemist after all.

14

I rang the doorbell of 35 Alder Way. I was about to give up when the door opened. I realized why it had taken so long. The harassed-looking young woman who stood in the doorway had identical toddlers clinging on to each leg of her jeans. As a handicapping system, it beat anything the Jockey Club has ever come up with. The twins stared up at me and conducted a conversation with each other in what sounded like some East European language, all sibilants and diphthongs. 'Yes?' the woman said. At least she spoke Mancunian.

'Sorry to bother you,' I said. 'I'm looking for a guy called Richard Barclay. The address I've got for him is next door at number thirty-seven. But there doesn't seem to be anybody in.'

She shook her head. 'There's nobody by that name next door,' she said with an air of finality, her hand rising to close the door.

'Are you sure?' I said, looking puzzled and refer- ring to the piece of paper in my hand where I'd just written my lover's name and Sandra Bates's address. I waved it at her. 'I was supposed to meet him here. About a job.'

She took the paper and frowned. 'There must be some mistake. The bloke next door's called Simon. Simon Morley.'

I sighed. 'I don't suppose he's the one taking people on, then? I mean, I've not got the right address and the wrong name?'

One of the twins detached itself from the woman's jeans and lurched towards me. Without looking down, she stuck her leg out and stopped its progress. 'I shouldn't think so, love,' she said. 'Simon got made redundant about six months ago. He's only started working himself a couple of months back, and judging from the overalls he goes in and out in, he's not hiring and firing.'

I did the disappointed look, but it was wasted on the hassled woman. The pitch of the twins' dialogue had risen to a level she couldn't ignore. 'Sorry,' she said, closing the door firmly in my face.

'Don't be sorry,' I said softly as I walked back to the Rover. 'Lady, you just made my day.' Simon Morley's name had rung so many bells my head felt like the cathedral belfry.

By three o'clock, everything was in place. Shelley and I had driven across the Pennines on the M62, to the Bradford exit, the first past Hartshead Services. We'd turned off on the Halifax road, where I remembered there was a lay-by just after the motorway roundabout. I left Shelley there in her Rover while I zoomed back down the motorway, doubling back so I ended up on the correct side of the sprawling service area. I parked away from the main body of cars and teetered up the car park on the white stilettos I keep in the bottom of the wardrobe for days like these.

I went to the ladies' room to check that I still looked like a tarty blonde. I don't often go in for disguises that involve wigs, but a couple of years before, I'd needed a radical appearance change, so I'd spent a substantial chunk of Mortensen and Brannigan's petty cash on a really good wig. It was a reddish blonde, which meant it didn't look too odd against my skin, which is the typically yellow-based freckle-face that goes with auburn hair. Coupled with a much heavier make-up than I'd normally be seen dead in, the image that peered out of the mirror at me was credible, if a bit on the dodgy side. I'd dressed to emphasize that impression, in a black lycra mini-skirt and a cream scoop-necked vest under my well-worn brown leather blouson. My own mother would have thrown me out of the house.

I touched up the scarlet lipstick and gave myself a toothy grin. 'Show time, Brannigan,' I muttered as I walked back across the car park and leaned against the door of my coupé.

He was right on time. At precisely 3.30, a metallic green Mercedes appeared at the entrance to the car park. He cruised round slowly, before purring to a halt next to my car. The driver was indeed fortyish, though calling him bald on top seemed to be a euphemistic description for someone well on the way to the billiard-ball look. I opened the passenger door and sank into the leather seat. 'Pleased to meet you,' I said.

'Dennis tells me you have something I might be interested in,' he said without preamble. His voice was nasal, the kind that gets on my nerves after about five minutes. 'I don't normally deal with people on a freelance basis,' he added, glancing at me for the first time.

'I know. Dennis explained how you like to work. But I thought that if I showed you what I can do, you might put some work my way,' I said, trying to sound hard-bitten.

'Let's see what you've got, then.' He turned in his seat towards me. His eyes were grey and cold, slightly narrowed. When he spoke, his mouth moved asymmetrically, as if he were gripping an imaginary cigarette in one corner.

'What about the colour of your money?' I demanded.

He leaned across. For a wild moment, I thought his hand was heading for my legs, but he carried on to the glove box. It fell open to reveal bundles of notes. I could see they were fifties, banded into packs of a thousand. There were ten of them. He picked one up and riffled it in my face, so I could see it was fifties all the way through.

Then he slammed the glove box shut again. 'Satisfied?'

'You will be,' I said, reaching into my bag. I took out the buckle, wrapped in an ordinary yellow duster. I opened it up and displayed the buckle. 'Anglo-Saxon,' I said. 'From High Hammerton Hall.'

'I know where it's from,' he said brusquely, taking a loupe out of his pocket and picking up the buckle. I hoped he couldn't hear the pounding of the blood in my ears as he examined it. I could feel a prickle of sweat under the foundation on my upper lip. 'Is this the real thing or is it a fake?' he asked.

I pointed to the twenty-grand car sitting next to us. 'Is that a real Leo Gemini turbo super coupé or is it a fake? Behave. It's the business,' I said aggressively.

'There's been nothing in the papers,' he said.

'I can't help that, can I? What do you want me to do, issue a press release?'

A half-smile twitched at the corners of his mouth. 'You done much of this sort of thing?' he asked.

'What d'you want, a fucking CV? Listen, all you need to know is that I can deliver the goods, and I haven't got a record, which makes me a damn sight better bet than Dennis and Frankie. D'you want this or not?' I held my hand out for the buckle.

'Oh, I think my clients will be happy with this,' he said, pocketing the buckle and the loupe. 'Help yourself.' He gestured towards the glove box, at the same time taking a card out of his inside pocket. I grabbed the money and stuffed it in my bag.

'Cheers,' I said.

He handed me the card. It was one of those ones you get made up on those instant print machines at railway stations and motorway services. I'd passed one minutes before. All it had on it was his mobile number. 'Next time, phone me before you do the job and I'll tell you whether we want the piece or not.'

'No sweat,' I said, opening the door. 'I like a man who knows what he wants.' I closed the door with a soft click and got behind the wheel of the coupé. The fence showed no sign of moving, so I started the engine and drove off. As I joined the motorway, I clocked him a few cars behind me. I stayed in the inside lane, and he made no move to catch me up, never mind overtake me. I left the motorway at the next junction, going round the roundabout twice to make certain he wasn't following me, then I turned down the Halifax road. Shelley got out of the Rover as I pulled in behind her. I jumped out of the coupé and raced for the Rover, pulling off my jacket as I ran. Shelley had left the engine running, as I'd asked her to.

'Speak to you later,' I shouted as I put the car in gear, did an illegal U-turn at the first opportunity and tore back to the motorway. The receiver for the bug beeped reassuringly. He was already five kilometres away from me, and climbing. I floored the accelerator as I rejoined the M62. The car seemed sluggish after the coupé, but it didn't take long to push it up to ninety. I pulled off the wig and ran a hand through my hair. I'd left a packet of moist tissues on the passenger seat of the Rover, and I used a handful of them to scrub the make-up off my face.

According to the tracer screen, the fence's direction had changed slightly. As I'd expected, he'd turned off on the M621 for Leeds. I followed, noting that I'd narrowed the distance between us. He was only 2.7 kilometres ahead of me now. I really needed to be a lot closer before he turned off and lost me in a maze of city streets. Luckily, the M621 runs downhill, and he was sticking to a speed that wouldn't get him picked up by the speed cameras. By the time we came to the Wetherby and Harrogate slip road, I was close enough to glimpse his pale green roof leave the motorway. Fortunately, there was a fair bit of traffic, so I was able to keep a couple of cars between us. In the queue at the Armley roundabout, I pulled on my denim shirt over the vest, completing the transformation from the waist up.

I had a momentary panic when he entered the tunnels of the inner city ring road and the signal disappeared from the receiver. But as soon as we emerged into daylight, the beep came back. I kept him in sight as we approached the complex confluence of roads at Sheepscar, one car behind as he swung right into Roundhay Road. I reckoned he had no idea that he was being followed, since he wasn't doing any of the things you do when you think you've got a tail; no jumping red lights, no sudden turns off the main road, no lane switching.

He stayed on Roundhay Road, then, just by the park, he turned left and drove up Prince's Avenue, through the manicured green of playing fields and enough grass to walk all the dogs of Leeds simultaneously. Where the avenue shaded into Street Lane, he turned right into a drive. I cruised past with a sidelong glance that revealed the Merc pulling into a double garage, then found a place to park round the corner. I kicked off the stilettos and pulled on the leggings I'd left in the car. I wriggled out of the lycra mini and got out of the car, stuffing my feet into my Reeboks. Then I strolled back along Prince's Avenue. Clearly, being a fence was a lot more lucrative than being a private eye. Baldy's house was set back from the road, a big detached job in stone blackened with a century and a half of industrial pollution. Not much change out of a quarter of a million for that one, by my reckoning. Probably the most popular man in the street too; they say good fences make good neighbours! I carried on down the road and bought an ice cream from one of the vans by the park gates. I sat on a wall and ate my cornet, keeping an eye on Baldy's house all the while.

Five minutes later, an Audi convertible pulled in to the drive. A blonde woman got out, followed by two girls in the kind of posh school uniform that has straw boaters in the summer term. From where I was sitting, the girls looked to be in their early teens. The woman left the car on the drive and followed the girls into the house. I finished my ice cream and walked back to the car. I drove around for a few minutes, trying to find a suitable place for a stakeout. Eventually, I parked just round the bend on the forecourt of a row of shops. I couldn't see the whole house from there, but I could see the door and the drive, and I hoped that by not parking outside anyone else's house, I'd escape the worst excesses of the neighbourhood watch. If I was going to have to come back tomorrow, I'd ring the local police and tell them I was in the area on a surveillance to do with a non-criminal matter. What's a few white lies between friends?

I took out the phone and rang the local library and asked them to check the address on the electoral roll. They told me the residents listed at that address were Nicholas and Michelle Turner. At last, I had a name that hadn't come from the pages of Ian Fleming.

Just after six, the woman came out again with the girls, each carrying a holdall. They drove off, passing me without a glance. They came back after eight, all with damp hair. I deduced they'd been indulging in some sporting activity. That's why I'm a detective. At half past eight, I phoned the Flying Pizza, a few hundred yards up the road, and ordered myself a takeaway pizza. Ten minutes later, I walked up and collected it, using their loo at the same time. I ate the pizza in the car, taking care not to drop my olives on Shelley's immaculate carpet and upholstery. At nine, my phone rang. 'Kate? It's Michael Haroun,' the voice on the other end announced.

I jerked upright, ran a hand through my hair and smiled. As if he could see me. Pathetic, really. 'Hello, Michael,' I said. 'What can I do for you?'

'I wondered if you were free for a drink this evening? You could give me a progress report.'

'No, and no. I'm working, and you're not my client. Not that that means we can't have a friendly drink together,' I added hastily, in case he thought I was being unfriendly.

'You can't blame me for trying,' he said. 'I do have an interest.'

'In the case or in me?' I asked tartly.

'Both, of course. When are you going to finish work?'

'Not for a while yet, and I'm over in Leeds.' I hoped the regret I felt was being transmitted through the ether.

'In Leeds? What are you doing there?'

'Just checking out an anonymous tip-off.'

'So you're making progress? Great!'

'I never said I was working on Henry's case,' I said. 'We do have more than one client, you know.'

'OK, OK, I get the message. Keep your nose out, Haroun. I'm sorry you can't make it tonight. Maybe we could get together soon?'

'Why don't you give me a ring tomorrow? I might have a clearer idea what my commitments are then.'

'I'll do that. Nice to talk to you, Kate.'

'Ditto.' After that little interlude, my surveillance seemed even more unbearably tedious. When the radio told me it was time for a book at bed-time, I decided to call it a day. It didn't look like Nicholas Turner or my buckle were going anywhere tonight.

When I got home, I picked up the Kerrchem file I'd left there when I'd got changed earlier. I skimmed the list of former employees, and one name jumped straight out at me. I hadn't been mistaken about Simon Morley. He'd been a lab technician at Kerrchem, made redundant with golden handcuffs six months before. He'd been the one I hadn't been able to contact because he'd moved. At least I knew where he was now. And I had a funny feeling that I knew just what he was doing in his overalls.

15

I pulled up on the forecourt of the shops in Street Lane at five to seven in Bill's Saab turbo convertible. One of the first rules of surveillance is to vary the vehicle you're sitting around in. Luckily, when Bill had gone off to Australia, he'd left me with a set of keys for his house and the car. I'd left Shelley's Rover in Bill's garage, with a message on the office answering machine telling her to hang on to the coupé for the time being. I felt sure this was a hardship she'd be able to bear, always supposing she didn't leap to the conclusion that the reason I wasn't back with her Rover was that her beloved heap was in some garage being restored to its former glory.

It had been a toss-up whose house I was going to sit outside this morning. On the one hand, if I didn't keep close tabs on Nicholas Turner, having the buckle bugged would have been a complete waste of time. On the other hand, Simon Morley's little adventures in cleaning had already cost a man his life. I'd lain awake, tossing and turning to the point where Richard, who normally sleeps like a man in persistent vegetative state, had sat up in bed and demanded to know what was going on. He'd eventually persuaded me to talk the dilemma over with him, something I always used to do but had been avoiding since his involvement in the car fraud case caused us both so much grief.

'You've got to go after the fence,' he finally said.

'Why?'

'Because if you lose him this time, you'll never get a second bite of the cherry. Sooner or later, someone's going to spot that your buckle isn't just a fake but a bugged fake, and then you're going to be on someone's most wanted list. And if this Simon Morley really has killed some bloke accidentally, he's going to be a damn sight more careful what he puts in his chemical soup in future. I'd be surprised if he's still at it. Maybe I should give him a bell; if he's such a shit hot chemist, I know some people who'd be delighted to have him on the payroll.'

I smacked his shoulder. 'I've told you before about the people you hang out with.'

He grinned. 'Only joking. You know I'm allergic to anything stronger than draw. Anyway, Brannigan, you should go for the fence.'

'You sure?' I asked, still doubtful.

'I'm sure.'

'And what about the ten grand?'

Richard shrugged. 'Hang on to it for now. We all need walking-around money.'

'It's a lot to be walking around with. Shouldn't I be paying it back to the insurance company, or somebody?'

'They don't know you've got it, they're not going to miss it. Maybe you should just look on it as an early Christmas bonus for Mortensen and Brannigan.'

'I don't know . . .'

'Trust me. I'm not a doctor,' he said, wrapping his arms around me and nuzzling the back of my neck. Instant goose-flesh. You can't fight your gonads. I hadn't even wanted to try. Michael who?

The Turner household came to life around half past seven. The curtains in the master bedroom opened, and I caught a glimpse of Nicholas in his dressing gown. This time I'd come fully equipped for surveillance. I had a video camera in the well of the passenger seat, cunningly hidden in a bag made of one-way fabric which allowed the camera to see out but prevented anyone seeing in. I had a pair of high-powered binoculars in my bag, and my Nikon with a long lens attached sitting on the passenger seat. And five hundred quid of walking-around money in the inside pocket of my jacket. I'd left the other nine and a half grand with Richard, who had strict instructions to pay it into a building society account which I hold in a false name for those odd bits and pieces of money that it's sometimes advisable to lose for a while.

At quarter past eight, Mrs Turner and her two daughters emerged, the girls in the same smart school uniform. The Audi drove off. Two hours later, the Audi came back. Mrs Turner staggered indoors with enough Tesco carrier bags to stock a corner shop. Then nothing for two more hours. At a quarter to one, Mrs T came out, got into the Audi and drove off. She came back at ten past two, when I was halfway through my Flying Pizza special. If something didn't happen soon, I was either going to die of boredom or go home. Apart from anything else, Radio Four loses its marbles between three and four in the afternoon, and I didn't think I could bear to listen to an hour of the opinions of those who are proof positive that care in the community isn't working.

Half an hour later, the front door opened, and Nicholas Turner came out. He was carrying a brief-case and a suit carrier. He opened the garage, dumped the suit carrier in the boot and reversed out into the road. 'Geronimo,' I muttered, starting my engine. Within seconds, the screen told me that he had the buckle with him. I eased out into the traffic and followed him back through the park.

The traffic was pretty much nose to tail as we came down the hill towards the city centre so it wasn't hard to stay in touch with the Mercedes. I kept a couple of cars between us, which meant I got snagged up a couple of times at red lights, but there wasn't enough free road for him to make much headway. I realized pretty soon he was heading for the motorways, which took some of the pressure off. I caught up with him just before he hit the junction where he had to choose between the M621 towards Manchester and the M1 for the south and east. He ignored the first slip road and roared off down the M1. In the Saab, it was easy to keep pace with him, which was another good reason for having swapped the Rover. I kept about half a mile behind to begin with, since I didn't want to lose him at the M62 junction. Sure enough, he turned off, heading east towards Hull.

We hammered down the motorway, the speedo never varying much either side of eighty-five. He'd obviously heard the same rumour I had about that being the speed cameras' trigger point. When we hit Hull, he followed the signs for the ferry port. I followed, with sinking heart. At the port, he parked and went into the booking office. I got into the queue in time to hear him book the car and himself on to that night's ferry. I didn't have any choice. I had to do the same thing.

By the time I emerged, he'd disappeared. I ran to the car, and saw that the buckle was moving away from the ferry port. He was either going to dispose of it now, or it was going on the ferry with him. Either way, I needed to try and follow him. I drove off in the direction the receiver indicated, grabbing my phone as I went and punching in Richard's number. The dashboard clock told me it was five past four. I prayed. He answered on the third ring. 'Yo, Richard Barclay,' he said.

'I need a mega favour,' I said.

'Lovely to hear your voice too, Brannigan,' he said.

'It's an emergency. I'm in Hull.'

'That sounds like an emergency to me.'

'I've got to be on the half past six ferry to Holland. My passport's in the top drawer of my desk. Can you get it, and get here by then?'

'In my car? You've got to be kidding.'

I could have wept. He was right, of course. Even though it's pretty souped up, his Volkswagen just couldn't do the distance in the time. Then I remembered the coupé. 'Shelley's got the Gemini,' I told him. 'I'll get her to meet you outside the office in five minutes with it. Can you do it?'

'I'll be there,' he promised.

I rang the office, one eye on the monitor, one eye on the road. I was probably the most dangerous thing on the streets of Hull. We seemed to be heading east, further down the Humber estuary. Shelley answered brightly.

'Don't ask questions, it's an emergency,' I said.

'You've been arrested,' she replied resignedly.

'I have not been arrested. I'm hot on the trail of a team of international art thieves. Some people would be proud to work with me.'

'OK, it's an emergency. What's it got to do with me?'

'Hang on, I think I'm losing someone . . .' We'd cleared the suburbs of Hull, and the receiver was registering a sharp change in direction. Sure enough, about a kilometre up the road, there was a right turn. Cautiously, I drove into the narrow road then pulled up. The distance between us remained constant. He'd stopped.

And the phone was squawking in my ear. 'Sorry, Shelley. OK, what I need is for you to meet Richard downstairs in five minutes with the Gemini. He'll leave you his car so you won't be without wheels,' I added weakly.

'You expect me to drive *that*?'

'It'll do wonders for your street cred,' I said, ending the call. I was in no mood for banter or argument. I put the car in gear and moved slowly down the lane, keeping an eye open for Turner's car. The tarmac ended a few hundred yards later in the car park of a pub overlooking the wide estuary. There were only two cars apart from Turner's Merc. There was no way I was going in there, even if he was offering the buckle to the highest bidder. With so few customers, I'd be painfully obvious. All I could do was head back to the main road and pray that Turner would still have the buckle with him.

I fretted for an hour, then the screen revealed signs of activity. The buckle was moving back towards me. Moments later, Turner's car emerged from the side road and headed back into Hull. 'There is a God,' I said, pulling out behind him. We got back to the ferry port at half past five. Turner joined the queue of cars waiting to board, but I stayed over by the booking office. The last thing I wanted was for him to clock me and the Saab at this stage in the game.

Richard skidded to a halt beside me at five to six. He gave me a thumbs-up sign as he got out. He picked up my emergency overnight bag from the passenger seat and came over to the Saab. He tossed the bag into the back and settled into my passenger seat. 'Well done,' I said, leaning across to give him a smacking kiss on the cheek.

'You'll have to stand on for any speeders I picked up,' he said. 'It really is a flying machine, that coupé.'

'You brought the passport?'

Richard pulled out two passports from his inside pocket. Mine and his. 'I thought I'd come along for the ride,' he said. 'I've got nothing pressing for the next couple of days, and it's about time we had a jaunt.'

I shook my head. 'No way. This isn't a jaunt. It's work. I've got enough to worry about without having to think about whether you're having a nice time. I really appreciate you doing this, but you're not coming with me.'

Richard scowled. 'I don't suppose you know where this guy's going?'

'I've no idea. But where he goes, I follow.'

'You might need some protective colouring,' he pointed out. 'I've heard you say that sometimes there are situations where a woman on her own stands out where a couple don't. I think I should come along. I could share the driving.'

'No. And no. And no again. You don't expect me to interview spotty adolescent wannabe rock stars, and I don't expect you to play detectives. Go home, Richard. Please?'

He sighed, looking mutinous. 'All right,' he said, sounding exactly like his nine-year-old son Davy when I drag him off the computer and tell him ten is not an unreasonable bedtime. He flung open the door and got out, turning back to say, 'Just don't expect me to feed the cat.'

'I haven't got a cat,' I said, grinning at his olive branch.

'You could have by the time you get back. Take care, Brannigan.'

I waved as I drove off, keeping an eye on him in my rear-view mirror. As I took my place in the slowly moving queue, I saw him get in the car and drive off. Half an hour later, I was standing in the stern of the ship, watching the quay recede inch by inch as we slowly moved away from the dock and out towards the choppy, steel grey waters of the North Sea.

I spent almost all of the trip closeted in my cabin with a spy thriller I'd found stuffed into the door pocket of Bill's car. The only time I went out was for dinner, which comes included in the fare. I left it to the last possible moment, hoping Turner would have eaten and gone by then. I'd made the right decision; there was no sign of him in the restaurant, so I was able to enjoy my meal without having to worry about him clocking me. I was certain he wouldn't recognize me as the tart with the buckle, but if this surveillance lasted any length of time, the chances were that he'd see me somewhere along the line. I didn't want him connecting me back to the ferry crossing.

On the way back to the cabin, I changed some money; fifty pounds each of guilders, Belgian francs, Deutschmarks, French francs, Swiss francs and lire. Nothing like hedging your bets. The sea was calm enough for me to get a decent night's sleep, and when we docked at Rotterdam, I felt refreshed enough to drive all day if I had to. From where I was placed on the car deck, I couldn't actually see Turner, and the steel hull of the ship didn't do a lot of favours for the reception on the tracking monitor.

Once I was clear of the ship, however, the signal came back strong and clear. For once, Bill's mongrel European ancestry worked to my advantage. He makes so many trips to the continent to visit family that he has serious road maps and city street plans for most of northern Europe neatly arranged in a box in his boot. I'd shifted the box to the back seat and unfolded a map of Holland and Belgium on the passenger seat. Comparing the map to the monitor, I reckoned that Turner was heading for Eindhoven. As soon as I got on the motorway, I stepped on the gas, pushing my speed up towards a ton, trying to close the distance between us.

Within half an hour, I had Turner in my sights again. He was cruising along just under ninety, and there was enough traffic on the road for me to stay in reasonably close touch without actually sitting on his bumper. He stayed on the motorway past Eindhoven. The next possible stop was Antwerp. From my point of view, there couldn't be a better destination. Bill's mother grew up in the city and he still has a tribe of relations there. I've been over with him on weekend trips a couple of times, and I fell in love with the city at first sight. Now, I feel like I know it with the intimacy of a lover.

It was my lucky day. He swung off the E34 at the Antwerp turn-off and headed straight for the city centre. He seemed to know where he was going, which made following him a lot easier than if he'd kept pulling over to consult a map or ask a passer-by for his destination. Me, I was just enjoying being back in Antwerp. I don't know how it manages it, but it still manages to be a charming city even though it's the economic heartbeat of Belgium. You don't normally associate culture with huge docks, a bustling financial centre and the major petrochemical industries. Not forgetting Pelikaanstraat, second only to Wall Street in the roll of the richest streets in the world. Come to think of it, what better reason could a fence have for coming to Antwerp than to do a deal in Pelikaanstraat, since its diamonds are the most portable form of hard currency in the world?

It began to look as if that was Turner's destination. We actually drove along the street itself, diamond merchants lining one side, the railway line the other. But he carried on up to the corner by Central Station and turned left into the Keyserlei. He slipped into a parking space just past De Keyser, the city centre's most expensive hotel, took his briefcase and suit carrier out of the car and walked inside. Cursing, I made a quick circuit of the block till I found a parking garage a couple of hundred metres away. I chose one of the several bars and restaurants opposite the hotel and settled down with a coffee and a Belgian waffle. I was just in time to see a liveried flunkey drive off in Turner's car, presumably taking it to the hotel garage.

I was on my third coffee when Turner re-emerged. I left the cup, threw some money on the table and went after him. He crossed over to the square by the station and walked towards the row of tram stops on Carnotstraat. He joined the bunch of people waiting for a tram. I dodged into a nearby tobacconist and bought a book of tram tickets, praying he'd still be there when I came out.

He was, but only just. He was stepping forward to board a tram that was pulling up at the stop. I ran across the street and leapt on to the second of the two carriages just before the doors hissed shut. Turner was sitting near the front, his back to me. He got off near the Melkmarkt, and I had no trouble following him past the cathedral and into the twisting medieval streets of the old town. He was strolling rather than striding, and he didn't look like he had the slightest notion that he might be followed. That was more than I could say for myself. I kept getting a prickling sensation in the back of my neck, as if I were aware at some subconscious level of being watched. I kept glancing over my shoulder, but I saw nothing to alarm me.

Eventually, we ended up in the vrijdag markt. Since it was too late for the twice-weekly second-hand auction, I could only assume Turner was heading for the Plantin-Moretus Museum. I'd tracked him all the way round Antwerp just so we could go round a printing museum? I hung back while he bought a ticket, then I followed him in. While it was no hardship to me to revisit one of my favourite museums, I couldn't see how it was taking me any nearer my art-racket mastermind.

The Plantin-Moretus house and its furnishings are just as they were when Christopher Plantin was Europe's boss printer back in the sixteenth century. But Nicholas Turner didn't seem too interested in soaking up the paintings, tapestries, manuscripts and antique furniture. He was moving swiftly through the rooms. Then I realized he was heading straight for the enclosed garden at the heart of the rectangular house. Rather than follow him out into the open air, I stayed put on the first floor where I could see what was going on.

Turner sat down on a bench, appearing to be simply enjoying the air. After about five minutes, another man joined him. They said nothing, but when the stranger moved on a few minutes later, he left his newspaper beside Turner's briefcase. Another few minutes went by, then Turner picked up the paper, placed it in his briefcase and started for the exit. The man had definitely been watching too many James Bond films.

I hurried back through the rooms I'd already visited and made it into the street in time to see Turner hail a cab. I ran up the square after him, but there wasn't another cab in sight. I ran all the way up to the Grote Market before I could get a cab to stop for me.

Luck was still running my way. As we turned into the Keyserlei, Turner was walking into the hotel. I paid off the cab and chose another bar to watch from. I'd eaten a bucket of mussels and drunk three more coffees before I saw any action. This time, he walked round the corner into the Pelikaanstraat. A couple of hundred yards down the street, he turned into a diamond merchant's. I wasn't too happy about staking the place out; it's an area where people are understandably suspicious of idle loitering. I'd noticed a slightly seedy-looking hotel on the way down the street, so I doubled back and walked into the foyer. It seemed as handy a place as any to spend the night, so I booked a room. I settled down on a sofa near the door and waited.

I was beginning to think Turner had gone off in the other direction when he finally walked past just before six. This time, I followed him into the hotel, where he headed for reception to pick up his key. I picked up a brochure about daily excursions to Bruges, managing to get close enough to hear him book a table for one in the restaurant at seven and an early-morning call at six. It sounded like he wasn't planning on anything more exciting than an early night. It sounded like a good idea to me.

I had one or two things to see to before I could crash out, but by half past seven, I was sorted. I'd used the hotel phone to check in with Shelley, since my mobile isn't configured to work with the continental system. She was singularly unimpressed with where I was, what I was doing and Richard's car. She was even less impressed when I confessed that her own car was less than a couple of miles from her house, locked safely inside Bill's garage, since I had the keys for the garage lurking somewhere at the bottom of my bag.

Thanks to the wonders of car hire, I was better off than she was. I had my very own Mercedes stashed in the parking garage round the corner. The Saab was safely parked behind a high fence at the Hertz office, and I'd dined on a giant slab of steak with a pile of crisp chips and thick mayo. I hadn't eaten so well on a job for years.

By nine, I was watching CNN in my hotel room, a large vodka and grapefruit juice sweating on the bedside table next to me. I was just about to get up and run a bath when I heard the unmistakable sound of a key fumbling into the lock of my bedroom door.

16

I was off the bed in seconds and in through the open door of the bathroom, hitting the light switches on the way. Whoever was outside the door would have to pass me on their way into the room itself, with only the flickering light of the television screen to guide them. The scrabbling stopped, and an arc of light from the hallway spilled across the carpet as the door opened. A shadow crossed the light, then the arc narrowed and disappeared as the door closed. I tensed, ready to come out kicking.

A hand groped along the far wall, followed by a shoulder. I leapt through the doorway, pivoted on one foot and put all my weight behind a straight kick at stomach level, yelling as loudly as I could to multiply the fear and surprise. My foot made contact with flesh and the body staggered back against the door with a heavy crash, the air shooting out of him in a groaning rush as he crumpled on the floor. I stepped back, keeping my weight on the balls of my feet, and reached for the lights.

Richard was doubled up on the carpet, arms folded defensively over his guts. For once, I was lost for words. I relaxed my fighting stance and stood staring at him.

'Fucking hell,' he gasped. 'Was that some traditional Belgian greeting, or what?'

'It's a traditional private eye's greeting for uninvited visitors,' I snarled. 'What the hell are you doing here?'

Richard struggled to his feet, still clutching his stomach. 'Nice to see you too, Brannigan.' He pushed past me and stumbled on to the bed, where he curled into a ball. 'Oh shit, I think you've relocated my stomach somewhere around my left shoulder blade.'

'Serves you right,' I said heartlessly. 'You scared me shitless.'

'That why you were in the bathroom?' he said innocently.

'What was wrong with the phone? Was it too much for you to handle, a foreign phone system? Besides, how did you get here? How did you find me? Did Shelley tell you where I was?'

Richard stopped rubbing his stomach and eased up into a sitting position. 'I thought I'd surprise you. I don't know, call yourself a detective? I've been tailing you ever since you got off the ferry, and you didn't even notice,' he said proudly.

I moved across the room to the only chair and sat down heavily. 'You've been tailing *me*?'

'Piece of piss,' he said.

He had me worried now. If I'd been so busy watching Nicholas Turner that I hadn't spotted a car as obvious as a snazzy UK-registered coupé on my own tail, it was time I gave up detective work and settled for something like social work where I could get away with a complete lack of observational skills. 'I don't believe you,' I said. 'Shelley told you where I was and you got a flight over here.'

He grinned. For once, it made me want to hit him, not kiss him. 'Sorry, Brannigan. I did it all by myself.'

'No way. I couldn't have missed seeing the coupé on the ferry,' I said, positive now. The Saab had been one of the last cars to board. He simply couldn't have got the coupé on board without me spotting it.

'That's what I thought too,' he said complacently. 'That's why I left it at Hull. I travelled as a foot passenger, which meant I got off the ferry before you. I hired a Merc at the ferry terminal and picked you up as you came off. Then I followed you here. I thought I'd lost you when you got on the tram, but I managed to get a taxi and he followed the tram. Just like the movies, really. I waited outside while you were in that museum, and I hung about just inside the station when you came in here first time around.'

I shook my head in bewildered amazement. 'So how did you get a key for the room?'

His grin was beginning to infuriate me. 'I had a

word with the desk clerk. Told him my girlfriend was here on business and I'd come to surprise her. It cost me two thousand francs. Most I've ever paid for a good kicking.'

Forty quid. I was impressed. 'I suppose you're potless now, are you?' I said sternly.

He looked sheepish. 'Not as such. I forgot to go to the building society with the nine and a half grand, so I brought it with me.'

I didn't know whether to be furious or impressed. There was no doubt the money would come in handy, at the rate I was spending, but I didn't want Richard around on the chase. I had enough to worry about keeping tabs on Turner without having to be constantly aware of what Richard was up to. 'Thanks,' I said. 'I was wondering what to do when I ran out of cash. You can leave it with me when you go home tomorrow.'

He looked crestfallen. 'I thought you'd be pleased to see me,' he said.

I got up and sat down beside him on the bed. 'Of course I'm pleased to see you. I just don't need to have to worry about you while I'm trying to do my job.'

'What's to worry about?' he demanded. 'I'm not a kid, Kate. Look, these are heavy people you're after, there's no two ways about it. You could use an extra pair of eyes. Not to mention an extra set of wheels. If he's going on a long haul, you can't use the same car all the way, and you could lose him while you're swapping over at some car-hire place.

If I stay, we can rent a couple of mobile phones and that way one of us can stay with him while the other one does things like fill up with petrol or stop for a piss.'

The most irritating thing was that he was right. I'd been worrying about that very thing myself. 'I don't know,' I said. I wanted to say, this is my territory, my skill area, my speciality and you're just an amateur. But I didn't want to throw that down on the bed for both of us to look at. The thing that worried me most was that after the debacle when he'd last tried to help me out, Richard felt he had something to prove. And there's nothing more dangerous on a job that needs patience than someone with something to prove.

At quarter past six the following morning, I was sitting in the dark in my rented Mercedes on Pelikaanstraat. Richard was on the Keyserlei, a couple of hundred yards up from the hotel. Whichever way Turner went, one of us would pick him up. I checked the equipment on the passenger seat one more time. Richard hadn't been strictly honest with me the previous evening. Once I'd reluctantly agreed to let him tag along, he confessed that he'd already hired a pair of mobile phones, so convinced was he that I'd see what he called sense.

We'd already agreed on a modus operandi. I would use the bugging equipment to keep tabs on Turner. Richard would sit tucked in behind me. If I wanted to stop to change cars, fill up with petrol or go to the loo, I'd phone him and he'd overtake me. Then, when he had Turner in sight, he'd call me and I'd go and do whatever I needed to. Once I was back on track, Richard would fall back behind me again. That was the theory. I'd put money on it working like a wind-up toy with a broken spring.

I sipped the carton of coffee I'd bought from the vending machine in the station and watched the screen. The buckle wasn't moving yet. I ate one of the waffles I'd bought the evening before. I could feel my blood sugar rising with every mouthful. The combination of sugar and caffeine had me feeling almost human by the time the phone rang at five to seven. 'Yes?' I said.

'Z-Victor one to BD,' Richard said. 'Target on move. I've just pulled out in front of him. Heading for the traffic lights. He's staying in the left-hand lane. Roger and out.'

If he carried on like this all day, I might just kill him by dinner time, I decided. I stepped on the accelerator and swung round the corner. I was just in time to see the two cars turn left at the traffic lights. No way was I going to catch them, so I settled for watching the screen. I caught up with them about a mile from the motorway. It looked like we were heading southeast, towards Germany.

Once we hit the motorway, I called Richard and told him to fall back behind me. I kept a steady two kilometres behind Turner, which was far enough at a hundred and forty kph, and five minutes later Richard appeared in front of me, slowing down enough to slide into my slipstream with a cheery wave. By nine, we'd sailed past Maastricht and Aachen, the bug had seen us safely through the maze of autobahns round Köln, and Bonn was fast approaching on the port bow as we rolled on to the west of the Rhine. The boring flat land of Belgium was a distant memory now as the motorway swept us inexorably through rolling hills and woodland. Somehow, the motorways in Europe seem to be much more attractively landscaped than ours do. Maybe it's just the indefinably foreign quality of the scenery, but I suspect it's more to do with the fact that the Germans in particular have had to take Green politics seriously for a few years longer than we have.

Just before eleven, we crossed the Rhine north of Karlsruhe, with no sign of slowing up. I rang Richard and told him to overtake me and get on Turner's back bumper again. The motorway split just south of the city, the A5 carrying on south and the A8 cutting off east. Unlike Köln, there was no quick way to double back if we made the wrong decision. A few minutes later, he called telling me to stay on the A5. We carried on down the river valley, the wooded hills on the left starting to become mountains, the occasional rocky peak flashing in and out of sight for seconds at a time.

A few kilometres before the Swiss border, the blip on the screen started moving towards me. It looked like Turner had stopped. Judging by the state of my fuel gauge, he was probably buying petrol. I rang Richard and told him to pull off at the approaching services while I carried on across the border. I stopped as soon as I could after waving my passport at Swiss customs and poured petrol into my tank till I couldn't squeeze another drop in. I bought a couple of sandwiches, bars of yummy Swiss chocolate and cans of mineral water, then rushed back to the car. The buckle was still behind me, but closing fast. I rang Richard.

'We both filled up with petrol,' he reported. 'I waited till he'd cleared the shop before I went in to pay, then I followed him through the border. Where are you?'

'In the service area you're about to pass,' I told him. 'You can let Turner get away from you now. If you drive into the services, you can fall in behind me again.' I couldn't believe it was all going so well. I kept waiting for the other shoe to drop.

We carried on past Basel and on to Zürich. By now, we were properly into the Alps, mountains towering above us on all sides. If I hadn't been concentrating so hard on staying in touch with Turner and the buckle, I'd have been enjoying the drive. As it was, I felt as stressed as if I'd been sitting in city rush-hour traffic for the five and a half hours it had taken us to get this far.

We skirted the outskirts of the city and drove on down the side of Lake Zürich. About halfway down the lake, the blip on the screen suddenly swung off to the right. 'Oh shit,' I muttered. I stepped on the accelerator, checking in my mirror that Richard was still with me. The motorway exit was only seconds away, and I swung off on a road that led into the mountains. I grabbed the phone, punched the memory redial that linked me to Richard and said, 'Wait here. Turn round to face the motorway so you can pick him up if he heads back.'

'Roger wilco,' Richard said. 'Call me if you need back-up.'

I carried on, checking the blip on the screen against the road map. Cursing the fact that I didn't have a more detailed map of Switzerland, I swung the car through the bends of what was rapidly becoming a mountain road. A couple of miles further on, I realized that staying on the main road had been the wrong decision, as the buckle was moving further away from me at an angle. Swearing so fluently my mother would have disowned me, I nearly caused a small pile-up with a U-turn that took a thousand miles off the tyres and hammered back down the road and on to a narrow, twisting side road. About a kilometre away from the main drag, the screen suddenly went blank.

I panicked. My first thought was that Turner had met someone or picked someone up who had taken one look at the buckle, spotted the bug and disabled it. Then logic kicked in and told me that was impossible in so short a time. As I swung round yet another bend with a sheer rock wall on one side and a vertiginous drop on the other, I twigged. The mountains were so high and so dense that the radio signal was blocked.

I raced the car round the bends as fast as I could, tyres screaming on every one, wrists starting to feel it in spite of the power steering. I was concentrating so hard on not ending up as a sheet of scrap metal on the valley floor that I nearly missed Turner. With the suddenness of daylight at the end of a tunnel, the road emerged on to a wide plateau about halfway up the mountain. In the middle of an Alpine meadow complete with cows that tinkled like bass wind chimes stood an inn, as pretty as a picture postcard, as Swiss as a Chalet School novel. On the edge of the crowded car park, Turner's pale green Mercedes was parked. And the screen flashed back into life.

Heaving a huge sigh of relief, I drove to the far end of the car park and tried to ring Richard and let him know everything was OK. No joy. I supposed the mountain was in the way again. I got out of the car, took a black beret and a pair of granny glasses with clear lenses out of my stakeout-disguises holdall and walked into the inn. Inside, it was the traditional Swiss chalet, wood everywhere, walls decorated with huge posters of Alpine scenery, a blazing fire in a central stone fireplace. The room was crammed with tables, most of them occupied. A quick scan showed me Turner sitting alone at a table for two, studying the menu. A waitress dressed in traditional costume bustled up to me and said something in German. I shrugged and tried out my school French, saying I wanted to eat, one alone, and did they have a telephone?

She smiled and showed me to a table near the fire and pointed out the phone. I got change from the cashier and gave Richard a quick call. For some reason, he was less than thrilled that I was sitting down to some Tyrolean speciality while he was stuck on the verge of the road with nothing in sight but the motorway and a field of the inevitable cows. 'Go and get some sandwiches or something,' I instructed him. 'I'll let you know when we set off.'

I went back to my table. Out of the corner of my eye, I could see Turner tucking into a steaming bowl of soup, a stein of beer beside him, so I figured I'd have time to eat something. I ordered Tiroler gröstl, a mixture of potatoes, onions and ham with a fried egg on top. It looked like the nearest thing to fast food on the menu. I was right. My meal was in front of me in under five minutes. I was halfway through it before Turner's main course arrived. Judging by the pile of chips that was all I could identify, he was eating for two. Frankly, I could see why he'd made the detour. The food was more than worth it, if my plateful was anything to go by. Definitely one to cut out and keep for next time we were passing Zürich.

By the time I'd finished and lingered over a cup of coffee, Turner had also demolished a huge wedge of lemon meringue pie. If I'd scoffed that much in the middle of the day, I'd have been asleep at the wheel ten miles down the road. I hoped he had a more lively metabolism. When he called for the bill, I took mine to the cashier, rang Richard to warn him we were on the move, and headed back to the car. Minutes later, Turner was heading back down the road, with me a couple of bends behind him.

As we hit the motorway, I had another panic. Where I'd expected to see Richard in his Mercedes, there was a black BMW. As I sailed past, I glanced across and saw the familiar grin behind the thumbs-up sign. Moments later, as he swung in behind me, the phone rang. 'Sierra 49 to Sierra Oscar,' he said. 'Surprise, surprise. I nipped back to Zürich and swapped the cars. I thought it was about time for a change.'

'Nice one,' I conceded. Maybe he wasn't the liability I'd feared he'd be after all. And there was me thinking that he was as subtle as Jean Paul Gaultier. This wasn't the time to reassess the capabilities of the man in my life, but I filed the thought away for future scrutiny.

I figured we must be heading for Liechtenstein, haven for tax dodgers, fraudsters and stamp-collecting anoraks. No such luck. We carried on south, deep into the Alps. Richard was in front of me again, keeping tabs on Turner. The bug kept cutting out because of the mountains, and I was determined that we weren't going to lose him after coming this far. Now Richard was in another car, I felt happy about him staying in fairly close touch.

A few miles down the road, my bottle started twitching. There was no getting away from it. We were heading for the San Bernardino tunnel. Ten kilometres in that dark tube, aware of the millions of tons of rock just sitting above my head, waiting to crush me thin as a postage stamp. Just the thought of it forced a groan from my lips. I'm terrified of tunnels. Not a lot of people know that. It doesn't sit well with the fearless, feisty image. I've even been known to drive thirty miles out of my way to avoid going through the tunnels under the Mersey.

With every minute that passed, that gaping hole in the hillside was getting closer and my heart was pounding faster. Desperately, I rattled through the handful of cassettes I'd grabbed when I'd picked up Bill's car. Not a soothing one among them. No Enya, no Mary Coughlan, not even Everything But The Girl. Plenty of Pet Shop Boys, Eurythmics and REM. I settled for Crowded House turned up loud to keep the eerie boom of the tunnel traffic at bay and tried to concentrate on their harmonies.

Two minutes into the tunnel and the sweat was clammy on my back. Three minutes in and my upper lip was damp. Four minutes in and my forehead was slimy as a sewer wall. Six minutes in and my knuckles were white on the steering wheel. The walls looked as if they were closing in. I tried telling myself it was only imagination, and Crowded House promised they could ease my pain. They were lying. Ten minutes and I could feel a scream bubbling in my throat. I was on the point of tears when a doughnut of light appeared around the cars in front of me.

As soon as I burst out again into daylight, my phone started ringing. 'Yeah?' I gasped.

'You OK?' Richard asked. He knows all about me and tunnels.

'I'll live.' I swallowed hard. 'Thanks for asking.'

'You're a hero, Brannigan,' he said.

'Never mind that,' I said gruffly. 'You still with Turner?'

'Tight as Jagger's jeans. He's got his foot down. Looks like we're heading for *la bella Italia*.'

At least I'd be somewhere I could speak the language, I thought with relief. I'd been worried all the way down Germany and Switzerland that Turner was going to end up in a close encounter that I couldn't understand a word of. But my Italian was fluent, a hangover from the summer before university, when I'd worked in the kitchens of Oxford's most select trattoria. It was learn the language or take a vow of silence. I'd prevented it from getting too rusty by holidaying in Italy whenever I could.

I drove cheerfully down the mountain, glad to be out in the open air again, relieved that we were gradually leaving the mountains behind us. We worked our way round Milan just after five, Richard back behind me, and by seven we were skirting Genoa. This was turning into one hell of a drive. My shoulders were locked, my backside numb, my hips stiff in spite of regular squirming. If they ever start making private eyes work with tachographs, I'm going to be as much use to my clients as a cardboard chip pan. I shuddered to think what this overtime was going to look like on Henry's bill. He'd run out of buckshee hours a while back.

At Genoa we turned east again on the A12, another one of those autostradas carved out of the side of a mountain. I kept telling myself the little tunnels were just like driving under big bridges, but it didn't help a lot, especially since the receiver kept cutting out, giving me panic attacks every time.

Three quarters of an hour past Genoa, the screen told me Turner was moving off to one side. First, he went right, then crossed back left. I nearly missed the exit, I was concentrating so hard on the screen, but I managed to get off with Richard on my tail. We were on the outskirts of some town called Sestri Levante, but according to my screen, Turner was heading away from it. Praying I was going the right way, I swung left and found myself driving along a river valley, the road lined with shops and houses. Sestri Levante shaded into Casarza Ligure, then we were out into open country, wooded hills on either side of the valley. We hit a small village called Bargonasco just as the direction changed on the receiver. A couple of kilometres further up, there was a turning on the left. It was a narrow, asphalt road, with a sign saying Villa San Pietro. The blip on the screen stayed steady. A kilometre away, straight up the Villa San Pietro's drive.

Journey's end.

17

'What now, Sam Spade?' Richard asked as we both bent and stretched in vain attempts to restore our bodies to something like their normal configuration.

'You go back to the village and find us somewhere to stay for the night, then you sit outside in the car in case Turner comes back down the valley,' I told him.

'And what are you doing while I'm doing that?' Richard asked.

'I'm going to take a look at the Villa San Pietro,' I told him.

He looked at me as if I'd gone stark staring mad. 'You can't just drive up there like the milkman,' he said.

'Correct. I'm going to walk up, like a tourist. And you're going to take the receiver with you, just in case the buckle's going anywhere Turner isn't.'

'You're not going up there on your own,' Richard said firmly.

'Of course I am,' I stated even more firmly. 'You are waiting down here with a car, a phone and a bug receiver. If we both go and Turner comes driving back down with the buckle while we're ten minutes away from the cars, he could be outside the range of the receiver in any direction before we get mobile. I'm not trekking all the way across Europe only to lose the guy because you want to play macho man.'

Richard shook his head in exasperation. 'I hate it when you find a logical explanation for what you intend to do regardless,' he muttered, throwing himself back into the driver's seat of the BMW. 'See you later.'

I waved him off, then moved the Merc up the road a few hundred yards. I scuffed some dust over my trainers, put on a pair of sunglasses even though dusk was already gathering, hung my camera round my neck and trudged off up the drive.

There was a three-foot ditch on one side of the twisting road, which appeared to have been carved out of the rough scrub and stunted trees of the hillside. Ten minutes' brisk climbing brought me to the edge of a clearing. I hung back in the shelter of a couple of gnarled olive trees and took a good look. The ground had been cleared for about a hundred metres up to a wall. Painted pinkish brown, it was a good six feet high and extended for about thirty metres either side of a wrought iron gate. Above the wall, I could see an extensive roof in the traditional terracotta pantiles.

Through the gates, I could just about make out the villa itself, a two-storey white stucco building with shutters over the upper-storey windows. It looked like serious money to me.

I would have been tempted to go in for a closer look, except that a closed-circuit video camera was mounted by the gate, doing a continuous 180-degree sweep of the road and the clearing. Not just serious money, but serious paranoia too.

Staying inside the cover of the trees and the scrub, I circled the villa. By the time I got back to the drive, I had more scratches than Richard's record collection, and the certainty that Nicholas Turner was playing with the big boys. There were video cameras mounted on each corner of the compound, all programmed to carry out regular sweeps. If I'd had enough time and a computer, I could probably have worked out where and when the blind spots would occur, but anyone who's that serious about their perimeter security probably hasn't left the back door on the latch. This was one burglary that was well out of my league.

I found Richard sitting on the bonnet of his car on the forecourt of a building with all the grace and charm of a Sixties tower block. Green neon script along the front of the three-storey rectangle proclaimed Casa Nico. Below that, red neon told us this was a Ristorante-Bar-Pensione. The only other vehicles on the parking area were a couple of battered pickups and a clutch of elderly motor scooters. So much for Italian style.

'This is it?' I asked, my heart sinking.

'This is it,' Richard confirmed gloomily. 'Wait till you see the room.'

I gathered my overnight bag, the video camera bag and my camera gear and followed Richard indoors. To get to the rooms, we had to go through the bar. In spite of the floor-to-ceiling windows along one wall, it somehow managed to be dark and gloomy. As soon as we walked through the bead curtain that separated the bar from the fore-court, the rumble of male voices stopped dead. In a silence cut only by the slushy Italian Muzak from the jukebox, we crossed the room. I smiled inanely round me at the half-dozen men sprawled around a couple of tables. I got as cheerful a welcome as a Trot at a Tory party conference. Not even the human bear leaning on the Gaggia coffee machine behind the bar acknowledged our existence. The minute we left by a door in the rear, the conversation started up again. So much for the friendly hospitality of the Italian people. Somehow, I didn't see myself managing to engage mine host in a bit of friendly gossip about the Villa San Pietro.

The third-floor room was big, with a spectacular view up the wooded river valley. That was all you could say for it. Painted a shade of yellow that I haven't seen since the last time I had food poison-ing, it contained the sort of vast, heavy wooden furniture that could only have been built *in situ*, unless it was moved into the room before the walls went up. Above the double bed was a crucifix, and the view from the bed was a massive, sentimental print of Jesus displaying the Sacred Heart with all the dedication of an offal butcher.

'Bit of a turn-off, eh?' Richard said.

'I expect Jeffrey Dahmer would love it.' I sat down on the bed, testing the mattress. Another mistake. I thought I was going to be swallowed whole. 'How much is this costing us?' I asked.

'About the same as a night in the Gritti Palace. Mind you, that also includes dinner. Not that it'll be edible,' he added pessimistically.

After we'd had a quick shower, I set the bug receiver to auto-alert, so that it would give a series of audible bleeps if the buckle moved more than half a kilometre from its current relative position. Then we went in search of food. Richard had been right about that too. We were the only two people in the cheerless dining room, which resembled a school dining room with tablecloths. The sole waitress, presumably the wife of Grizzly Adams behind the bar, looked as if she'd last laughed somewhere around 1974 and hadn't enjoyed the experience enough to want to repeat it. We started with a platter of mixed meats, most of which looked and tasted like they'd made their getaway from the local cobbler. The pasta that followed was *al dente* enough to be a threat to dentistry. The sauce was so sparing that the only way we could identify it as pesto was by the colour.

Richard and I ate in virtual silence. 'What was that you said about it being time we had a bit of a jaunt?' I said at one point.

He prodded one of the overcooked lamb chops that looked small enough to have come from a rabbit and scowled. 'Next time, I won't be so bloody helpful,' he muttered. 'This is hell. I haven't had proper food for two days and I'd kill for a joint.'

'Not many Chinese restaurants in Italy,' I remarked. 'It's on account of them inventing one of the world's great cuisines.' Richard took one look at my deadpan face and we both burst out laughing. 'One day,' I gasped, 'we'll look back at this and laugh.'

'Don't bet on it,' he said darkly.

We passed on pudding. We both have too much respect for our digestive tracts. At least the coffee was good. So good we ordered a second cup and took it upstairs with us. The one good thing about the bed was the trough in the middle that forced us into each other's arms. After the day we'd had, it was more than time to remind each other that the world isn't all grief.

My eyelids unstuck themselves ten hours later. The bleeding heart on the wall wasn't a great sight to wake up to, so I rolled over and checked the receiver sitting on the bedside table. No movement. By nine, we were both showered, dressed and back in the dining room. Breakfast was a pleasant surprise. Freshly baked focaccia, three different cheeses and a choice of jam. 'What's the game plan for today?' Richard asked through a mouthful of Gorgonzola and bread.

'We stick with the buckle,' I said. 'If it moves, we follow. If it stays put and Turner moves, we stay put too and follow Plan B.'

'What's Plan B?'

'I don't know yet.'

After breakfast, Richard took his BMW up the valley past the drive. I'd told him to park facing up the valley and to follow anything that came down the drive, unless I called him and told him different. I sat on a bench on the forecourt of Casa Nico, reading Bill's thriller, the receiver in my open bag next to me. I hoped that anyone passing would take me for a tourist making the most of the watery autumn sunshine. I only had thirty pages to go when the receiver bleeped so loudly I nearly fell off my seat.

I picked it up and stared at the read-out. The buckle was moving steadily towards me. I leapt to my feet and jumped into the car, gunning the engine into life. Still the buckle was drawing nearer. There was a sudden change of direction, which I guessed was the turn from the drive on to the main road. I edged forward, ready to pull out after the target vehicle had passed, one eye on the screen. Seconds later, a stretch Mercedes limo cruised past me, followed in short order by Richard in the BMW.

I slotted into place behind him, and our little

cavalcade made its way back down the valley and into Sestri Levante. The outskirts of the town were typical of northern Italy – dusty, slightly shabby, somehow old-fashioned. The centre was much smarter, a trim holiday resort all stucco in assorted pastel shades, green shuttered windows on big hotels and small *pensiones*, expensive shops, grass and palm trees. We skirted the wide crescent of the main beach and headed along the isthmus to the harbour. As the limo turned on to a quay, I dumped the car in an illegal parking space and watched Richard do the same. I ran up to join him, linked arms and together we strolled up the quay, our faces pointing towards the sea and the floating gin palaces lined up at the pontoons. The great thing about wrap-round sunglasses is the way you can look in one direction while your head is pointing in the other.

From the corner of my eye, I saw the stretch limo glide to a halt at the foot of a gangway. The boat at the end of it was bigger than my house, and probably worth as much as Henry's Monet. The driver's door opened and a gorilla in uniform got out. Even from that distance, I could see muscles so developed they made him look round-shouldered. He wore sunglasses and a heavy moustache and looked around him with the economical watchfulness of a good bodyguard. Martin Scorsese would have swooned.

Satisfied that there was no one on the quay more dangerous than a couple of goggling tourists, he opened the back door. By now, we were close enough for me to get a good look at the presumed owner of the Villa San Pietro. He wasn't much more than my own five feet and three inches, but he looked a hell of a lot harder than me. He was handsome in the way that birds of prey are handsome, all hooked nose and hooded eyes. His perfectly groomed black hair had a wing of silver over each temple. He was wearing immaculately pressed cream yachting ducks, a full-cut, canary yellow silk shirt with a navy guernsey thrown over his shoulders. He carried a slim briefcase. He stood for a moment on the quayside, shaking the crease straight on his trouser legs, then headed up the gangplank without waiting for Turner, who scrambled out of the car behind him.

I pulled Richard into a tight embrace as Turner and the bodyguard went on board, just in case Turner was looking. When they'd disappeared below, we carried on strolling past the *Petronella Azura III*. I can't say I was surprised to see that the expensive motor cruiser was registered out of Palermo.

'Fucking hell,' Richard murmured as we passed the boat. 'It's the Mafia. Brannigan, this is no place for us to be,' he said, casting a nervous look back over his shoulder.

'They don't know we're here,' I pointed out. 'Let's keep it that way, huh?' At the end of the quay, we stared out to sea for a few minutes.

'We're going to pull out now, aren't we?' Richard

demanded. 'I mean, it's time to bring in the big battalions, isn't it?'

'Who did you have in mind?' I asked pointedly. 'This isn't Manchester. I don't know the good cops from the bad cops. From what I've heard of Italian corruption, I could walk into the nearest police station and find myself talking to this mob's tame copper. Can you think of a better short cut to a concrete bathing suit?'

Richard looked hurt. 'I was only trying to be helpful,' he said.

'Well, don't. When I want help, I'll ask for it.' I can't help myself. The more scared I get, the more I bite lumps out of the nearest body. Besides, I didn't figure I was obliged to feel guilty. As far as I was concerned, Richard had drawn the short straw from choice.

I got to my feet and started to stroll back down the quay. After a moment, Richard caught up with me. We were just in time to see the chauffeur and a young lad in shorts and a striped T-shirt trot down the gangplank and start unloading suitcases from the boot of the limo. They ferried half a dozen bags on board, not even giving us a second glance. We walked back to my car and stared at the receiver in a moody silence neither of us felt like breaking.

After about half an hour, Turner and the body-guard came off the yacht and got in the car. 'You want to follow them?' I asked Richard. 'I'll stay here and watch the boat.'

'No heroics,' he bargained.

'No heroics,' I agreed.

He just caught the lights at the end of the road where the limo had turned right. It looked like the chauffeur was taking Turner back to the villa. And judging by the screen, the buckle was now aboard the yacht. One of two things was going to happen now. Either the yacht was going to take off, complete with buckle, or some third party was going to come to the yacht and get the buckle. My money was on the former, but I felt duty-bound to sit it out. The phone rang about twenty minutes later. 'They're back at the villa,' Richard reported. 'Do you want me to wait and see if Turner takes off?'

'Please,' I said. 'Thanks, Richard. Sorry I bit your head off earlier.'

'So you should be. You're lucky to have me.' He ended the call before I could find a retort.

Suddenly the receiver screen went blank. I sat bolt upright. I pulled the connector out of the cigarette-lighter socket where I'd been recharging the batteries and slid the power compartment cover off. I broke one of my nails getting the batteries out in a hurry, and stuffed replacements in. But when I switched on again, the screen was still blank. Given that it wasn't the batteries and the yacht hadn't moved out of range, there was only one possible reason why my screen was blank. Someone had discovered the bug and put it out of action. I took a deep breath and thanked my lucky stars that my name wasn't Nicholas Turner.

Ten minutes later, the lad in the shorts was back on the quayside, casting off. Within twenty minutes, the *Petronella Azura III* had disappeared round the point. Pondering my next step, I drove back up the valley and found Richard sitting in the BMW a couple of hundred yards up the road from the turn-off to the drive. I parked my Merc at Casa Nico and walked up to join him. I filled him in on the latest turn of events. It didn't take long.

'So do we go home now?' he asked plaintively.

'I suppose so,' I said reluctantly. 'I'd like to get inside that villa, though.'

'You said yourself it was impregnable,' he pointed out.

'I know, but I never could resist a challenge.'

Richard took a deep breath. 'Brannigan, you know I never try to come between you and your job. But this time, you've got to back off. Go home, tell the police what you've got so far. They can pick up Turner and they can talk to the good cops over here and get them to look at the villa and the boat. There's nothing more you can do here. Besides, you've got another investigation you're supposed to be working on, in case you'd forgotten.'

Part of me knew he was right. But there is another part of me that responds to being told what to do by doing just the opposite. It overrides all my common sense, and it's one of the reasons why I prefer to work alone. Besides, I knew that all we had was an address and the name of a boat. That wouldn't necessarily take the authorities anywhere at all. I wanted more. But I didn't want to get into that right then. 'Let's book in at Casa Nico for another night,' I said. 'We might as well get an early start tomorrow and shoot straight back to Antwerp in a oner,' I said. 'We don't have to eat there,' I added hastily. 'Sestri Levante looked like it might have a few decent restaurants.'

Richard scowled. 'So why don't we go the whole hog and book in at a decent hotel too?'

'I'd like to stay up here, keep an eye on the place, see if there are any more comings and goings,' I told him. 'You can go down to Sestri and potter round the shops if you want.'

The scowl deepened. 'I'm not some bloody bimbo,' he complained. 'If you're waiting here, I'll keep you company.'

It was a long afternoon. I finished the thriller and Richard started it. We played I-Spy. We played Bonaparte. We played 'I went to the doctor's with . . .' right through the alphabet. The only break was when I nipped back to the Casa Nico to book us a room for the night. I was about to give in to Richard's pleas to call it a day when there was movement. An Alfa Romeo sports saloon shot out of the drive heading up the valley. Even at the speed it was travelling, I recognized the bodyguard behind the wheel. 'Move it,' I told Richard. He pulled the BMW round in a tight arc and shot after the Alfa.

We didn't have far to go. A few miles up the road was a bar whose owner could have taught Nico a thing or two. Even from our slow cruise past, it was obvious that Bar Bargonasco made Nico's look like a funeral parlour. The music was loud and cheerful, the car park didn't look like an apprentice scrapyard and there were more than six people in there. 'Pull up round the corner,' I said.

When the car stopped, I opened the door. 'Where are you going?' Richard said, panic in his eyes.

'I'm going to get into that villa one way or another. If I can't do it Dennis O'Brien style, I'm going to do it Kate Brannigan style. I'm going to chat up the bodyguard.' I shut the door and took off the shirt I was wearing over the cotton vest that was tucked into my jeans. As I was stuffing the shirt into my handbag, Richard jumped out of the driver's seat.

'You're out of your mind,' he yelled at me. 'Have you seen the size of that guy?'

'That's the whole point. He's obviously been hired for his size, not his brains. He probably keeps them in his trousers, which gives me a head start.'

'You'll never get his keys off him,' Richard exploded. 'For fuck's sake, Kate. This is madness.'

'I'm not planning on getting his keys off him. I'm planning on getting him to take me home with him,' I said, starting off towards the bar.

Richard caught up with me two steps further on and grabbed my arm. 'No way,' he shouted.

Mistake, really. In one short, sharp move, I freed myself and left Richard white-faced and clutching his wrist. 'Never, never grab me like that,' I said softly. 'You don't own me, Richard, and you don't tell me what to do.'

For a long moment we stood in a silent standoff. 'I love you, you silly bitch,' Richard finally said. 'If you want to go off and get yourself killed, you'll have to knock me out first.'

'I'll do it if I have to. You better believe me. This is my job, Richard. I know what I'm doing.'

'You'd fuck that gorilla because you think it'll help you nail some mafioso?'

I snorted. 'Is that what this is about? Sexual jealousy? What do you think I am, Richard? A tart? I never said I was going to fuck the guy. If he thinks that's on the agenda, that'll be his first mistake.'

'You think you can sort out a fucking monster like that with a bit of Thai boxing? Brannigan, you're off your head!' Richard was scarlet by now, his hands bunched into fists by his side.

I was inches away from completely losing control, but I had enough sense left not to flatten him. That would be one move that our relationship wouldn't survive. 'Trust me, Richard,' I said quietly. 'I know what I'm doing.'

He laughed bitterly. 'Fine,' he spat at me. 'Treat me like an idiot. I'm used to it, after all. That's what you all think I am anyway, isn't it? Richard the wimp, Richard the pillock, Richard the doormat, Richard the wanker, Richard who lets Kate do his thinking for him, Richard the limp dick who can't be trusted to do the simplest of jobs without ending up in the nick,' he ranted.

'Nobody thinks you're a wimp. I don't think you're a wanker, or any of the other things,' I shouted back at him. 'What happened to you with the car could have happened just as easily to me.'

'Oh no, it couldn't,' he screamed back at me. 'Clever clogs Brannigan would have phoned the police as soon as she found the car. Clever clogs Brannigan would have checked the car to see if there was anything in it there shouldn't have been. Clever clogs Brannigan and the girls would never have got themselves banged up. Because the girls are smart, and I'm just a fucking stupid arsehole *man* who gets put up with because he's marginally more fun than a vibrator.' He stopped suddenly, out of steam.

'I love you, Richard,' I said quietly. It's not an expression I'm given to, but extreme circumstances demand extreme responses.

'Bollocks,' he shouted. 'I'm a fucking convenience. You don't know what love is. You never let anyone close enough. It's all a fucking game to you, Brannigan. Like your fucking job. It's all a game. Nothing ever gets you in here,' he added, thumping his chest like an opera buffa tenor.

He looked so ridiculous, I couldn't help a smile twitching at the corners of my mouth. 'This isn't the time for this,' I said, trying to make my amusement look like conciliation. 'I'd no idea you felt this bad about what happened, and it's important that we sort it out. But we're both tired, we're both under a lot of pressure. Let's leave it till we get home, OK? Now, let me do what I've got to do. I'll see you back at Casa Nico later, OK?'

Richard shook his head. 'You really are a piece of work, Brannigan. You think you can just sweep all this aside like that? Forget it. You can go back to Casa fucking Nico if you want. But I won't be there.'

He turned on his heel and stormed back to the car. As he opened the door, he said, 'You coming?'

I shook my head. He slammed the car door behind him, swung the car round and headed back down the valley. I watched him go, my stomach feeling hollow, my eyes suddenly swimming with tears. Impatiently, I blinked them away. I tried to convince myself that Richard would be back at Casa Nico once he'd calmed down.

In the meantime, I had work to do. Besides, now I needed a lift back down the valley.

18

No woman is a heroine to her dentist. Along with my phobia about tunnels goes my paralysing fear of needles and drills. As a result, I knew I wasn't going to have to rely on anything as crude as physical strength to beat the bodyguard. If Richard hadn't pissed me off so much, I'd have explained it to him. But Watsons who scream at their Holmeses don't get the inside track on methodology.

Picking up the bodyguard was a doddle. Any man who spends as much time as he obviously did on keeping his body in peak condition has to have a streak of vanity a mile wide. He fully expected that if an attractive foreign woman walked into a bar where he was drinking, he'd be the one she'd inevitably be drawn to. And in a country where the native women are so sexually constrained by religion, it's equally inevitable that foreign women who walk into bars alone and with bare shoulders must be whores. My target thought it was his lucky night as soon as I settled on the bar stool next to him and smiled as I ordered a Peroni.

On the short walk to the bar, I'd come up with the cover story that I was a professional photographer, in Italy to take pictures for a coffee-table book of Italian church bell towers. Gianni the bodyguard and his drinking companions fell for it hook, line and sinker, with much nudging in the ribs about women who liked big ones. I suppose they thought my Italian wasn't up to mucky innuendo. By the time I'd finished my first beer, they were competing over who was going to buy the next one. By the time I'd finished my second, his heavy, muscular arm was draped over my naked shoulders and his equally heavy cologne had invaded my nostrils. The hardest part of the whole production number was hiding my revulsion. If there's one thing I hate it's hairy men, and this guy was covered like a shag pile carpet. Just the thought of his shoulders was enough to make me feel queasy.

I was on my fourth beer when I casually let slip that I was staying at Casa Nico and that I'd left my car down there while I walked up the valley. Immediately, Gianni volunteered to drive me back down. Then, of course, he suddenly remembered how terrible the cooking was at Casa Nico. Cue for nods of agreement from his buddies, coupled with nudges and winks acknowledging the cleverness of Gianni's moves. Why, he asked innocently, didn't I come back to the villa with him for some genuine

Italian home cooking. His boss was away, and he was a dab hand with the spaghetti sauce. We could eat on the terrace like the rich folks do, and then, later, he could run me back down to the *pensione*.

I looked up adoringly at him and said how delightful it was to meet such hospitable people. We left a couple of minutes later, accompanied by whoops and grunts from his cronies. In the car, he put a proprietary paw on my knee between gear changes. I fought the urge to lean over and grip his balls so tight his eyes would pop from their sockets like shelled peas. He was the driver, after all, and I didn't want to end up on the river bed looking like spaghetti sauce.

As we approached the villa, he pulled a little black electronic box out of his tight jeans and punched a button. The gates swung open, the Alfa shot through and I got my first full frontal view of the Villa San Pietro. It was magnificent. A modern villa in the style of the traditional houses that front every fashionable resort in Italy. Immaculate pink stucco, green louvred shutters. And a satellite dish the size of a kid's paddling pool. '*Molto elegante,*' I said softly.

'Good, huh?' Gianni said proudly, as if it were all his. The drive swung round the side of the house, past a tennis court and swimming pool and over to a separate, single-storey building. As we drew near, Gianni hit the button on the box again and an up-and-over garage door opened before us. Inside the garage was the stretch limo, Turner's Merc and a small green Fiat van. At the sight of Turner's car, I started to get a bad feeling in the pit of my stomach. Gianni had said we'd have the place to ourselves. But Turner had come back to the villa with him in the afternoon, and his car was still here as proof positive that he hadn't left. Maybe he'd nipped into Sestri for the evening in a taxi. Somehow, I didn't think so. For the first time since I'd started this crazy expedition, I allowed a trickle of fear to creep in. Maybe I should have listened to Richard after all.

We got out of the car and Gianni folded me into a bear hug, his tongue thrusting between my teeth. It felt like my tonsils were being raped. 'What happened to dinner?' I asked as soon as I could get my mouth clear. 'I don't know about you, but I can't think about having fun when I'm hungry.'

Gianni chuckled. 'OK, OK. First the food, then the fun.' He leered and gestured with his thumb towards a door at the side of the garage. 'That's my apartment over there. But we'll go over to the house to eat. My boss has better food and drink than me.'

We walked over to the house, his arm heavy across my shoulders. We crossed a marble patio, complete with built-in barbecue and pizza oven, and entered the kitchen through tall french windows. It was like a temple to the culinary arts. There was a free-standing butcher's block in the middle of the floor, complete with a set of Sabatier knives in their slots. Above it hung a batterie de cuisine. On the blond wooden worktops, there was every conceivable kitchen machine from ice-cream maker to a full-sized Gaggia espresso machine. Bunches of dried herbs hung from the walls, while pots of fresh basil, coriander and parsley lined a deep windowsill to the side. 'He likes to cook,' Gianni said. 'He likes me to cook too, when we have guests.'

'Nice one,' I said. 'Where's the drink?'

He nodded towards a door. 'Through there. There's a wet bar in the dining room. It's got everything. There's white wine in the fridge, and red wine in the cupboard here. Why don't you help yourself?' He moved towards me again and clutched me close, his huge hands cupping my buttocks. 'Mmm, gorgeous,' he growled.

I reached round and let my fingers stray up and down his back. That way I stopped myself thrusting my thumbs into his eyeballs. 'Tell you what,' I whispered, 'I'll fix us some cocktails. I might not be much good in the kitchen, but I'm terrific with a cocktail shaker.'

He released me and leered again. 'I can't wait to experience your wrist action.'

I giggled. 'You won't be disappointed, I promise you.'

I left him staring into a big larder fridge. He hadn't lied about the wet bar. It did have everything. The first thing I did was dredge my phial of Valium out of the bottom of my bag. I'm pretty hostile to pharmaceuticals in general, but without the Valium, I'd have blackened stumps where my teeth should be. I tipped the tablets out. There were six. I hoped that would be enough on an empty stomach to knock Gianni out before I had to test whether I really did have the skills to stop a man in his tracks. I spotted a sharp knife by a basket of lemons and oranges, and quickly crushed the tablets with the blade. Then I took a quick inventory of the bar. What I needed was a cocktail that was strong and bittersweet.

I found the measure and the shaker sitting on a shelf behind me. A small fridge contained a variety of fruit juices, and a couple of bags of ice. I settled on a Florida. Into a cocktail shaker I put three measures of gin, six measures of grapefruit juice, three measures of Galliano, and one and a half measures of Campari. I tossed in a couple of ice cubes, closed the shaker and did a quick salsa round the bar with the shaker providing the beat. 'Sounds good,' Gianni shouted from the kitchen.

'Wait till you taste it,' I called back. I chose a couple of tall glasses and scraped the Valium powder into one. I topped it up with about two thirds of the cocktail mixture and stirred it vigorously with a glass rod. I poured the rest into the other glass and topped it up with grapefruit juice and a dash of grenadine syrup to make the colours match. I swallowed hard, picked up both glasses and walked through to the kitchen. Gianni was chopping red onions with a wide-bladed chef's knife. 'A very Italian cocktail,' I announced, handing the drugged glass to him.

He took it from me and swigged a generous mouthful. He savoured it, swilling it round his mouth before swallowing it. 'You're right. Bitter and sweet. Like love, huh?' The leer was back.

'Not too bitter, I hope,' I giggled, moving behind him and hugging him from behind.

'Not with me, baby. With me, it'll be sweeter than sugar,' he said arrogantly.

'I can hardly wait,' I murmured. I wasn't exactly lying. I moved away and perched on a high stool, watching him cook. The onions went into a deep pan with olive oil and garlic. Next, he chopped a fennel bulb into thin slices and added them to the stewing onions. He took a punnet of wild mushrooms from the fridge, washed them under running water, patted them dry lovingly with paper towels and chopped them coarsely. Into the pan they went along with a torn handful of coriander leaves.

'It smells wonderful,' I said.

'Wait till you taste it,' he said. 'There's only one thing tastes better.' Time for another leer. The temperature was rising in more ways than one. The only good thing about that was the speed at which he was drinking his cocktail.

'No contest,' I said, watching him measure out round grains of risotto rice. He tipped the rice into the pan, stirred it into the mixture for a couple of minutes, then took a carton out of the freezer.

'Chicken stock,' he said, tossing the solid lump into the pan amidst much hissing and clouds of steam. He kept stirring till the stock had defrosted and the pan was bubbling gently. Then he put a lid on, set the timer for twelve minutes and drained his glass.

'How about a salad to go with it?' I asked hastily as he started to move towards me. 'And I'll mix you another drink, OK?'

His eyes seemed to lose focus momentarily and he shook his head like a bull bothered by flies. He rubbed his hands over his face and mumbled, 'OK.' I'd reckoned about twenty minutes for the drugs to take effect, but maybe the amount he'd had to drink on an empty stomach was accelerating things.

I'd barely got the cap off the gin bottle when there was a sound like a tree falling in the kitchen. I tiptoed back to the doorway to see Gianni spread-eagled on the marble floor. For one terrible moment, I thought I'd killed him. Then he started to snore like a sawmill on overtime. I ran across to the butcher's block and picked up the knife. It took seconds to saw off the electric cable from a couple of the kitchen appliances. Tying him up took quite a bit longer, but the snoring didn't even change in note while I was doing it. I took the black box out of his pocket and tucked it in my bag.

I found the cellar door on the second try. A wide flight of stairs led down into the depths. One thing about marble floors is that they make shifting heavy loads a lot easier. I got down on my knees behind Gianni and shoved with all my strength.

Foot by foot, we slid across the gleaming tiles to the doorway. One last push sent him skidding over the first step, feet first. He bounced down the stairs like a sack of potatoes, still snoring. I staggered to my feet. For the first time, I was grateful that Gianni's boss was security conscious. The cellar door had bolts top and bottom as well as a lock on the door. I slid the bolts home and leaned against the door to get my breath back.

When the timer went off, I nearly jumped out of my skin. Automatically, I turned off the gas under the pan. Now the adrenaline surge was slipping away, I realized that I was in fact ravenous. I shrugged. The food was there, I might as well eat. I didn't think Gianni was going to be knocking at the door demanding his share in a hurry.

He might have been the world's worst lecher, but he was a fabulous cook. I shovelled the risotto down, savouring every delicious mouthful. Now I needed coffee. It was going to be a long night. I wished I hadn't chopped the lead off the Gaggia. A search of the cupboards eventually turned up a jar of instant and a Thermos jug. I brewed up and, armed with jug, mug and shoulder bag, I set off to explore.

Whatever Gianni's boss was, he wasn't short of a bob. The public rooms on the ground floor were all marble floored, with expensive Oriental rugs scattered around. The furniture was upmarket repro, all polished to a mirror finish. There was nothing in the dining room, drawing room, morning room or the TV lounge to indicate that this was anything other than the home of a successful businessman. Even the videos lined up in the cabinet by the oversized TV were completely innocuous.

Cautiously, I made my way up the stairs. It was always possible that Turner was a prisoner somewhere inside the villa rather than the victim of my worst imaginings. Six doors opened off the long landing. The first two were lavish guest bedrooms, complete with *en suite* bathrooms. If Gianni's boss ever set up in competition with Casa Nico, the *pensione* down the valley would go out of business within hours. The third door opened on what was clearly the master bedroom. The wardrobes were filled with designer suits and shirts, the drawers with silk underwear and the kind of leisure wear that has the labels on the outside. No trace of a woman in residence. No trace of any papers, either.

The fourth door opened on to a library. It was obviously a reader's library rather than one where the books had been bought by the yard. Modern hardbacks lined the shelves. I noticed a sizeable chunk of crime fiction, but most of the books were by authors I'd never heard of. There was also a whole section of legal textbooks, mostly covering commercial and international law. But again, there were no papers anywhere, unless some of the books were dummies. If they were,

237

they'd be hanging on to their secrets. There was no way I had time to go through that lot book by book.

The fifth door was locked. I left it for a moment and tried the sixth. Another guest bedroom. That told me that either Turner was behind the locked door, or something significant was. Unfortunately, I didn't have my set of picklocks with me. I don't carry them routinely, and when I'd set off on my pursuit of Turner, I hadn't expected to be doing any burglaries. I could of course simply smash the lock with one of the dozens of marble statuettes that hung around in niches all over the place. But I didn't want the villa's owner to know the extent to which he'd been turned over unless I could possibly help it.

I looked up at the door lintel. Gianni's boss was not much bigger than me, so the chances were that the key wasn't sitting up there. I went back to the master bedroom and began a proper search. I got lucky in the bathroom. I'd taken the contents of the bathroom cupboard off the shelves one by one, just to make sure there was nothing behind them. There were two aerosol cans of Polo shaving foam, and one was a lot lighter than the other. I looked more closely at the heavier of the two. Gripping it tightly, I twisted the bottom of the can. It unscrewed smoothly, revealing a compartment lined with bubble wrap. Inside was what looked like a handkerchief. I pulled it out and a bunch of keys tumbled to the floor. 'Gotcha!' I murmured.

The longest of the keys opened the locked door. Inside was a starkly functional office, a sharp contrast to the luxurious appointments of the rest of the villa. I switched the light on, closed the shutters and took a good look around. A basic desk stood against one wall with a computer, a modem, and a fax machine on it. To one side there was a photocopier and a laser printer. Automatically, I switched them on. I noticed a shredder under the desk as I sat down and hit the computer's power button. The machine booted up and I called up the directories. Ten minutes later, my jubilation had given way to depression. Every single data file I'd tried to access was password protected. I couldn't get in to read them. All it would let me do was print out a list of all files, which I duly did.

Muttering dark imprecations, I returned to the main directory. Time for some lateral thinking. In the years since I first started working at Mortensen and Brannigan and discovered the wonderful world of electronic mail, the Internet had grown from the home of academics and a handful of computer loonies like me to the world's bulletin board. The communications software that was running on this machine was a standard business package that I'd used dozens of times before. Even if the files were password protected, I reckoned that the communications program would still be able to transmit them intact to somewhere I could retrieve them later and pass them on to someone who could crack the passwording. All I needed was a local number for the Internet. If I was lucky, there would be one already loaded in the comms program. I started it running and called up the telephone directory screen.

It was my lucky night. Right at the top of the list was the number for the local Internet node – the E-mail equivalent of a postal sorting office. The way the Net works is simple. It's analogous to sending a letter rather than making a phone call. The network is connected by phone lines, and works on what they call a parcel switching system. What happens is you dial a local number and send your data to it. The computer there reads the address and shunts your data down the network, section by section, till it arrives at its destination. But unlike a letter, which takes days if you're lucky, this takes less time than it takes to describe the process.

I used the edit mode to discover Gianni's boss's login and password, then I instructed the computer to connect me to the Internet. Less than a minute later, we were in. I typed in the electronic mail address of the office, then I started sending the files one by one. An hour and a mug of coffee later, I'd sent a copy of every data file in the machine back to Manchester.

Breathing a deep sigh of relief, I switched off the machine. Now it was time for the desk drawers. I unlocked each drawer with the remaining keys on the bunch. The first drawer held stationery. The second held junk – rubber bands, spare computer disks, a couple of computer cables, a half-eaten chocolate bar and a box of Post-it notes. The bottom drawer looked more promising, with its collection of suspension files. No such luck. All the files held was the paperwork for the house: utility bills, receipts for furniture, building work, landscaping, pool maintenance. The only interesting thing was that everything was in the name of a company – Gruppo Leopardi. There was no clue as to who was behind Gruppo Leopardi. And I didn't have the time for the kind of thorough search that might reveal that. I'd already been there too long, and I was getting too tired to concentrate. It was time to make tracks.

I went back over to the window, to open the shutters again. I wanted to leave everything exactly as I'd found it. As I turned back, clumsy with exhaustion, I caught the Thermos jug with my elbow. It sailed off the desk and bounced off the panelled wall under the window. It landed on its side on the floor, apparently undamaged. Not so the wall. The wood panelling where the jug had hit had slowly swung away from the wall, revealing a safe. Eat your heart out, Enid Blyton. If preposterous coincidence is good enough for the Secret Seven, it's good enough for me.

19

If the Brannigans were posh enough to have a
family motto, it would go something like, 'What
do you mean, I *can't*?' Just because I've never
learned how to crack a safe didn't mean I was
going to close the panel and walk away. I sat on
the floor opposite the safe and studied it. There
was a six-digit electronic display above a keypad
with the letters of the alphabet and the numbers
zero to nine. Beside the keypad were buttons that
I translated as 'enter code', 'open', 'random reset',
'master'. That didn't take me a whole lot further
forward.

I checked my watch. Ten o'clock. Not too late
to make a call. I took the mobile out of my bag
and rang Dennis. It would have been cheaper to
use the fax phone, but I'd already noticed that
Gruppo Leopardi had itemized billing on their
phone account and I didn't want to leave a trail
straight back to Dennis, especially given that he
already had connections with these people via

Turner. Dennis answered his phone on the second ring. 'Hi, Dennis,' I said. 'I'm looking at the outside of a safe and I want to be looking at the inside. Any ideas?'

'Kate, you're more of a villain than I am. You know I haven't touched a safe since Billy the Whip dropped one on my foot in 1983.'

'This isn't the time for reminiscing. This call's costing me a week's wages.'

He chuckled. 'Then somebody else must be paying for it. What does this safe look like?'

I described it to him. 'You're wasting your time, Kate. Beast like that, you've got no chance unless you know the combo,' he said sorrowfully.

'You sure?'

'I'm sure. He might be a sloppy git though, this guy you're having over. He might have gone for something really stupid like the last six digits of the phone number. Or the first six. Or his date of birth. Or his girlfriend's name. Or some set of letters and numbers he sees in his office every day.'

I groaned. 'Enough, already. You sure there's no other way?'

'That's why they call them safes,' Dennis said. 'Where are you, anyway?'

'You don't want to know. Believe me, you don't want to know. I'll be in touch. Thanks for your help.'

I went back to the domestic files and tried various combinations of the phone number and any other number I could find, including the vehicle registrations. No joy. I sat in the boss's chair and looked around me. What would he see from here that would be a constant *aide-mémoire*? I got up and tried the model numbers of the fax machine, the modem and the photocopier. Nothing. I didn't know the boss's birthday, but I had a feeling that a man as security conscious as him wouldn't have gone for anything that obvious.

It was last resort time. What would *I* do if I wanted a code that was random enough for no one to guess, but accessible to me whenever I forgot it? Acting on pure instinct, I hit the power button on the computer again and watched the screen, looking for any six digit combinations that came up during the boot process. I ended up with two, MB 4D33 was part of the operating system ident. And the CD-ROM drive's device model number was CR-563-X. The first string did nothing. But when I entered the second set of digits, the display changed from red to green. I couldn't believe it.

Holding my breath, I hit the 'open' button. There was a soft click and the door catch released. 'There is a God, and she likes me,' I said softly. I opened the safe and stared in at the contents. There was a stack of papers about half an inch thick. On top of them sat a loose-leaf folder, slightly bigger than a Filofax. I took everything out of the safe and moved back to the desk. I started with the folder. First there was a list of names, with dates and figures next to it. Following that were half a dozen pages listing numbered locations. Some of them had ticks beside them, and a couple were crossed out. Castle Dumdivie was on the list, with a tick. So were a few other names I recognized. Next came a list of dates and places followed by a number and letter code – 20CC, 34H, 50,000E, that sort of thing. The fourth column was a number. A little bit of crosschecking, and I realized that the numbers corresponded to ticked locations on the list, and, in the cases I knew about, the dates were all two to four weeks after the burglaries. Finally, there were several pages of names, addresses and phone numbers. Halfway down the third page, I spotted Turner. I wasn't sure what all of this meant, but I was beginning to have the glimmerings of an idea.

I opened the clasps of the folder and put the pages through the photocopier. While they were feeding through, I looked at the other papers. Some of them were legal contracts, and I couldn't make head nor tail of them. Others were handwritten notes which seemed to refer to meetings, but although I understood most of the words, I couldn't get a lot of sense out of them. There were a few business letters, mostly of the 'thank you for your letter of the fifteenth, we can confirm the safe arrival of your consignment' type. The final bundle of papers were draft accounts of Gruppo Leopardi. I copied the lot.

Once I'd finished, I replaced everything in the safe, exactly as I'd found it. I had the papers, but I wanted a little bit of insurance, just in case anything happened on the way home to deprive me of my photocopies. The fax machine was the best source of that insurance, but I didn't want to send the stuff to my office number for the same reason I'd used the mobile to phone Dennis. It needed to go somewhere secure, but somewhere large enough for it not to be obvious who specifically it had gone to. Ideally, it also had to go somewhere that even the Mafia would think twice about storming mob-handed.

There was only one place and one person I could think of that fitted the bill. Detective Chief Inspector Della Prentice, top dog on the Regional Crime Squad's fraud task force. This wasn't her bailiwick, but Della's still the only copper I'd trust with anything that might put me at risk. I'd worked with Della a couple of times now since we'd first been introduced by Josh Gilbert. They'd been at Cambridge together, and although their fascination with finance high and low had taken them in radically different directions, they'd stayed close enough for Josh to recognize that Della and I are kindred spirits. Since our first encounter, we'd become close friends. I knew if I faxed this wodge of incomprehensible paperwork to Della, she'd tuck it away safely in her drawer till I turned up to explain its significance.

I took a sheet of paper out of the stationery drawer and scribbled a cover sheet. 'Fax for the urgent and confidential attention of DCI Prentice, Regional Crime Squad. Dear Della, Vital evidence.

Please keep safe until I can fill you in on the deep background. I'll call you as soon as I get back. Thanks. KB.' That should do it, I thought, dialling her departmental fax machine. God knows what the duty CID would make of a hundred-page fax from Italy in the middle of the night.

By the time I'd finished, it was after two. I bundled up my photocopies, stuffed them in an envelope and tucked the lot into my bulging bag. Time to get the hell out of here, as far away as possible. I had a horrible feeling that I knew what had happened to Nicholas Turner, probably because of my bug, and I didn't want to end up the same way. There wasn't a trace of the guy in any of the spare bedrooms, which put paid to any comforting ideas about him having nipped into Sestri in a taxi for dinner.

I switched everything off and locked the desk drawers again. Satisfied that it all looked just as it had when I'd walked into the office, I got out, locking the door behind me. I replaced the keys in the dummy can, hoping that my memory of how the contents of the cabinet had been arranged was accurate. I trotted down the stairs and back to the kitchen. I put my ear to the cellar door. Silence. I had a momentary pang of conscience, wondering what would happen to the big man when he came round and found himelf tied up in the dark for an indefinite period of time. Then I reminded myself that he was probably directly responsible for whatever had happened to Turner, and I stopped feeling guilty. Besides, judging by the pristine condition of the villa, I reckoned there must be a maid who came in every day to polish the floors, the furniture and the kitchen equipment. By the time she arrived, Gianni would probably be bellowing like a bull.

I let myself out of the French windows and stood on the patio, weighing up what to do next. I had the black box that would open the gates for me, but I didn't know where the security system was controlled from, and the cameras would still be rolling. I wasn't keen on finding myself the star of the Mafia equivalent of *Crimewatch*, so I decided to help myself to one of the vehicles, just to keep myself hidden from the all-seeing eyes by the gate. You can only do so much with computer enhancement, and I reckoned the combination of the darkness and the obscurity of being inside a car would make sure I couldn't be identified.

A quick sortie in the garage revealed that the keys for all the vehicles were hanging on the board where Gianni had deposited his set earlier. I settled on the van, on the basis that it was the least memorable of the three. I opened the door, threw my bag on the passenger seat and climbed behind the wheel. I was just about to stick the key in the ignition, when something stopped me.

I don't believe in sixth sense or second sight or seventh sons of seventh sons. But something was making the hair on the back of my neck stand up, and it wasn't love at first sight. I took a deep breath and looked over my shoulder into the back of the van.

At once I wished I hadn't. There's only one thing comes in a six-feet-long, heavy-duty black bag with a zipper up the front. It didn't take many of my detective skills to decide that I'd probably solved the mystery of Nicholas Turner's disappearance.

I was out of the van in seconds. I stood in the garage, leaning against the wall for support, my breath coming fast, clammy sweat in my armpits. The combination of shock and exhaustion was making my limbs tremble. I don't know how long I stood there like that, frozen in horror, incapable of movement, never mind decisive action. It's one thing to think somebody might be dead. It's another thing entirely to find yourself sitting in a van with their mortal remains. Especially when you're the one who's responsible for their present state.

It was only fear that got me moving again. Hanging around the Villa San Pietro was about as clever a move as a mouse going walkabout in a cattery. My first instinct was to dive into the Alfa and put as much distance between me and the villa as fast as I could. I was halfway across the garage when I realized that wasn't an answer I could live with. It was my bug and my fake that had got Nicholas Turner murdered. I couldn't just walk away and let the people who'd had him killed dispose of the body and wash their hands of the whole business. If I left him here, that's exactly what would happen. I couldn't just drive to the nearest police station and tell them what I knew. They might be on the villa's payroll, for a kickoff. And even if they weren't and I did get them to believe me, I couldn't think of a cover story that wouldn't leave me facing charges of false imprisonment, assault, deception, breaking and entering, and probably the murder of Aldo Moro.

I thought about waking Della and bringing her up to speed so we could do it through official channels, but by the time we'd got the wheels of justice rolling, there would be no evidence of murder at the villa, the body would be miles away, and even if it did eventually turn up, there would be nothing to connect it to Gianni and his boss.

Taking a deep breath, I opened the back of the van. Before I did anything else, I needed to be sure it really was Turner in the bag. Gingerly, I reached out for the tab of the zip and pushed it away from me. It wouldn't budge. I could feel my stomach begin to turn over as I gripped the slick, rubberized bag with one hand and forced the zip down. A few inches was all I needed. Nicholas Turner's eyes stared up at me out of a face grey in the stark fluorescent light of the garage. I gagged and whipped round just in time for the contents of my stomach to miss the van and hit the floor. I stood there, hands on my knees, throwing up till my stomach and throat were raw. Shaking and sweating, my fingers slippery on the body bag, I managed to pull up the zip. Turner's face showed no signs of how he had met his end, but

I'd have been willing to bet it hadn't been a brain tumour.

I don't remember how I managed it, but somehow I got back behind the wheel and drove out of the garage. All I could think of was getting out of there and putting some distance between me and the Villa San Pietro. I hurtled down the drive, punching the steering wheel in frustration as the gates took their time opening. I shot down the track so fast I nearly lost it on one of the bends. The shock of that sobered me enough to slow me down to a more reasonable speed. As I hit the main road, I realized I'd have to move the Mercedes away from Casa Nico, since Gianni knew that was where I was staying, and I couldn't guarantee I'd get back to the car before he was released from his prison.

I left the van parked on the verge by the villa turn-off and jogged the couple of kilometres back to the *pensione*. There was no sign of the BMW. So much for expecting Richard to see sense and come back. I drove the Merc back up the valley, past the van, looking for somewhere to stash it. About a kilometre further on, there was a cluster of houses and a mini-market. I left the car just off the main road and half jogged, half staggered back to the van. I didn't pass another car the whole hour.

I turned the van round and headed back towards Sestri Levante. I reckoned I needed to leave the van somewhere no one would notice if it was parked for a few days. I thought about finding some remote forest track in the mountains, but I vetoed that. It would be difficult to find the right place in the dark, it would be impossible for me to remember where it was with pinpoint accuracy, and it wouldn't be easy for me to make my way back to the Merc. I didn't want to leave it parked on a street, because I didn't know how long it was going to take to get anyone to listen to my tale, and after a day or two in Italian sunshine, the van wasn't going to smell too appetizing. What I needed, ideally, was an underground car park where no one would pay attention.

Either I needed a big city, or a swanky resort where people left their cars in the hotel car park for a few days. The solution popped out of my memory just as the autostrada junction hove into sight. The picture postcard village of Portofino, star of a thousand jigsaw puzzles, its harbour lined with picturesque houses painted every colour of the ice-cream spectrum. I'd been there a couple of years before with Richard, and remembered the big car park, half underground, where tourists left their cars to avoid completely choking the centre of the former fishing village.

I drove into Portofino just after 5.00 a.m. It's probably the only time of day when there isn't a queue to get into the village. I drove straight into the car park, taking a ticket at the automatic barrier. I left the van on the lowest level and walked up the stairs to the street. The pale light of dawn was just beginning to brighten the eastern sky as I strolled down to the harbour. There were a few boatmen around in the harbour, but I didn't want to draw too much attention to myself by asking any of them how soon I could get out of the place. I tried to look like an insomniac tourist enjoying the peace and quiet, and wandered down the quayside to where the pleasure boats departed. I was in luck. At nine, there was a boat that went to Sestri Levante and on to the Cinque Terre beyond.

I walked on round the harbour and found a bench that overlooked the bay. Using my bag as a pillow, I put my head down and managed to doze off. Strange dreams featuring Gianni's chef's knife and bodies that climbed out of bags and into passenger seats prevented it from being a restful sleep, but I was so exhausted that even the nightmares couldn't wake me up. The sound of a pleasure steamer's hooter jerked me into wakefulness just after eight, and I staggered back into the village, bought myself a couple of sandwiches and a cappuccino from a café and headed for the pleasure boat.

I don't remember much about the sail. I was too jittery from lack of sleep and the horrors of the night. I kept nodding off, and starting awake, nerves jangling and eyes staring in paranoia. I couldn't stop thinking about Turner's wife and those two daughters. Not only had they lost a husband and father, but they were going to find out about it in a blitz of police and media activity.

In spite of the fact that arriving on dry land brought me nearer to the enemy, I was glad to be off the boat. Somehow, I felt more in control. In Sestri, I found the tourist office and discovered where I could catch a bus up the valley. The next one left in twenty minutes, and I was first on it, complete with brand-new sun hat. I sat at the back, slouched low in my seat. As Casa Nico approached, I put my sunglasses on and pulled the hat forwards. The bus was so much higher off the road than a car would have been that I was able to look right down on Casa Nico. As the bus rounded the bend beyond the *pensione*, I looked back. Parked behind the building, where I wouldn't have been able to spot it in a car, was Gianni's Alfa.

I got off at the next stop and walked cautiously past the alley where I'd left the Merc. It was still there, and no one seemed to be watching it. I doubled back behind the houses and came up the alley from the far end. I crept into the car, not even slamming the door shut until I had the engine running. Then I shot out on to the main road and headed up the valley, away from Casa Nico and the Villa San Pietro, my foot hard on the accelerator, my eyes on the rear-view mirror. As I joined the autostrada, I wondered how long Gianni would stake out the *pensione*. It was worth the loss of my overnight bag not to have him on my tail.

Nigel Mansell couldn't have got to Milan airport faster than I did that day. I dumped the car with the local Hertz agent and headed for the terminal. I'd just missed a flight to Brussels, but there was one to Amsterdam an hour later. If I could only stay awake, I could pick up Bill's Saab in Antwerp, catch the night ferry from Zeebrugge and be home the following morning some time. Frankly, I couldn't wait to feel British soil under my feet.

I had half an hour to kill in the international departure lounge. I thought I'd better give Shelley a ring before she decided tracking me down was a job for Interpol. She answered on the first ring, and I could hear relief in her voice. I knew then it must be bad, since Shelley never lets on that anything's beyond her competence.

'Thank God it's you,' she said. 'Where are you? You've got to get back here. There's been another death.'

20

I nearly dropped the phone. My first thought was, how the hell had Shelley found out about Nicholas Turner? Her voice cut through my panic. 'Kate? Are you still there? I said there's been another death involving KerrSter.' This time round, I heard the whole sentence.

'Oh fuck,' I groaned.

'Where *are* you? Trevor Kerr is reading me the riot act every ten minutes. I've managed to stall him so far, but if you don't speak to him soon, he's threatening to sack us and go to the press saying the reason for the second death is your dereliction of duty,' Shelley continued, her voice betraying an agitation I'd never heard from her before.

'I'm at Milan airport. On the way to Amsterdam, *en route* for Antwerp. I'll have to leave Bill's car in Belgium and get a flight straight back to the UK. When did this happen?'

'This morning. An office cleaner. They found her dead beside a new drum of KerrSter. It looks like another case of cyanide poisoning, according to Alexis. Incidentally, she wants to talk to you too.'

I glanced over at the gate. They hadn't started boarding us yet. 'Is Kerr still in his office?'

'He was five minutes ago,' Shelley said. 'He's had the Merseyside police all over his factory this afternoon.'

'I'll call him and stall him,' I said. 'I'm sorry you've had all this shit to deal with on your own. If it's any consolation, this trip's been a nightmare. I've already had one close encounter with death today. I'm not sure if I'm up to another one.'

'You're all right?' Shelley demanded anxiously.

'I wouldn't pitch it that high. I'm in one piece, which is more than I can say for Turner.'

'Oh my God,' she said, sounding stricken.

'Look, it's OK. Let me talk to Kerr. I'll call you from Amsterdam. There's a flight gets in to Manchester about half-seven tonight. See if you can get me a seat on it. I don't care if it's business class, club class or standing in the toilet, just get me on it.'

'Will do. I'll hang on here till I hear from you,' she promised. 'For God's sake, be careful.'

It was a bit late for me to take heed of that warning. I took a deep breath, bracing myself for battle, and rang Trevor Kerr. Not even my powers of imagination had prepared me for his onslaught. For two straight minutes he ranted at me, with a string of obscenities that would have won him admiration on the football terraces but didn't do a lot for me. I made a mental note to bump that surliness surcharge up to ten per cent. When he paused to regroup for a second outpouring, I cut in decisively. 'I'm sorry you've had a difficult day, but you're not the only one,' I said grimly. 'I have been pursuing my inquiries into your problem as fast as I can. I've made a lot of progress, but I needed a crucial piece of information that I've not been able to get hold of yet. Now, I'm meeting someone in an hour's time who can tell me what I need to know,' I continued, raising my voice to cut through his crap.

'Bullshit!' he hollered like a bear with its leg in a gin. 'You've been doing fuck all. Give me one good reason why I shouldn't fire you this fucking minute.'

'Because if you do, some other private eye with half my talent is going to have to start from square one because you'll have to sue me to get one single scrap of the information I've already uncovered.'

That silenced him for all of ten seconds. 'I'll tell the police you're withholding information,' he blustered.

'Tell them. Inspector Jackson knows me well enough to realize that shoving me in a cell won't make a blind bit of difference to what I have to say for myself.'

'You can't treat me like this,' he howled, the ultimate spoilt bully.

'If you want us to discuss this like reasonable adults, you can meet me this evening in the bar of the Hilton at the airport at eight o'clock,' I said. 'Otherwise, I'm taking my bat and ball home, Mr Kerr.' Out of the corner of my eye, I could see my fellow passengers disappearing through the gate. 'It's up to you,' I said, replacing the phone.

The flight to Amsterdam seemed never ending. I stared gloomily out of the window, feeling more guilty than a Catholic in bed with a married man. My meddling had cost Nicholas Turner his life. Meddling I'd done while I should have been nailing down my suspicions about the product-tampering racket. If I'd done that job properly, the culprits would be answering Inspector Jackson's questions now and maybe the woman who had died would still be alive. I should never have taken Trevor Kerr's case on when I was in the middle of another demanding investigation. But I had to be smart, prove to the world that I was twice as good as any reasonable private investigator needed to be. I'd been trying to show Bill that I was more than capable of being left to run the agency single-handed. All I'd done so far was get two people killed.

Not only that, but I'd fractured my relationship with Richard, perhaps beyond repair this time. All because I was determined to be the big shot, doing things my way. I began to wonder why I was bothering to go back. On my present form, the only people I'd be keeping satisfied were the undertakers. I had the best part of nine grand in my bag, a car waiting at Antwerp. In all my working life, I've never been closer to running away.

When it came to the crunch, I couldn't do it. Call it duty, call it stubbornness, call it pure bloody-mindedness. Whatever it was, it propelled me off that plane and over to the check-in desk for the flight to Manchester. Shelley had come up trumps. I was booked on a seat in business class. I had ten minutes to give her a quick ring and tell her I was meeting Kerr at the airport hotel. Slightly reassured, she told me again to take care. She was warning the wrong person.

They had that evening's *Chronicle* on the plane. CLEANER'S MYSTERY DEATH hit me like a stab in the guts. Even though she'd died in Liverpool, Mary Halloran had made the front page in Manchester because of the KerrSter connection and because it gave the paper the chance to rehash the Joey Morton story. Feeling accused by every word, especially since they came under the by-line of Alexis Lee, I read on. Mrs Halloran, forty-three, a mother of two (oh God, another two kids I'd deprived of a parent . . .), had started her own commercial cleaning firm after she was made redundant by the city council. The business had grown into a real money-spinner, but Mrs Halloran liked to keep her hand in on the office floor, presumably to stay in touch with her roots. She had a regular stint three mornings a week in a local solicitor's office, where she started work at half past five. Normally, she worked with another woman, but her partner had been off sick that week. Mrs Halloran's body had been found outside the cleaning cupboard on the first floor by one of the solicitors who had come in just after seven to catch up on some work. She was slumped on the floor beside an open but full container of KerrSter. The police had revealed that the postmortem indicated Mrs Halloran had died as a result of inhaling hydrogen cyanide gas.

The pathologist must have been quick off the mark, I thought. Not to mention in possession of a nasty, suspicious mind. After Joey Morton's death I'd checked my reference shelves, which had confirmed what I'd already thought – death by cyanide's a real pig to diagnose. It happens almost instantaneously, and there's not much to see on the pathologist's slab. Maybe a trace of frothing round the mouth, possibly a few irregular pink patches on the skin like you get with people who suck too long on their car exhausts. If you get the body open quickly, there might be a faint trace of the smell of bitter almonds in the mouth, chest and abdominal cavity. But if you don't get your samples pdq, you're knackered because the cyanide metamorphoses into sulphocyanides, which you'd expect to find there anyway. The only reason they'd picked up on it right away in Joey's case was that the barman who discovered his body noticed the smell and happened to be a keen reader of detective fiction.

The Merseyside police were being pretty cautious, and there was a stonewalling quote from

Jackson, but reading between the lines, you could see they were talking to each other already. Trevor Kerr was on the record as saying he was confident that there was no problem with the products leaving his factory and he was sure that any investigation would completely vindicate Kerrchem. Never one to miss the chance for a bit of speculation, Alexis had flown the kite of industrial sabotage, but she had no quotes to back her up. No wonder she wanted to talk to me. I wondered if Trevor Kerr had told her I was working for him as part of his attempt to get out from under.

By the time the plane landed, I could have done with a couple of lines of speed. I'd had a stressful couple of days with almost no sleep, and the coffee I'd been mainlining in the air was starting to give me the jitters rather than simply keeping me awake. I was just in the mood for Trevor Kerr.

I reclaimed my bags by ten to eight and pushed them through customs on a trolley, like a sleep-walker. Halfway down the customs hall, I felt a hand on my shoulder and heard a voice say, 'Step this way, madam.' I looked up blearily at the customs officer, inches away from tears. The last thing I needed right now was to explain my bizarre assortment of possessions, ranging from a box of maps to a wad of cash and a radio receiver.

'What's going on?' I asked.

'Just follow me, please,' he said, leaving me no choice. We walked across the hall to a door on the far side. I was aware of several curious stares from my fellow passengers. The customs man showed me into a small office and closed the door behind me. Leaning against the wall, exhaling a mouthful of smoke, stood Detective Chief Inspector Della Prentice, a wry smile on her lips. Her chestnut hair was loose, hanging round her face in a shining fall. Her green eyes were clear, her skin glowing. She'd clearly had more than two hours' sleep in the last thirty-six. I hated her.

'You look like you had a rough flight,' she said.

'The flight was fine,' I told her, slumping into one of the room's plastic bucket chairs. 'It's just the last two days that have been hell.'

'Anything to do with the collected works that was waiting on my desk this morning?' she asked.

I groaned. 'More than somewhat. I realize it won't have made a word of sense to you, but I needed to send it somewhere safe.'

'Come on,' Della said, shrugging away from the wall. 'I'll drive you home and we'll talk.'

'I'm meeting a client at the Hilton,' I said, glancing at my watch. 'Two minutes from now. On a totally unrelated matter,' I added.

Della looked concerned. 'You sure you're up to that?'

I laughed affectionately. 'The copper in you never quite goes off duty, does it? I'm in a fit state for you to give me the third degree, but let me near a client? Oh no, I'm far too knackered for that.'

Della gave me a playful punch on the shoulder. 'I can't imagine that your client's planning to run you a hot bath laden with stimulating essential oils or to cook you a meal while you luxuriate with a stiff Stoly and grapefruit juice. And if he is, maybe I should call Richard and let him know the competition's hotting up.'

My head fell into my hands. 'Not one of your better ideas, Della,' I sighed.

'Oh God, you've not been checking out the insurance man's endowments, have you?' she giggled.

'Thank you, Alexis,' I said, getting wearily to my feet. 'And thank you for your confidence in me, Della. Come on, then. You can give me a lift over to the Hilton so I can talk to the client. Then you can take me home and I'll tell you all about it.'

One of the good things about having the cops meet you at the airport is that they get to park right outside the door without the traffic wardens turning their windscreens into scrapbooks. We drove across to the Hilton in blissful silence, and I left Della in reception with strict instructions to get me out of there in no more than ten minutes.

Trevor Kerr was planted in an armchair in the corner with a brandy glass in front of him. I sat down opposite him. He didn't offer me a drink. 'So what have you got to say for yourself?' he demanded by way of greeting. 'I've had a hell of a day thanks to your incompetence. The police have turned my bloody factory upside down, questioning everybody. God knows what today's production figures will be like.'

'Somebody is making fake KerrSter. They're releasing it on to the market via a little scam they've got going with one of the major wholesale chains. I know how the scam works and I know who's pulling it. The only thing I don't yet know is where they're manufacturing the stuff,' I said in an exhausted monotone. I just didn't have the energy to let Trevor Kerr wind me up.

His red face turned purple. 'Who is it? Who's doing this to me?' he shouted, leaning forward and banging the table with his fist. Several distant drinkers turned towards us, curious. The Hilton's bar isn't a place that's used to raised voices that early in the evening.

'It's a former employee, who clearly wasn't too impressed with the golden handcuffs you slapped on him,' I said.

'I want a name,' he demanded, his voice lower but his expression no less menacing. 'And an address. I'm going to break every bone in his fucking body when I get my hands on him.'

I shook my head, weary of his incontinent anger. 'No way.'

'What the hell do you think I'm paying you for, girl? Give me the name and address!'

'Mr Kerr, shut up and listen to me.' I'd reached the end of my rope and I suspect it showed. Kerr fell back in his seat as if I'd hit him. 'A client hires me to do a job, and I do that job. Sometimes I come up against things that make people want to take the law into their own hands. Part of my job is stopping

265

them. If I give you that name and address, and you go round there and give this bloke a good seeing to, you won't thank me tomorrow when you're in a police cell and he's sitting in his hospital bed free and clear because there isn't a shred of tangible evidence to tie him to the fake KerrSter or these killings. Sure, he'll have a sticky couple of hours down the nick, but unless we find where this stuff is being made and connect him directly to it, all we have is a chain of circumstantial evidence.' Kerr opened his mouth to speak, but I waved a finger at him and carried on. 'And I have to tell you that because of the way I've collected some of that circumstantial evidence, we're not going to be able to produce it for the police. We can tell them where to look, but we can't show them all we've got. We *need* the factory. I'm not keeping the name from you out of bloody-mindedness. I'm doing the job you paid me for, and I intend to finish it before somebody else dies. Do you have a problem with any of that?' I challenged him.

'Your name will be mud in this town,' he blustered.

'For what? Keeping my client out of jail? Mr Kerr, if I ever get the faintest whiff that you have bad-mouthed me to a living soul, our solicitors will slap a writ on you so fast it'll make your eyes water. If you want this case clearing up, and your good name restored, you'll give me till this time tomorrow to come up with the final piece of evidence that we need to hand this mess over to the police.'

Before he could answer, the barman appeared at his shoulder. 'Excuse me? Miss Brannigan?'

'That's me,' I said wearily.

'Phone call for you. You can take it at the bar.'

Thank you, Della. Without a word to Kerr, I got up and went to the phone. 'Time to go,' Della said.

'I'll be right with you.' I replaced the phone and returned to the table. 'I have to go now,' I said. 'Frankly, Mr Kerr, there are plenty more productive things for me to be doing than talking to you. I'll be in touch.'

Della was as good as her word. While I soaked in a bath laced with refreshing essential oils, a cold drink sweating on the side, she knocked together a chicken and spinach curry from the contents of the freezer. Wrapped in my cuddly towelling dressing gown, I curled up in a corner of one of the sofas and tucked in. I hadn't been able to face food on the flight, and as soon as the first forkful hit my mouth, I realized I was absolutely ravenous. As we ate, I gave Della the rundown on the case. 'And so I sent you the stuff from the safe,' I ended up.

Della nodded. 'I've been through it, as far as I could get with an Italian dictionary. What's your conclusion?'

'Drugs,' I said. 'They're swapping art for drugs. Those number and letter combinations – 20CC, 34H, 50,000E. I make that twenty kilos crack cocaine, thirty-four kilos heroin, fifty thousand tabs of Ecstasy. Once you've taken a painting out of its frame, it's a lot more portable than the cash equivalent, and a lot easier to smuggle. It's costing them next to nothing to acquire the stolen art, and it's got a sizeable black-market value, so they can swap it for a much greater value in drugs than they've initially laid out to have it stolen.'

Della nodded. 'I think you're right. Kate, you know I'm going to have to pass all this on to other teams, don't you? It's not my field.'

I sighed. 'I know. And somebody's going to have to liaise with the Italians so they can send someone to pick up Nicholas Turner's body. But I can't handle going through all this with some sceptical stranger tonight.'

'Of course you can't. And before you talk to any other coppers, you need to have Ruth with you. They're going to put a lot of pressure on you to come up with the original source that put you on to Turner in the first place. I've got a shrewd idea who that might be, but I don't see any need to pass my suspicions on.'

I smiled gratefully. She was right about Ruth. I'd broken the law too many times in the previous couple of days to be prepared to talk to the police without a solicitor. And my buddy Ruth Hunter is the best criminal solicitor in Manchester. 'Thanks, Della,' I said. 'Can you start the ball rolling tomorrow? I warn you now that I'm not going to be available for questioning till the day after. I've got something else to chase that I can't ignore.'

Della looked doubtful. 'I don't know if they'll want to wait that long.'

'They'll have to. Watch my lips. I'm not going to be available. I won't be in the office, I won't be here, I won't be answering my mobile.'

Della grinned. 'I hear you. I'll leave a message on the machine.' She gave me the copper's once-over look. 'You need to sleep, Kate. Speak to me tomorrow, OK?'

After Della had gone, I went next door. No sign of the coupé, which wasn't surprising if Richard had chosen to drive back. He might have made tonight's ferry out of Rotterdam, or he might have decided to take the long way home. I was still furious with him, but something inside me didn't want it to end here. I climbed into his bed, drinking in the smell of him from his pillows.

Call me sentimental. On the other hand, if you've just handed the police a stack of information pointing straight to a Mafia-style drug-running operation, sleeping in your own bed might not seem to be the safest option.

21

Some mornings you wake up ready to take on the world, feeling invincible, immortal and potentially omniscient. This wasn't one of them. I'd set Richard's *Star Trek* alarm clock for seven, which meant I'd had a straight eight hours' sleep before Captain James T. Kirk intoned, 'Landing party to *Enterprise*, beam us up, Scotty,' but I was in no mood to boldly go. I felt rested, but the hangover you get from guilt is infinitely worse than the one that comes from drink.

I dragged myself next door, called a cab and dived into the shower. I dressed in the last clean pair of jeans, a dark blue shirt and the new navy blazer, and managed half a cup of instant before the taxi pulled up outside. I picked up Shelley's Rover from Bill's garage, making a mental note to ring Hertz in Antwerp and ask them to hang on to Bill's car till I could get back over to pick it up. I was parked at the end of Alder Way by eight.

For once, I didn't have long to wait. At ten past,

Sandra Bates left the house with a tall, skinny bloke in overalls. She passed me without a glance in her little Vauxhall Corsa. Clearly her feminism didn't extend to boycotting products that indulge in blatantly sexist advertising. The man I took to be Simon Morley followed in a two-year-old Escort. I slipped into the traffic a couple of cars behind him.

When we reached Kingsway, he turned left, heading away from the city centre. I had no trouble staying in touch with him as we drove down the dual carriageway. We went out through Cheadle, past Heald Green, and on into Handforth. He turned left in the centre of the village, out past the station. We drove through a housing estate, then, just as we reached open country, he turned right. A couple of hundred yards down the road, there was a turning on the right, leading to a small industrial estate. I pulled up and watched as he parked outside a unit that wasn't much bigger than a double garage.

As he disappeared inside, I cruised into the estate and parked further down the road, outside a company that made garden sheds. Just after nine, a battered Transit van pulled up behind Morley's car. The two lads in overalls who got out looked as if they should still be in school. You know you're getting old when even the villains start looking young. I gave it another ten minutes, then I grabbed my clipboard and the bag containing the video camera, and headed for the unmarked warehouse.

I knocked on the door and marched straight in.

At one end of the room were a couple of tall vats with taps on the bottom of them. On a platform behind them, one of the lads was emptying the contents of a white plastic five-gallon drum into a vat. The other lad was halfway down the room, pushing a trolley that held gallon drums identical to the ones Kerrchem used for KerrSter. Simon Morley had his back to me, doing something at a bench on the far wall. Compared to the high-tech world of Kerrchem, this was a medieval alchemist's cell.

The lad pushing the trolley looked over at me, and called, 'Can I help you, love?'

At the sound of his voice, Simon Morley whirled round, consternation written all over his face. 'Who are you?' he demanded, crossing the room towards me.

'Is this Qualcraft?' I asked, casually swinging my bag through a gentle arc, hoping the video was getting the full flavour of the premises. 'Only, there's no name on the door, and I've got an order for Qualcraft, and I can't seem to find them.'

By now, Simon Morley was feet away from me. He looked like the classroom swot twenty years on, gangling limbs, acne scars and glasses that were constantly slipping down his sharp nose. 'You've come to the wrong place,' he said nervously. 'This isn't Qualcraft.'

If I hadn't stepped backwards, he'd have trodden on my trainers. 'Sorry,' I said. 'You don't know where Qualcraft is, do you?'

'No,' he said.

I smiled. 'Sorry to have bothered you.' I carried on backing out the door. Morley closed it firmly behind me, and I heard a key turn in the lock.

I pressed my ear to the door and heard him say, 'How many times have I told you to keep the door locked?' He said something more, but he was obviously moving back to his workbench, since I couldn't make out the words.

Back at the car, I checked the video on playback. The picture was slightly hazy, but the vats and the gallon drums were clearly discernible, along with a nice clear shot of Morley's face. I set the video camera up on the dashboard and waited. I rang Shelley and filled her in on what had happened to me in Italy and told her to call me as soon as she heard from Richard. 'Don't worry if you get diverted to the message service,' I added. 'I'm trying to avoid the cops, so I won't actually be answering the phone.' Wonderful thing, technology. If I don't want to take calls on my mobile, I can divert them to an answering machine. Then, when I want to pick the messages up, I simply dial a number and it plays them over to me.

By eleven, I'd had messages from Della, Mellor from the Art Squad, a superintendent from the Drugs Squad, Alexis and Michael Haroun. I didn't feel like talking to any of them, but I made myself ring Michael. I still had a client, after all, something I'd kind of lost sight of as I'd chased across Europe. And Henry needed insurance. If I could convince

Michael Haroun that the art thieves' racket was over for the time being, maybe he'd be a little more flexible about Henry's premium.

Michael was in a meeting, but I made an appointment with his secretary for three o'clock. I figured I'd be through here by then. Next, I took out my micro-cassette recorder and dictated a full report on the KerrSter scam. I'd drop it off with Shelley on my way to meet Michael so I could hand the client a copy this evening. I'd also be dropping off a copy with Inspector Jackson, just so Clever Trevor couldn't go taking the law into his own hands.

There was movement at the warehouse just after noon. I hit the record button on the video and taped Simon Morley and the two lads loading up the van with pallets of schneid KerrSter. Simon went back indoors with one of the lads, and the van took off. I followed at a discreet distance. I needn't have bothered. If I'd just driven straight to Filbert Brown's Manchester HQ, I'd have been able to film them arriving just as easily.

I was gobsmacked at their sheer cheek. Two people had died because of their crazy product tampering, yet they were still milking the racket for all it was worth. The more I thought about it, the more disturbing I found that. Simon Morley might well be crazy enough to carry on putting people's lives at risk in his vendetta against Kerrchem. But Sandra Bates hadn't struck me as a woman who would go along with random murder. I know people do ridiculous things for love, but I couldn't get the scenario into a credible shape at all.

But if Sandra Bates and Simon Morley weren't bumping people off, who was? It went beyond the bounds of credibility to imagine two lots of blackmailing saboteurs. I know coincidences do happen, but this wasn't one I could buy into. I closed my eyes and groaned. All this time and effort and I had a horrible feeling I wasn't any nearer the killer than I had been at the start.

Michael looked delighted to see me, greeting me with an unprofessional kiss on the lips. The tingle factor was still firing on all four cylinders, I noted as I moved away and sat demurely on the opposite side of the table from him. 'You've been keeping a very low profile,' he complained jocularly. 'I've been trying to reach you for days. Your secretary keeps telling me you're unavailable. I was beginning to think you'd gone off me.'

'She wasn't bullshitting,' I said. 'I genuinely have been unavailable. I've been out of the country. The good news is that you're not going to have any more trouble from this particular gang of art thieves.'

He leaned forward, his eyes surprised and interested. 'Really? They've been arrested?'

'Let's just say the market's collapsed,' I replied. 'Take it from me, the racket's over and done with. So you can safely reinsure Henry Naismith's property. They won't be back for a second bite of the cherry.'

Michael ran a hand through his dark hair and shook his head. 'This is incredible. What on earth have you been up to? It all sounds very unorthodox.'

'That's a word,' I said.

'You're going to have to tell me more than that,' Michael said, his face and voice equally determined. 'It's not that I don't believe you. But I have to explain myself to higher powers, and they're not going to be overly impressed if I tell them I've taken a particular course of action on the say-so of a private eye who isn't even our employee.'

I was growing bored with this story already, and I was still going to have to repeat it more times than the sole survivor of an air crash. 'Look, I can't go into great detail. I've still got a lot of talking to do to the police, and there are going to be arrests to come. The bare bones go like this. I got a tip-off from a good source as to who was fencing the goods. I tracked him back to an international criminal consortium who have been using art works as payment in kind for drugs. The fence is out of the game for good, and the police will be closing in on the rest of the syndicate. Without a guaranteed market, the thieves won't be doing any more robberies. I promise you, Michael, it's all over.'

He looked up from the pad where he'd been taking notes. 'You're sure? You don't think the fence is going to start up again once everything quietens down?'

I closed my eyes briefly. 'Not unless you believe in communications from beyond the grave,' I said.

Michael's mouth opened as he stared at me with new eyes. 'He's dead?' His voice was incredulous.

'Very.'

'You didn't . . . ? It wasn't . . . ?' A flicker of fear showed in his eyes.

I snorted with ironic laughter. 'Please,' I said. 'I didn't kill him, Michael, I only set him up. And my payoff was getting to discover the body.'

He looked faintly queasy. I can't say I blamed him. 'Is there any chance of recovering any of the stolen paintings?' he asked.

I shrugged. 'I shouldn't think so. I'm afraid you're going to have to bite the bullet and cough up. But like I said, you won't be having any repeat business from this team.'

'What can I say?' He spread his hands. 'I'm impressed. Look, I can't make any promises at this stage, but I'd be interested in working with you in future. On a more official basis.'

'Fine by me. Anything you need sorting, give us a call and we'll talk.' Normally, I'd have been punching the air in jubilation at landing a client as major as Fortissimus. Today, all I could muster was a moment's satisfaction. Fortissimus had been too expensive an acquisition.

I got to my feet. 'And on a personal note,' Michael added, his eyes crinkling in a smile, 'when can I see you again?'

'Tomorrow night?' I suggested. 'Meet me in the

bar at the Cornerhouse at half past seven?'

'Fine. See you then.'

I sketched a wave and moved towards the door. He bounded to his feet and caught up with me on the threshold. He tried to put his arms round me in a hug, but I backed off. 'Not in business hours,' I said defensively. 'If we're going to work together, we need some ground rules. Rule one, no messing about on the company's time.'

His mouth turned down ruefully. 'Sorry. You're absolutely right. See you tomorrow. Stay lucky.'

I stopped off at the Cigar Store café for a bite to eat and a cappuccino, then went back to the office to pick up the Kerrchem reports from Shelley. 'Nice work,' she remarked as she handed me two neatly bound copies.

'Yeah,' I said, my lack of conviction obvious.

'So what's the problem?'

I told her my reservations about Sandra Bates and her boyfriend. At the end of my tale, Shelley nodded sympathetically. 'I see what you mean,' she said. 'Are you going to front them up and see what they've got to say for themselves?'

'I hadn't planned on it,' I said. 'I was just going to hand over the reports to Trevor Kerr and the cops and let them get on with it. I can't pretend murder isn't police business, can I?'

'No, but if they're not the killers, maybe you should go and talk to them. They might have some useful ideas as to who actually is doing the killing.'

She was right, of course. Before I blew their lives out of the water, I should at least talk to Sandra Bates and Simon Morley. 'What if they leg it?' I protested weakly.

'If you drop off the reports with Kerr and Jackson and go straight round there, they won't have time to leg it, will they? This isn't a lead that Jackson's going to sit on till morning, is it?'

Half an hour later, I was walking up the path of 37 Alder Way. I'd sent Kerr's copy of the report round by motorbike courier, and I'd left Jackson's copy with his sergeant. I estimated I probably had a maximum of half an hour before the police came knocking.

Sandra Bates opened the door. Her first reaction was bemused bewilderment, then, clearly remembering what I'd been asking about, she tried to close the door. I stepped forward, shoving my shoulder between the door and jamb. 'What's going on?' she demanded.

'Too slow, Sandra,' I said. 'An innocent woman would have spoken sooner. We need to talk.'

'You're not a student,' she accused me, eyes narrowing.

'Correct.' I handed her one of my business cards. 'I'm Kate Brannigan. I'm working for Kerrchem, and we need to talk.'

'I've got nothing to say to you,' she said desperately, her voice rising.

From inside the house, Simon Morley's voice

joined in. 'What's going on, Sandra?'

'Go *away*,' she said to me, shoving the door harder.

'Sandra, would you rather talk to me about industrial sabotage or to the police about murder?' I replied, leaning back against the door. 'You've got ten seconds to decide. I know all about the scam. There's no hiding place.'

Simon's tall figure loomed behind Sandra in the hall. 'What's . . . ? Wait a minute, you were at the factory this morning.' He looked down at Sandra. 'What the hell's going on?'

'She's a private detective,' Sandra spat out.

'Simon, we need to talk,' I said, struggling to maintain a responsible façade with my shoulder jammed painfully between two bits of wood. 'I know about the fake KerrSter, I've got videos of your factory and your delivery run this morning, I know exactly how Sandra's working the fiddle at her end. You're already in the frame for product tampering and attempted blackmail. Do you really want two counts of murder adding to the list?'

'Let her in,' Simon said dully. Sandra looked up pleadingly at him, but he simply nodded. 'Do it, love,' he said.

I followed them into a living room that came straight from Laura Ashley without any intervening application of taste. I chose an armchair upholstered in a mimsy floral chintz, and they sat down together on a matching sofa. Sandra's hand crept out and clutched Simon's. 'There's no way you can wriggle out of the scam,' I said brutally. 'But I don't think murder was on the agenda.'

'I haven't killed anybody,' Simon said defiantly, pushing his glasses up his nose.

'It doesn't look that way,' I said.

'Look, I admit I wanted to get my own back on Kerrchem,' he said.

'The golden handcuffs?' I asked.

He nodded. 'That was bad enough, but then I found out they were refusing to give me a proper reference.'

I frowned. Nobody at Kerrchem had indicated that anyone had left under a cloud. 'Why?' I said.

'It was my department head, Keith Murray. He screwed up on a research project I was working on with him and it ended up costing the company about twenty grand in wasted time and materials. It was just before the redundancies were going to be announced and everybody was twitchy about their jobs, and he blamed me for the cockup. Now, because of that, personnel say I can't have a good reference. So I've ended up totally shafted. Never mind waiting six months, I'll be waiting six years before anybody gives me a responsible research job again. Kerrchem owes me.' The words spilled out angrily, tumbling out in the rush of a normally reticent man who's had enough.

'So you decided to take it out in blackmail?'

'Why not?' he asked defiantly.

'Apart from the fact that it's illegal, no reason

at all,' I said tartly. 'What about the two people who died?'

'That's got nothing to do with us,' Sandra butted in. 'You've got to believe us!' She looked as if she was about to burst into tears.

'She's right,' Simon said, patting Sandra's knee with his free hand. 'The papers said they'd died from cyanide poisoning – that's right, isn't it?' I nodded. 'Well, then,' he said. 'All the stuff I've been using is over-the-counter chemicals, mostly ones Sandra's picked up through work. I've got no access to cyanide. I've got none in the warehouse or here. You can search all you like, but you can't tie us in to any cyanide. Look, all we wanted was to get some money out of Trevor Kerr. Why would we kill people if that was what we were trying to do? It'd be daft. You pay off somebody who's wrecking your commercial operation, you do it quiet so the opposition don't get to hear about it. You don't go to the police. You don't pay off murderers. You can't hide murder.'

'What about the note? The one that came after the first death? That implied there would be more if Kerrchem didn't pay up,' I said.

This time, Sandra did start crying. 'I said we shouldn't have sent that one,' she sobbed, pulling her hand away from Simon and punching ineffectually at his chest.

Gently, Simon gripped her wrists, then pulled her into a tight hug. 'You were right, I'm sorry,' he told her. Then he turned back to me. 'I thought if we pretended to be more ruthless than we were, Kerr might cough up. It was stupid, I see that now. But he got me so mad when he just ignored the first note and nobody seemed to notice what we were doing. I had to make him pay attention.'

'So if you're not doing the killings, who is?' I demanded, finally getting round to the reason why I'd put myself through another harrowing encounter.

I was too late. Before Simon could answer, the doorbell rang, followed by a tattoo of knocking. 'Police, open up,' I heard someone shout from the other side of the door. I thought about making a run for it through the back door, but the way my luck had been running lately, I'd probably have been savaged by a police dog.

The pair on the sofa had the wide-eyed look of rabbits transfixed by car headlights. By the time they got it together to let the cops in, their front door was going to be matchwood. With a sigh, I got to my feet and prepared for another jolly chat with Detective Inspector Cliff Jackson.

22

My encounter with Jackson reminded me of the old radical slogan: help the police, beat yourself up. After listening to the usual rant about obstructing the police, withholding evidence and interfering with witnesses, I needed a drink. I was only a couple of miles away from the Cob and Pen, the pub where Joey Morton had breathed his last, which clinched the decision.

If they'd gone into mourning over the death of mine host, it hadn't been a prolonged period of grief. It was pub quiz night, and the place was packed. In the gaps between the packed bodies, I got the impression of a bar that had been done out in the brewery version of traditional country house: dark, William Morris-style wallpaper, hunting prints, and bookshelves containing all those 1930s best sellers that no one has read since 1941, not even in hospital out-patients' queues. No chance of anyone nicking them, that was for sure.

I bought myself a vodka and grapefruit juice

and retreated into the furthest corner from the epicentre of the quiz. I squeezed on the end of a banquette, ignored by the other four people surrounding the nearby table. They were much too involved in arguing about the identity of the first Welsh footballer to play in the Italian league. There was no chance of engaging any of the bar staff in a bit of gossip, not even lubricated with the odd tenner. They were too busy pulling pints and popping the caps off bottles of Bud. I sipped my drink and waited for an interval in the incessant trivia questions. Eventually, they announced a fifteen-minute break.

The foursome round my table sat back in their seats. 'John Charles,' I said. They looked blankly at me. 'The first Welshman to play in Italy. John Charles.' Amazing the junk that invades your brain cells when you live with a football fan.

'Really?' the lad with the pen and the answer sheet said.

'Truly.'

The one who'd been rooting for Charles against the other three grinned and clapped me on the back. 'Told you so,' he said. 'Can I get you a drink?'

I shook my head. 'I've got to get off. But thanks all the same. I'm surprised you didn't all know the answer. I'd have thought anybody who was a regular in Joey Morton's pub would have been shit hot on all the football questions.'

They all looked momentarily embarrassed, as if they'd caught me swearing in front of their mothers. 'Did you know Joey, then?' the penpusher said.

'We met a couple of times. My fella's a journalist. Bad business.'

'You're not kidding,' another said with feeling. 'Now, if you'd said it was Mrs M. that took a breadknife to him, I wouldn't have been half as surprised. But dying like that, a casual bystander in somebody else's war, that's seriously bad news.'

'You thought his wife had done it?' I asked, trying to keep my voice light and jokey.

They all snorted with laughter. 'Gail? Get real,' Penpusher said scornfully. 'Like Tez said, if it had been a breadknife job, nobody would have been gobsmacked. Them two fighting behind the bar's the nearest thing you used to get to cabaret in here. But rigging up a drum of cleaning stuff with cyanide? Nah, Gail's too thick.'

'When Gail writes the daily specials up on the board, there's more spelling mistakes than there are hot dinners,' another added. 'She probably thinks cyanide's a perfume by Elizabeth Taylor.'

'Must have been a hell of a shock, then. I guess it hit her hard,' I said.

The one I'd backed up gestured over his shoulder with his thumb towards the bar. 'Looks like it, doesn't it?'

I looked across. 'Which one's Gail? I never met her, just Joey.'

'The bottle blonde with the cleavage,' Penpusher said.

I didn't have to ask for more details. Gail Morton's tumbled blonde mane looked as natural as candy-floss, and the bra under her tight, V-necked T-shirt didn't so much lift and separate as point and aim. As I looked she served a customer, giving a laugh that revealed perfect teeth and healthy tonsils. 'A bit of a merry widow,' I remarked.

'Widow's weeds up until the funeral, then back to normal.'

I began to wonder if my eager inquiries down the line of industrial sabotage had shunted Jackson off the right track. After all, it's one of the great truisms that when wives or husbands die of unnatural causes, the prime suspect is the spouse. I was going to have to eat more than my usual portion of humble pie with Jackson if Gail Morton turned out to be Joey's killer. But that didn't explain why Mary Halloran had died. Time to go and pick some more brains.

I made my excuses and left. I headed east out of Stockport, and soon I was on the edge of the Pennine moors. About a mile before I hit Charlesworth village, I turned right on to a narrow road whose blacktop had been laid so recently it still gleamed in my headlights. The road climbed round the side of a hill and emerged in what had originally been a quarry. In the huge horseshoe carved out of the side of the hill stood ten beautiful stone houses, each individually designed by Chris.

For as long as I'd known them, Chris and Alexis had cherished the dream of building their own home, designed by Chris to their own specifications. They'd joined a self-build scheme a few years back, and, after a few hiccups, the dream had finally become a reality. Chris had swapped her architectural skills for things like plumbing, bricklaying, carpentry and wiring, while Alexis had served as everybody's unskilled labourer. The site was perfect for people who get off on a spectacular view, looking out through a gap in the Pennines to the Cheshire plain. There isn't a pub within three miles, the nearest decent restaurant is ten miles away, and if you run out of milk at half past nine at night, you're drinking black coffee. Me, I'd rather live in a luggage locker at Piccadilly Station.

The house wasn't quite ready to be inhabited yet. A small matter of connection to the main gas, electricity, telephone and sewage systems. So for the time being Alexis and Chris were living in an ugly little caravan parked in their drive. It must have been a bit like going out for dinner to the best restaurant in town with your jaw wired up.

The light was on in their van, so I knocked. Chris opened the door in her dressing gown, blonde hair in a damp, tousled halo round her head. Seeing me, a broad grin split her face. 'Kate!' she exclaimed, then made a point of leaning out and scanning the area beyond me. 'And you made it without a team of native bearers and Sherpa guides.'

'Sarcasm doesn't become you,' I muttered as I followed her into the claustrophobe's nightmare. The caravan was a four-berth job which might

conceivably have contained a family for a fortnight's holiday. Right now, it was bursting at the
seams with the worldly goods that Chris and Alexis
simply couldn't do without. Once they'd packed in
their work clothes, their casual clothes, a couple
of shelves of books, a portable CD player with the
accompanying music library, two wine racks, a
drawing board for Chris and the files Alexis deemed
too sensitive to trust to her office drawers, there
wasn't a lot of room left for bodies.

Alexis was sprawled on the double bed watching
the TV news in a pair of plaster- and paint-stained
jogging pants and a ripped T-shirt, her unruly hair
tied back in a ponytail with an elastic band. She
greeted me with a languid wave and said, 'Kettle's
just boiled. Help yourself.'

I made a cup of instant and joined the two of
them on the bed. It wasn't that we were planning
an orgy; there just wasn't anywhere else to sit. 'So
what brings you up here in the hours of darkness,
girl?' Alexis asked, leaning across me to switch off
the TV. 'You finally decided to tell me why you've
been doing a Cook's tour of the EC?'

'I bring greetings from civilization,' I told her.
'Cliff Jackson's just arrested two suspects in the
Kerrchem product-tampering scam.'

I had all her attention now. Alexis pushed herself
into an upright position. 'Really? He charging them
with the murders?'

'I don't know. If he does, he'll be making a
mistake,' I said.

'So, spill,' Alexis urged.

I gave her the bare bones of the tale, knowing she wouldn't be able to say much in the following day's paper because of the reporting restrictions that swing into place as soon as suspects are charged with an offence. But the details would be filed away in Alexis's prodigious memory, to be dragged out as deep background when the case finally came to court. And she wouldn't forget where the information came from.

'And you believe them when they say they had nothing to do with the two deaths?' Chris chipped in.

'Actually, I do,' I said. 'Breaks my heart to say so, but I don't think the job's finished yet, whatever Cliff Jackson decides to charge them with.'

Alexis lit a cigarette. Chris pointedly cracked the window open an inch and moved out of the draught. 'I know, I know,' Alexis sighed. 'But how can I possibly be a labourer without a fag hanging out of my mouth and a rolled up copy of the *Sun* stuffed in my back pocket? Anyway, KB, I suppose this means that you're here for access to the Alexis Lee reference library?'

'You can see why she's an investigative reporter, can't you?' I said nonchalantly to Chris.

'So what do you want to know?' Alexis asked.

'Tell me about Joey Morton,' I said. First rule of murder investigation, according to all the detective novels I've read: find out about the victim. Embarrassing that it had taken me so long to get there.

'Born and raised in Belfast. Came over here with a fanfare of trumpets that said he was going to be the next George Best. Unfortunately, the only thing Georgie and Joey had in common was their talent for pissing it all up against the wall. United took him on as an apprentice, but they didn't keep him on, and he never made it past the Third Division. Gail believed the publicity when she married him. She was expecting the days of wine and roses, and she never forgave him for not making the big time. So she gave him the days of bitter and thorns. They fought like cat and dog. When we were living in the Heatons, we used to pop into the Cob and Pen occasionally for a drink and the spectator sport of watching Joey and Gail tear lumps out of each other.'

'So why didn't she leave him?' I asked.

Alexis shrugged. 'Some people get addicted to rowing,' Chris said. 'You watch them at it and imagine how stressed it would make you to live like that, but then you realize they actually thrive on it. If they ever found themselves in agreement, the relationship would die on the spot.'

'Also, where would she go? It's not a bad life, being the *grande dame* of a busy pub like the Cob,' Alexis added. 'Besides, Joey was a staunch Catholic. He'd never have stood on for a divorce.'

'Now she's got it all,' I said. 'She's got her freedom, and presumably the brewery aren't going to chuck her out of the pub as long as it keeps making money.'

'And the insurance,' Alexis said. 'Word is, Joey was worth a lot more dead than he ever was in the transfer market.'

'All of which adds up to a tidy bit of motive for Mrs Morton,' I said. 'But if she's behind Joey's murder, how does Mary Halloran's death fit in?'

'Copycat?' Alexis suggested.

'Maybe, but cyanide isn't exactly a common household chemical. I wouldn't know how to get my hands on it. Would you?'

Alexis shrugged. 'I've never wanted to kill her enough,' she joked, grabbing Chris and hugging her. A sudden pang of envy took me by surprise. All too painfully, I could remember when Richard and I were as easy and warm together. It felt like a long time had passed since then. I wanted that back. I just didn't know any more if I could recover it with Richard or if I was going to have to start all over again on the wary process of love.

I must have shown something on my face, for Chris looked at me with a worried frown. 'You all right, Kate?' she asked.

'Not really,' I said. 'Me and Richard have had a major falling out. We parted company in Italy a couple of days ago, and I've not heard from him since. I'm just not sure if we can fix it this time.'

I could hardly bear the love and concern on their faces. Chris pulled free from Alexis and leaned over to hug me. 'He'll be back,' she said with more confidence than I felt.

'Yeah, but will he be back with a bricklayer to build a wall across the conservatory?' I asked bitterly.

'If Richard needed a brickie, he'd have to ask you where to find one,' Alexis said. 'You don't get rid of him that easy, girl.'

'He's obviously not very happy,' I told them. 'He said he's pissed off with everybody treating him like he's a pillock.'

'Maybe he should stop behaving like one, then,' Alexis said. 'Ever since he got himself arrested, he's been walking around like a dog waiting for the next kick. Wait till he comes back, girl, I'll take him out for a drink and put him right.'

I couldn't help smiling. That was one encounter I'd pay for a video of. 'Anyway, I don't want to talk about my troubles,' I said briskly. 'I've got too much to do trying to put right all the cockups I've made this week to worry about Richard. Did he have any dodgy contacts, this Joey Morton?'

'Not that I've heard. He hung out with one or two moody people, but that was probably for the so-called glamour as much as anything. He was probably into a few bits and pieces on the side, but he wasn't a player.'

So I wasn't looking for some gangster that Joey had double-crossed on a deal over stolen Scotch. 'What's the score with this Mary Halloran?' I asked.

'I haven't been over there myself, but I've still gorra few good contacts in Liverpool,' she said, becoming more Scouse by the syllable. 'This Mary

Halloran, she was a real grafter. The only out-of-the-way thing about her was that her staff actually liked her. They said she was a great boss, good payer, dead fair. According to them, she lived for her kids and her old man, Desmond. Our Desmond is apparently devastated. My mate Mo went round to try for a talk for the *Post*, but the guy was too distraught. She said he just burst into tears, then one of the relatives did the Rottweiler and saw her off.'

'This Desmond. Has he got a job?'

'He's got his own business too. Not as successful as Mary's by all accounts, but he does OK. He's a photographer. Does portraits mainly. Dead artistic, according to Mo. Specializes in unusual printing techniques and special effects stuff. Not your weddings and babies type. Charges about five hundred a shot, apparently. God knows where he gets clients. The only pictures I've ever seen of people in Liverpool with that kind of money are in police mugshots and wanted posters.'

'And no connection between the Hallorans and the Mortons?'

'Nothing that's come up so far. The only thing they've got in common, except for the way they died, is that they've left their surviving partners a lot better off than they were before. Mo says the girls that worked for Mary Halloran reckoned she was well insured. Had to be. If anything happened to her, the business was bound to suffer a bit, because Mary was one of those who had to take charge of everything herself.'

'Maybe they did a *Strangers on a Train*,' Chris volunteered. 'You know, I'll do your murder, you do mine.' We both looked at her, gobsmacked. 'It was only a suggestion,' she said defensively.

'The only point in doing something like that is when the murder method's one where having an alibi puts you in the clear. Like a shooting or a stabbing,' Alexis finally said. 'A delayed-action thing like this, there wouldn't be any point.'

'Nice idea, though,' I mused. Suddenly, a huge yawn crept up on me and shook me by the scruff of my neck. 'Oh God,' I groaned. 'I'm going to have to go, girls. If my overdraft was as big as my sleep deficit, the bailiffs would be kicking my door down.'

I leaned over and hugged the pair of them. 'You never know,' Chris said. 'He might be there when you get home.'

It's just as well Chris is such a good architect. She'd never make a living as a fortune teller.

23

The answering machine was flashing like a sex offender. I played back the long chain of messages against my better judgement. I'd had enough coppers on the line to staff my very own Tactical Aid Group minibus. But the one message I really wanted wasn't there. I hated myself for letting Richard's childish behaviour get to me, but that didn't make it any easier to escape. I ignored the rest of the messages and crashed out in my own bed. Deep down, I knew the Mafia weren't after me. Sleeping in Richard's bed the night before had been nothing but a self-indulgence I wasn't about to allow myself again.

I woke up just after eight, my head muzzy with the novel experience of a proper night's sleep. The phone was ringing already, but I had no problem ignoring it. I took a long, leisurely bath, deciding on my plans for the day. I'd told Della I'd be prepared to talk to the Art Squad and the Drugs Squad, but I had other ideas now. A few hours' delay wasn't going to make a whole lot of difference to their investigation, and I was determined to press on with my inquiries into the KerrSter murders as fast as I could. The last thing I wanted was another head to head with Cliff Jackson, and the best way to avoid that was to move as fast as I could while he was still working out what to do with Sandra Bates and Simon Morley.

After breakfast, I filled the washing machine with the first load of dirty clothes. Glancing out of the kitchen window, I noticed an unfamiliar car parked in one of the residents' bays. I didn't have to be Manchester's answer to Nancy Drew to work out that an unmarked saloon with a radio aerial and two men in it was a police car. The only thing left to wonder was which squad it belonged to. I wasn't about to pop over and ask a policeman.

I pulled the blonde wig out of its bag and arranged it on my head, adding the granny glasses with the clear lenses and a pair of stilettos to give me a bit of extra height. Then I nipped through the conservatory into Richard's house and out his front door. The two bobbies gave me a cursory glance, but they were waiting for a petite redhead from next door. That told me Della wasn't responsible, even indirectly, for their presence; she'd have told them about the conservatory. Which left Jackson.

Of course, the car was in the clear, since I was still driving Shelley's Rover. She'd tried the previous afternoon to persuade me to swap it for Richard's Beetle, but I played the card of professional necessity and managed to hang on to hers for the time being. I headed out of town towards Stockport and got to the Cob and Pen while the cleaners were still doing their thing. The bar stank of stale tobacco and sour beer, somehow more noticeable when the place was empty. 'I'm looking for Mrs Morton,' I told one of them.

'You from the papers?' she asked.

I shook my head. 'I'm representing Kerrchem, the company who manufacture the cleanser Mr Morton was using when he died.' Nothing like a bit of economy with the truth. Let them think I was here to talk about the compensation if they wanted.

The woman pursed her lips. 'You'd better go on up, then. It's going to cost your lot plenty, killing Joey like that.' She gestured towards a door marked 'Private'.

I smiled my thanks and opened the door on to a flight of stairs. The door at the top had a Yale, but when I tapped gently and turned the handle, it opened. 'Hello?' I called.

From a doorway on my left, I could hear a voice say, 'Hang on,' then the clatter of a phone being put down on a table. Gail Morton stuck her head through the doorway and said sharply, 'Who are you? What are you doing up here?'

'The cleaners sent me up,' I said. 'My name's Kate Brannigan. I'm a private investigator working for Kerrchem.'

She frowned and cast a worried glance back through the doorway. 'You'd better come through, then.' She moved back smartly into the room ahead of me and swiftly picked up the phone, swivelling so she could keep an eye on me. 'I'll call you back,' she said firmly. 'There's some private detective here from the chemical company. I'll ring you after she's gone . . . No, of course not,' she added sharply. Then, 'OK then, after one.' She replaced the phone and turned to face me, leaning against the table as if she were protecting the phone from hostile attack.

All my instincts told me that phone call was more than some routine condolence. Something was going on. Maybe it was nothing to do with anything, but my instincts have served me too well in the past to ignore them. I wanted to know just who she'd been talking to who needed to know a private eye was on the premises. 'Sorry to interrupt,' I said. 'Hope it wasn't an important call.'

'You'd better sit down,' she said, ignoring the invitation I'd dangled in front of her.

The room was as much of a cliché as Gail Morton herself. Dralon three-piece suite, green onyx and gilt coffee table and side tables, complete with matching ashtrays, cigarette box and table lighter. Naff lithographs in pastel shades of women who looked like they'd escaped from the pages of those true-romance graphic novels. The room was dominated by a wide-screen TV, complete with satellite decoder. I chose the chair furthest away from Gail.

She moved away from the telephone table and sat down opposite me. She leaned forward to take a cigarette from the box on the table, her deep-cut blouse opening to reveal the tanned swell of her breasts. Philip Marlowe would have been entranced. Me, I felt faintly repelled. 'So what have you come here for?' she asked. 'Have they sent you to make me an offer?'

'I'm afraid not,' I said. 'Kerrchem hired me to try to find out who tampered with their product.'

She gave a short bark of laughter. 'Trying to crawl out from under, are they? Well, they're not going to succeed. My lawyer says by the time we're finished with your bosses, they'll be lucky to have a pot to piss in.'

'I leave that sort of thing to the lawyers,' I said mildly. 'They're the only ones who can guarantee walking away rich after tragedies like this.' I thought I'd better remind her of her role as grieving widow.

'You're not kidding,' she said, dragging deep on her cigarette. In the unkind daylight coming through the window, I could see the incipient lines round her mouth as she kissed the filter tip. It wouldn't be long before her face matched her personality. 'So what do you want to know?'

'I've got one or two questions you might be able to help me with. First off, can you remember who actually bought the KerrSter?'

'It could have been me or Joey,' she said. 'We used to do the cash-and-carry run turn and turn about. KerrSter was one of the things that was always on the list, and we usually had a spare drum in the cupboard.'

'Who made the last trip?'

'That was Joey,' she said positively. Given when the affected batch had gone out, that meant Joey had purchased the fatal drum.

'Where are your cleaning materials kept?' I asked.

'In a cupboard in the pub kitchen.'

'Is it locked?'

She looked at me scornfully. 'Of course it's not. There's always spills and stuff in a pub. The staff need to be able to clean them up as and when they happen, not leave them for the cleaners.'

'So anybody who works in the pub would have access?'

'That's right,' she said confidently. 'That's what I told the police.'

'What about private visitors, friends or business associates? Would they be able to get to the cupboard?'

'Why would they want to? Do your friends come round your office and start nosing about in the cleaner's cupboard?' she asked aggressively.

'But in theory they could?'

'It'd be a bit obvious. When people come to visit, they don't usually swan around the pub kitchen on their own. You must know some really funny people. Besides, how would they know Joey was going to open that particular container?'

Before I could ask my next question, a voice from the stairwell shouted, 'Gail? There's a delivery down here you need to sign for.'

Gail sighed and crushed out her cigarette. 'I'll be back in a minute.'

As soon as she left the room, I was on my feet. I wouldn't be getting a second chance to check out what had set my antennae twitching. I took my tape recorder out of my bag and pressed the record button, then I picked up the phone and put the machine's in-built mike next to the earpiece. Then I hit last number redial. The phone clicked swiftly through the numbers, then connected. A phone rang out. I let it ring a dozen times, then broke the connection and gently replaced the phone.

I heard steps on the stairs and threw myself back into my chair. When Gail entered the room, I was sitting demurely flicking through the pages of the *TV Times*. 'Sorted?' I asked politely.

'I hate paperwork,' she said. 'But then, so did Joey, so we've got a little woman that comes in every week to keep the books straight.'

'Did your husband have any enemies?' I asked. Eat your heart out, Miss Marple.

'There were plenty of people Joey would happily have seen dead, most of them football managers. But people tended to like him. That was his big trouble. He was desperate to be liked. He'd never stand up for himself and make the bosses treat him properly. He just rolled over,' she said, years of bitterness spilling into her voice. 'I told him, you've got to show them who's in charge, but would he listen? Would he hell as like. Same with the brewery. I'd been on at him for ages to talk to them about our contract, but he just fobbed me off. Well, they'll know a difference now it's me they've got to deal with,' she added vigorously. Knowing the corporate claws of brewery chains, I thought Gail Morton was in for a nasty surprise.

'So, no enemies, no one who wanted him dead?'

'You're barking up the wrong tree,' she told me. 'You should be looking for somebody at that factory who has it in for their bosses. Joey just got unlucky.'

'You benefit from his death,' I commented.

Her eyes narrowed. 'It's time you were on your way,' she said. 'I'm not sitting here listening to that crap in my own living room. Go on, get out of it.'

I can take a hint.

When I walked into the office, Shelley had a look on her face I'd never seen before. After a couple of minutes of awkward conversation, I worked out what it was. The shifty eyes, the nervous mouth. She was feeling guilty about something. 'OK,' I said heavily, perching on the corner of her desk. 'Give. What's eating you? Is it having to lie to the police about where I am?'

'I don't know what you mean,' she said sniffily. 'Anyway, I'm black. Isn't lying to the cops supposed to be congenital?'

'Something's bothering you, Shell.'

'Nothing is bothering me. By the way, if you want your coupé back, it's on a meter round the corner. I wouldn't mind having my Rover back.' She couldn't meet my eyes.

'Has he been here?' Try as I might, I couldn't keep my voice cool.

'No. He came round the house about eight o'clock this morning. I asked him to talk to you, but you're too good a teacher. That man of yours has really learned how to ignore. I was going to phone you, but he was gone by then, so it wouldn't have been a whole lot of use.'

'Did he say where he was going?' There was a pain in my stomach which was nothing to do with what I'd had for breakfast.

'I asked him, but he said he wasn't sure what he was doing. He told me to tell you not to waste your time looking for him.'

I looked away, blinking back tears. 'Fine,' I said unsteadily. 'Though why he should think I can spare the time to chase him . . .'

Shelley reached out and gripped my hand. 'He's hurting in his pride, Kate. It's going to take him a bit of time, that's all.'

I cleared my throat. 'Sure. I should give a shit.' I walked through to my office. 'If anybody wants me, I'm not here, OK?'

I closed the door and sat down with the tape recorder. I'd recorded the number dialling on high speed, and now I played it back on the lower speed setting so I could more easily count the clicks. Given the way my luck had been running lately, the call I'd interrupted had probably been made *to* Gail, and all I was going to end up with was the number of her dentist.

I wrote the numbers down on a sheet of paper. Unless Gail made a round trip of eighty miles every time she wanted her teeth fixed, it looked like I'd struck gold. The number I'd recorded from her telephone was a Liverpool number. On an impulse, I marched through to Bill's office, where the phone books live, and picked out a three-year-old Liverpool directory. I looked up Halloran. There it was. Desmond J. Halloran, an address in Childwall. The number didn't match.

'It ain't over till it's over,' I said grimly, picking up the phone and calling Talking Pages. I asked for portrait photographers in Liverpool. The second number she gave me matched the number on the sheet of paper. DJH Portraits. I didn't think Ladbrokes would be offering me odds on those initials not standing for Desmond J. Halloran.

I shut myself back in my office and rang Paul Kingsley, a commercial photographer who occasionally does jobs for us when Bill and I are overstretched or we need pictures taking in conditions that neither of us feels competent to handle. Paul's always delighted to hear from us. I suspect he read too many Batman comics when he was a lad. I got him on his mobile. 'I need your help,' I told him.

'Great,' he said enthusiastically. 'What's the job?'

'I want to check out a photographer in Liverpool. I need to know how his business is doing. Is he making money? Is he on the skids? That kind of thing. Do you know anybody who could colour in the picture?'

'That's all you want?' He sounded disappointed. It was worrying. This is man whose assignments for us have included spending a Saturday night in an industrial rubbish bin, and standing for three days in the rain in the middle of a shrubbery. In his shoes, I'd have been delirious with joy at the news that his latest task for Mortensen and Brannigan involved nothing more hazardous to the health than picking up a phone.

'That's all I want,' I confirmed. 'Only I want it yesterday. DJH Portraits, that's the firm.'

'Consider it done,' he said.

My next call was to Alexis. 'All right?' she greeted me. 'Has dickhead turned up?' I told her about Shelley's encounter with Richard. 'That doesn't sound like goodbye to me,' she said. 'You want my advice, give your insurance man a bell. Show Richard you're not sitting around waiting for him to decide it's time to come home.'

'Strangely enough, I'm seeing him for dinner,' I told her.

'Nice one. Don't do anything I wouldn't do.'

'That doesn't give me a lot of scope on a date with a fella, does it?'

'Exactly. Now, what was it you wanted?'

'You still got your contact in Telecom accounts?' I asked her.

'You bet. Like the song says, once you have found her, never let her go. What are you after?'

'I want the itemized bills for the last six months on three numbers,' I said. 'One Manchester, two Liverpool. How much is that going to rush me?'

'It's usually fifty quid a throw. I'll ask her if she'll give you the three for a hundred and twenty.

You want to give me the numbers, I'll pass them on?'

I read the three numbers over to her. 'Soon as poss,' I said.

'If I catch her now, she'll fax them to you when she gets home tonight. That do you?'

'It'll have to.'

'Is this something I should know about, KB? I mean, I'm the woman you were pumping last night about mysterious deaths in Manchester and Liverpool.'

I chuckled. 'If I said it was a completely unrelated matter, would you believe me?'

'Girl, if the Pope himself told me it was a completely unrelated matter, I wouldn't believe him. You've got no chance. You want to share this with me?'

'Do your own investigations,' I told her.

'I'll catch up with you later. Have fun with the insurance man. I'll expect a full report tomorrow.'

'Only paying clients get full reports,' I laughed. I replaced the receiver and swung my feet up on to the desk. A vague shape was forming in my mind, but there were still too many questions that needed answering. Not least of them was the one Gail Morton herself had raised. If someone had been targeting Joey Morton specifically, how could they be sure he would be the person to open the fatal container?

I was still worrying at that point when Paul called back. 'DJH Portraits,' he said. 'Desmond Halloran. One-man band. He used to work with another guy, doing the usual weddings, babies and pets. But he fancied himself as a bit of an artist, so he set up on his own, doing specialist portrait work. I'm told his stuff is really good, but the problem is that using the kind of processes he does is very labour intensive, as well as costing a fair bit on the chemicals. He was keeping his head above water to begin with, but the way the recession's been biting, nobody's got the cash to spare for fancy photographs that come in at five hundred quid a throw. My contact says he reckons he must be running at a loss these days. That what you wanted to hear?'

'Smack on the button,' I said.

'This wouldn't have something to do with the fact that his wife has just popped her clogs, would it?' he asked eagerly, ever the boy detective.

'Now, Paul, you know I never divulge confidential client information.'

'I know. Only, my mate, he says Desmond only kept afloat because his wife's business was a raging success and she subsidized him. He was wondering how Desmond's going to go on now.'

Another piece of the jigsaw fell into place. 'Thank you, Paul,' I said. 'Send me an invoice.' It was a long shot, but if Desmond Halloran was having an affair with Gail Morton and they wanted to ditch their partners and run off together, they'd need something to live on. Quite a big something, if my impressions of Gail were accurate. But if Desmond divorced Mary, she'd doubtless hang on to the kids and to her business, leaving Desmond potless. And

I suspected that Desmond potless was a lot less attractive to Gail than Desmond loaded.

Before I could do anything more, the door to my office opened and Della walked in. She looked at me, eyes reproachful, and gently shook her head. 'Running out on Cliff Jackson I could understand,' she said. 'But running out on a promise you made to me? Kate, you checked your brains in with your bags at Milan and forgot to pick them up at the other end.'

She didn't need to say any more. I could beat myself up. She was right. When I start letting my friends down, I know my life's starting to spin out of control. I got to my feet. 'I'm sorry,' I said inadequately. 'You're right. You deserve better.'

'Shall we go?'

I nodded. On the way out, Shelley said, 'Sorry, Kate. I can lie to most people, but not to the rest of the team.'

'No need to apologize,' I said. 'I'm the one in the wrong. You better phone Ruth and tell her to meet me at . . . where, Della?'

'Bootle Street,' Della said.

'Oh, and Shelley? I think I might be a while. Better ring Michael Haroun at Fortissimus and tell him I need a rain check tonight.'

I followed Della out to the waiting police car. I knew I was damn lucky not to be under arrest. I just didn't feel like I could risk walking under ladders.

24

It seemed to take longer to recount Richard and Kate's excellent adventure than it had taken to experience it. Asking the questions were Inspector Mellor from the Art Squad, who remembered me from our earlier encounter at Henry's, and Geoff Turnbull from the Drugs Squad, who thankfully owed me one on account of information received in a previous investigation that had provided him with a substantial feather in his cap. Della sat in on the interview, probably to make sure my brief didn't change my mind and persuade me to opt for the Trappist approach.

Even so, by the time I'd answered everyone's questions, it was past midnight. I'd come clean about all of my nefarious activities, on the advice of Ruth Hunter, my nonpareil criminal solicitor and, incidentally, one of the tightknit group of my female friends which Richard refers to as the Coven-ment – witches who run the world. 'After all,' she pointed out drily, 'all your law-breaking took place outside their jurisdiction, and I rather think the Italian police are going to have enough to worry about without bothering you with such trivial charges as assault, kidnap, false imprisonment, burglary, data theft, concealing a body, and failing to report a murder.'

Ruth, Della and I ended up eating steak in one of the city's half-dozen casinos. The great advantage with them is that they stay open late and the food's cheap. It's supposed to act as an incentive to make people gamble. I don't know how effective it is; most of the gamblers that night were Chinese, and none of them looked like a juicy steak was on their agenda. Not as long as the roulette wheels were still spinning. 'Cliff Jackson's still going to want to talk to you,' Della pointed out after we ordered.

'I know. His goons were sitting on my doorstep this morning.'

Ruth groaned. 'What now, Kate? Haven't you broken enough laws for one week?'

'That's not why Cliff Jackson's after me,' I said stiffly. 'It's just that I've been doing his job for him, and now I've tracked down his saboteurs, he probably wants to know who the real murderer is.'

Della and Ruth both choked on their drinks. 'Oh ye of little faith,' I complained. 'Anyway, I want to stay out of his way until I've got the whole thing done and dusted. If I leave the job half done, he'll only mess it up and arrest the wrong person. He's got form for it.'

'Isn't it about time you went back to white-collar

crime and left the police to deal with these dangerous criminal types?' Ruth demanded. 'It's not that
I think you're incapable of looking after yourself.
It's just that you keep involving Richard, and he's
really far too accident-prone to be exposed to these
kinds of people.'

'I don't want to discuss Richard,' I said. 'Anyway,
Della, what have Mellor and Turnbull been doing
for the last forty-eight hours with the info I handed
them on a plate?'

'Luckily, Geoff's already had dealings with his
opposite numbers in Europe about organized drug
trafficking, so he was able to cut through a lot of
the bureaucratic red tape. It turns out his Italian
oppos have been taking a long hard look at Gruppo
Leopardi and its offshoots, so the info you brought
out of there has slotted in very nicely. You were
right, by the way. They've been organizing art
robberies all over Europe, not just in the UK,
and using the art works as payment for drug
shipments,' Della said. 'With the data you stole,
it looks like they'll be able to set up a sting that
will pull in some of the big boys, for a change.'

'What about Nicholas Turner?' I asked.

Della fussed with a cigarette and her Zippo. 'They
found his body in the van, where you left it. A
couple of the lads went over to Leeds this morning
and spoke to his wife. She's denying all knowledge
of anything shady, of course. She's going for the
Oscar as the grieving wife of a legitimate art and
antiques dealer. Grieving she may well be, but

nobody believes for a minute she's as innocent as she wants us to think. Apart from anything else, there's evidence that she's accompanied him on several of his trips to the Villa San Pietro.'

'He still didn't deserve to die,' I said.

Ruth shrugged. 'You take the money, you take the risks that go with it. How many lives have been destroyed by the drugs Turner was involved in supplying? Half the people I defend owe not a little of their trouble to the drug scene. I wouldn't lose any sleep over Turner, Kate.'

I didn't.

Jackson's goons were on my doorstep again the following morning. I figured that by now he'd probably be staking out the office as well. I rang Shelley. 'Have you got company of the piggy variety too?'

'Of course, sir. Did you want to talk to one of our operatives?'

That told me all I needed to know. 'Is it Jackson himself or one of his gophers?'

'I'm afraid our principal isn't in the office at present.'

I'll say this for Shelley, nothing fazes her. 'There should have been an overnight fax for me,' I said. 'Can you stick it in an envelope and have it couriered round to Josh's office? I'll pick it up there.'

'That's no problem, sir. I'll have Ms Brannigan call you when she comes back to the office. Good-bye now.'

Whoever said blondes have more fun obviously didn't garner the experience wearing a wig. I went through the disguise-for-beginners rigmarole again and made my exit through Richard's bungalow, pausing long enough to do a quick inventory of his wardrobe. If he'd been back, he hadn't taken any significant amount of clothing with him. His laptop was gone, though, which meant he was planning to be away long enough to get some work done.

I arrived at Josh's office ten minutes after the fax, and settled down at an empty desk to plough through the phone numbers. It was a long, tedious process of crosschecking, made worse by the fact that Alexis's contact had come up with a more detailed breakdown of calls than the customer receives. The fax she'd <u>sent listed every call</u> from all three numbers, even the quickies that don't cost enough to make it on to the customer's account. But at the end of it, I'd established that there were calls virtually every day between Desmond Halloran's office number and the private number of the Cob and Pen. There were also a couple of long calls from the Hallorans' home number to the pub.

There was one other curious thing. A Warrington number cropped up on both bills. I checked the dates. Every Monday, a call a few minutes long was logged on one bill or another. It appeared most often on Desmond's office bill, but it was there half a dozen times on the Cob and Pen's account too. Of course, I had to ring it, didn't I?

'Warrington Motorway Motel, Janice speaking, how may I help you?' the singsong voice announced.

'I'm meeting someone at the motel today. Can you give me directions?'

'Certainly, madam. Where are you coming from?'

'Manchester.'

'Right. If you come down the M62 and take junction nine, you go left as you come off the motorway and right at the first roundabout. We're the first turning on the left, just after the bridge.'

'Thank you,' I said. 'You've been most helpful.' If I had my way, Janice was going to be a lot more helpful before the day was out.

There was nothing to mark out the Warrington Motorway Motel from the dozens of others that sprang up around the motorway network in the late Eighties. A two-storey, sprawling red-brick building with a low-pitched roof, a car park and a burger joint next door, it could have been anywhere between the Channel Tunnel and that point on the edge of the Scottish highlands where the motorways run out. Rooms for around thirty quid a throw, TV but no phone, no restaurant, bar or lounge. Cheap and cheerless.

Late morning wasn't a busy time behind the reception desk. Janice – or someone who'd stolen her name badge – looked pleased at the sight of another human being. The reception area was so small that with two of us present, it felt intimate. On the way over, I'd toyed with various approaches. I'd decided I was too strung out to try for subtlety. Besides, I still had a wad of cash in my bag that had no official home.

I dropped one of my cards on the desk halfway through Janice's welcome speech. Her pert features registered surprise, followed by an air of suppressed excitement. 'I've never met a private detective before,' she confided, giving me the wide-eyed once-over. I hoped I wasn't too much of a disappointment.

I followed the card with a photograph of Gail I'd persuaded Alexis to lend me. 'This woman's a regular here,' I stated baldly. 'She comes here once a week with the same bloke.'

Janice's eyes widened. 'I'm not supposed to release information about guests,' she said wistfully.

I leaned on the desk and smiled. 'Forgive me being so personal, Janice, but how much do they pay you?'

Startled, she blurted out the answer without thinking. 'A hundred and seventy pounds a week.'

I opened my bag and took out the five hundred I'd counted out on the way. I placed it on the desk and pushed it towards her. 'Nearly three weeks' money. Tax free. No comebacks. I don't even want a receipt.'

Her eyes widened. She stared at the cash, then at me, consternation clear in her face. 'What for?'

'All I want to know is how often they come and how long they stay. I want to know when they're due here next. Then I want to book the room next door. Oh, and five minutes in their room before they arrive. There's no reason why anyone should know you've helped me.' I nudged the money nearer to her.

'It's for a divorce, isn't it?' she said.

I winked. 'I'm not supposed to release information either. Let's just say this pair shouldn't be doing what they've been doing.'

Suddenly, her hand snaked out and the dosh disappeared faster than a paper-wrapped prawn off Richard's plate. She tapped Gail's photograph with a scarlet fingernail. 'She's been coming here with this bloke for about a year now. They always book as Mr and Mrs Chester. It's usually a Wednesday. They arrive separately, usually about half past two. I don't know when they leave, because I go off at half past four.'

I nodded, as if this was exactly what I'd expected to hear. 'And when are they booked in next?'

'I think you've dropped lucky,' she said, consulting her screen. 'Yeah, that's right. They've got a room booked today.' She looked up at me, smirking. 'I bet you knew that, didn't you?'

Again, I winked. 'Maybe you could let me into the room they'll be in, then book me in next door?'

Eagerly, she nodded. Funny how excited people get when they feel like they're part of the chase. 'I'll give you their key,' she said. 'But bring it back quick as you can.'

I picked up the key and headed for the lift. Room 103 was a couple of doors down the corridor from the lift. The whole floor was eerily silent. I let myself in, and gave the room a quick scan. I could have drawn it from memory, it was so similar to every motel room I'd ever camped out in. Because I hadn't been able to get into the office to pick up proper surveillance equipment, I'd had to rely on what I could pick up from the local electronics store. A small tape recorder with a voice-activated radio mike hadn't made much of a dent in my payoff from Turner. I took out my Swiss Army knife and unscrewed the insipid seascape from above the bed. I stuck the mike to the back of the picture with a piece of Elastoplast, then screwed it back on to the wall. There was a gap of about a quarter of an inch between the picture and the hessian wallpaper, but I didn't think Gail and Desmond were there for the décor.

I quickly checked the mike was working, then I was out of there. I returned the key to Janice and went over to the burger joint for supplies. I settled down in my room with a giant cheeseburger, fries, a large coffee and a bag of doughnuts. I stuck the earpiece of the tape recorder in my ear and waited. I couldn't believe myself. I felt like I was playing the starring role in the worst kind of clichéd private-eye drama; staking out the seedy motel for the couple indulging in illicit sex. All I needed was a snap-brimmed trilby and a bottle of bourbon to feel like a complete idiot.

While I was waiting, I rang Michael Haroun. 'Sorry about last night,' I said. 'I was helping the police with their inquiries.'

'They *arrested* you?'

'Behave. They only wanted a friendly chat. They were just a little insistent about having it right that minute.'

'My God, you like to sail close to the wind, don't you?'

'My yachting friends tell me that's where you have to be if you want to travel fast,' I said. What was it about this man that brought out the portentous asshole in me?

'So is this a social or professional call?' he asked.

'Purely social. I wanted to offer you dinner tomorrow as a penance for cancelling yesterday.'

'You cook, as well as everything else?'

'I do, but that's not what I had in mind. How does the Market sound?'

'Fabulous. My favourite restaurant in town. What time?'

'I'll see you there about half past seven,' I promised. To hell with Barclay.

The feeling of wellbeing that I got from talking to Michael didn't last long. There's nothing more boring than sitting around in a featureless motel room waiting for something to happen. Patience and I aren't normally on speaking terms, so I always get really edgy on jobs like this. It's not so bad doing a stakeout in the car; at least I can listen to the radio and watch the world go by.

319

But here, there was nothing to do but stare at the walls.

The monotony broke around twenty past two. My earpiece told me that the door to the next room had closed. At once, I was on the alert, my free ear pressed to the wall. I heard the toilet flush, then, a few minutes later, the door closed again. There was a mumble of what sounded like greetings and endearments, irritatingly incomprehensible. At a guess, they were still in the passage by the bathroom, rather than in the room proper.

More mumblings, then gradually, I could make out what they were saying.

'. . . taking a risk,' a man's voice said.

'You said what I told you to, didn't you?' Gail's voice. Unmistakably.

'Yeah, I told my mother I needed some time on my own, that I was going for a drive and would she look after the kids.'

'And did she act like she thought you were behaving oddly?'

'No,' the man admitted.

'Well, then,' Gail said. There was the instantly recognizable sound of kissing, the groans of desire. 'I needed to see you,' Gail went on when she next surfaced. 'I wanted you so bad, Dessy.'

'Me too,' he said. More of the kind of noises you get in Tom Cruise movies. I half expected to hear 'Take my breath away' swelling in the background.

'We did it, you know,' Gail said exultantly in the

next break. 'We're going to get away with this. Nobody suspects a thing.'

'What about that private eye? You sure she doesn't know anything?'

'Positive. She was just on a fishing expedition, that was obvious. If she'd had anything solid to go on, she'd have let me know. Cocky bitch.'

I wasn't the only one who was cocky. Only I had better reason to be. I checked that the tape was still running.

'Have you seen the news?' Gail asked.

'What news?' Desmond said, sounding nervous.

'About the chemical company,' she said. 'It was all over the *Evening Chronicle* and the local TV news.'

'We haven't had the TV on much. We're supposed to be in mourning,' Desmond said cynically. 'What's been going on? Are they admitting liability?'

'Better than that,' Gail said. 'Apparently, somebody's been trying to blackmail Kerrchem. Product tampering, they said it was. The police have arrested a man and a woman. Hang on, I've got the paper in my bag.' There was the sound of rustling, then silence.

Then Desmond let out a low whistle. 'Fantastic!' he exclaimed. 'The icing on the cake. Nobody's going to look twice at us now, are they?'

Famous last words, I thought to myself.

'Exactly. It's turned out even better than we planned. The police might think I had a motive for wanting rid of Joey, but they're not going to bother digging around in my life when they've got a perfect pair of scapegoats.'

And even though his access to photographic chemicals meant Desmond Halloran could probably get his hands on cyanide without too much trouble, I reckoned the police weren't even going to think about suspecting him while they had Simon and Sandra behind bars. Besides, according to Alexis, the Hallorans were supposed to have an idyllic marriage. No one had an inkling that Desmond Halloran's Wednesday afternoons were spent in a motel room near Warrington.

The smooching noises had begun again. Then Gail said, 'In a year or so, when we've got to know each other because of the court cases we'll be filing against Kerrchem, no one will be surprised when we decide to get married. After all, we'll have had so much in common.'

Desmond giggled, an irritating, high-pitched whinny. Never mind his murderous instincts, that giggle alone should have put any reasonable woman off him for life. 'Talk about coincidence,' he cackled. 'I bet those two blackmailers are sweating.'

After that, things got a lot less interesting for me, though Gail and Desmond obviously thought different. There was a lot of kissing and groaning and embarrassing lines like, 'Give it to me, big boy'. Then they were grunting like a pair of Wimbledon champions. I pulled out the earpiece in disgust. It's not that I'm a prude, but it felt like this pair were shagging in an open grave. I sat patiently on the bed, watching the winking red light on the tape machine that told me it was recording. After an hour, I reckoned I'd got more than enough to nail the scumbags.

It was time to go and play at good citizens.

25

I dumped another oner on Janice's desk. 'You've got an office through the back?' I asked.

She nodded, never taking her eyes off the money. 'I'd like to use the phone there for a couple of minutes. I know you're not supposed to allow customers access to your phone, never mind your office, but if anyone kicks off, tell them I said it was an emergency.' I winked again. Strange how I develop that tic whenever I'm sharing my wealth with the less fortunate.

Janice lifted the access flap at the side of the reception desk and I went through to the tiny office, closing the door behind me. I rang the familiar number of Greater Manchester police and asked for the Stockport incident room. The detective who answered didn't seem very keen to put me through to Inspector Jackson. He told me firmly that anything I had to say to the boss could equally be said to him. Clearly a man desperate for Brownie points. 'I know he wants to talk to me,' I insisted.

'He wants to talk to me so badly that he's had two of his lads sitting outside my house for the last two days.'

'Hold on,' he said grudgingly. 'I'll see if he's free.'

Jackson came on the line immediately. 'At last,' he said grimly. 'Why have you been avoiding me, Miss Brannigan? I thought you were very hot on civic duty the last time we spoke.'

'I'm sorry, Inspector, I've been a bit busy. And I knew you wouldn't be very keen to take me seriously since the last criminals I handed over to you weren't exactly what you were looking for.'

He sighed. 'Cut the smartarse remarks and get to the beef,' he said. 'When are you coming in to talk to me?'

'I rather thought you might want to come to me,' I said sweetly. 'I have something I'd like you to hear. I'll happily play it over the phone, though I don't know how well you'll be able to hear it.'

'If you've been interfering with my case again . . .' he said heavily, letting some unspoken threat hang in the air. I wasn't scared; I've been threatened by experts.

'Just listen, please.' I pressed play and held the speaker of the cassette player up to the mouthpiece of the phone. I'd rewound to the crucial exchange where Gail had conveniently outlined the murder plan. I let the tape run for a few minutes, then clicked it off. 'The voices you just heard are Gail Morton and Desmond Halloran. I've only just made this recording. The pair of them are still in Room 103 at the Warrington Motorway Motel. If you hurry, you might just catch them at it.'

As I replaced the receiver, I heard a splutter of rage from Jackson. Like the man said, I'm into performing my civic duty. I didn't want him to waste time cursing me out when he should be jumping in a motor and shooting over here, sirens blaring and lights flashing.

I thanked Janice politely for the use of her phone and handed back my room key. I went out to the car park and sat in my car. I don't know what I was planning to do if they'd left before the police got there, but I didn't have to make any decisions. A bare twenty minutes after I'd called, a pair of unmarked police cars screamed into the car park. I was impressed. They must have really hammered it.

Jackson jumped out and ran across to my car. He looked as if he wanted to hit me. 'They still in there?' he demanded.

'Present and correct.'

'Wait here,' he commanded.

'My pleasure,' I said.

Jackson went back to his officers and the six of them went into a huddle. After a moment, the only woman there peeled off from the main group and walked across to my car. She opened the passenger door and plonked herself in the seat next to me. 'It's nice to be trusted,' I commented drily.

She grinned. 'After the way you've been giving

him the runaround, just be grateful you're not cuffed to the back bumper of his motor,' she said. 'I'm Linda Shaw, by the way. DC Shaw.'

'Kate Brannigan,' I said.

'Oh, I know exactly who you are, Ms Brannigan. My guv'nor says you've got something for us?'

I watched Jackson lead his troops into the motel. I had a momentary pang of sympathy for Janice. I hoped the six hundred would be enough to make her feel reasonably cheerful about having been had over. Once they'd gone inside, I took the tape out of the recorder and handed it to Linda Shaw. 'I take it this will come under the heading of anonymous tip-off when the case comes to court?'

'I'd imagine so. I don't think giving your agency good publicity is high on my guv'nor's Christmas list. Now, where else would you expect us to go looking for evidence that might strengthen our case?'

I liked Linda Shaw. She spoke my language. None of the bluster or intimidation of her boss had rubbed off on her. Like me, she'd developed her own style, complete with techniques that got quicker results than the heavy-handed approach without alienating everyone along the way. I made a mental note to mention her name to Della. Any woman trying to make it through the male-dominated hierarchy of the police needs all the help she can get. I stared straight ahead and said, 'For it to get as far as murder, this affair must have been going on for a while. I'd have thought the hotel records would indicate how long. So they must have had some means of communication. If I had access to that sort of information, I'd take a long hard look at the phone bills at the Cob and Pen and at DJH Portraits.'

Linda smiled and took out her notebook. As she scribbled a reminder to herself, she said, 'You do realize you're going to have to come back with us and give a full statement this time? Not just about this, but about the Kerrchem sabotage?'

I sighed, resigned to my fate. 'I spent yesterday evening in the nick helping the Art Squad and the Drugs Squad with *their* inquiries. Much more of this, and I'm going to be asking for overtime.'

Linda chuckled. 'You've got more chance of getting it out of your clients than out of our budget. Listen, would you prefer it if I took your statement?'

Another careerist. But this time, it suited me to go along. 'Do you really think Jackson's going to give up the opportunity to make my life seriously uncomfortable?'

Linda nodded towards the door of the motel. A man I took to be Desmond Halloran was stumbling towards the car park, wearing nothing but a pair of jeans and a policeman on each arm. 'I think Inspector Jackson's going to have his hands full with those two. Just thank your lucky stars that from here on in, you're a bit player.'

Next came Gail Morton, more respectable in leggings, scoop-necked T-shirt and the kind of fashion leather jacket that makes you angry on behalf of the cow. Jackson held her firmly by one arm, with the other two officers bringing up the rear. The lovers were each thrust into a separate car, and Jackson came over to us.

'I'll see you back in Stockport,' he said darkly to me, his eyes menacing behind the tinted lenses.

'I thought the police were supposed to be grateful for cooperation from members of the public,' I said airily.

'We are,' he snarled. 'What we don't like is smartarses who think they know how to do our jobs.'

He walked away before I could come up with a snappy rejoinder. Probably just as well. I didn't want to miss tomorrow night's date with Michael Haroun. I started the car and pulled in behind the two police motors. 'If they smash the speed limit on the way back, I want immunity from speeders,' I told Linda.

'You don't have to keep up with them,' she pointed out. 'I do know where we're going, even if you don't.'

'Listen,' I said. 'Your boss is so paranoid about me that if I disappear from his rear-view mirror he's going to put out an all-points bulletin to stop and shoot me on sight for abducting a police officer.'

'You're probably right. He's just brassed off because he was looking at the angle of possible collusion between the two bereaved spouses. Unfortunately, we're handicapped by having to operate inside the law, so we hadn't managed to make as much progress as you,' Linda said ironically.

'Touché. I'll remember that when I'm making my statement.'

'I would, if I were you. Certain of my colleagues would love to have something to charge you with.'

I reached over and pulled my mobile out of my bag. 'I'd better cover my back, then.' Ruth was going to be thrilled. Much as she loved me, holding my hand twice in two days was stretching our friendship more than somewhat.

For the second night running, I was in a police station past midnight. Most of the time had been spent hanging around while Linda Shaw acted as liaison with Jackson, returning every now and again to ask me fresh questions, most of which I didn't have the answers to. No, I didn't know how they met. No, I didn't know exactly what chemicals Halloran had used. No, I didn't know where he bought his chemicals. Eventually, in exasperation, Ruth said, 'Detective constable, do you believe in God?'

Linda frowned. 'What's that got to do with it?'

'Do you believe that my client is God?'

Linda tipped her head back, stared at the ceiling and sighed. 'No, Ms Hunter, I do not believe that your client is God.' Waiting for the punch line.

'Then why do you expect her to be omniscient?

We've been here for seven hours and my client has cooperated fully with you. Now we've reached the point where either you arrest her, or we're going home to bed. Which is it going to be, Ms Shaw?'

'Give me a minute,' she said. She was back in just over five. 'You can go now. But we may have some more questions for Ms Brannigan.'

'And she may or may not answer them,' Ruth said sweetly as we headed out the door.

When I got home, there was still no sign of Richard. I was too wound up to sleep, so I switched on the computer and played myself at snooker until my eyes were so tired I couldn't tell the reds from the black. I staggered off to bed then, only to dream of Gail Morton running naked across green fields pursued by a gigantic white cue ball.

The next morning, I had to deal with the depressing job I'd been avoiding ever since I'd got back from Italy. I drove out to Birchfield Place, noticing that the leaves were starting to fall. I hate the autumn. Not because it heralds winter or symbolizes the death of the year or anything like that. I just hate the way fallen leaves turn to slime on country roads and bring on four-wheel drift as soon as you corner at anything more than walking pace.

It was one of the days the house was open to the public, and I found Henry hiding from the masses in his little office in the private apartments. He didn't look particularly pleased to see me, which I put down to the pile of paperwork threatening to topple over and cover his desk. But the upper classes never let mere irritation interfere with their manners. 'Hello, Kate,' he said, pushing back his chair to stand up as I walked in. 'Good to see you.'

'And you, Henry.' I sat down opposite him.

'Mr Haroun from the insurance company tells me you've been having a rather exotic time lately,' he said. I thought I detected a slight note of reproach in his voice.

'Exotic. Now, there's a word,' I said. 'I'm sorry you heard it from him rather than directly from me, but I've been a bit hectic the last few days, and I thought the main priority was to make sure you could get reinsured at a decent premium as fast as possible.'

'Oh, absolutely, you did quite the right thing. And you must let me have your bill for your trip to Europe. It sounds utterly dreadful, but the one positive thing to come out of it is that Mr Haroun has agreed to pay some of your bill as a quid pro quo for your putting a stop to these burglaries.' All of a sudden, he'd gone motormouth on me.

I looked at him. 'Don't you want to know about your Monet?' I asked.

He flushed. 'Mr Haroun said you hadn't managed to recover it. I . . . I didn't want to remind you of your lack of success in that respect when you'd been so successful otherwise.'

The smell of bullshit filled my nostrils. 'What I didn't tell Mr Haroun is that the painting showed up in the paperwork,' I said. 'What it looked like to me was that the painting had been received by the drug runners, but hadn't yet been swapped for a consignment of drugs.' I sat back and let Henry work that one out for himself. Right from the start, I'd been convinced he was holding out on me, and an idea of why was starting to form at the back of my mind.

'You mean it might still turn up?' he asked. Too nervously for my liking.

'It's possible,' I said. 'But there could be another explanation.'

By now, he wasn't even trying to meet my eyes. 'I'm sorry, I'm not following you.' He looked up, caught my glance and looked away, his boyish smile self-deprecating. 'I'm obviously not as well up in the ways of criminals as you, Kate.'

'You want me to spell it out, Henry? You've been nervous about this investigation right from the start. I worked with you on the security for this place, and I think I got to know you well enough to realize you're not the sort of bloke who gets wound up about something like a burglary where no one's been hurt. So there had to be another reason. I only grasped it some time during the fourth hour of close questioning by the Art Squad. Henry, if what you had nicked off your wall is a Monet, I am Marie of Romania.'

26

There was a long silence after I dropped my bombshell. Henry stared blankly at the papers in front of him, as if they'd inspire him to an answer. Eventually, I said quietly, 'The rules of client confidentiality still apply. You'd be better off telling me what's going on. Then, if what they stole from you does turn up, we're ready with a story to cover your back.'

He glanced up at me quickly, then looked away again. He was pink to the tips of his ears. 'When my parents died, there wasn't a lot of money. I did my sums and realized that with a cash injection, I could make this place work. I was talking over my problem with an old friend who had had a similar dilemma himself. He told me what he'd done, and it seemed like a good idea, so I did the same thing.' More silence.

'Which was . . . ?' I prompted him.

'After I'd had the Monet authenticated for insurance purposes, I took it to this chap my friend knew. He's an awfully good copier of paintings. No talent of his own, just this ability to reproduce other people's work. Anyway, once I had the copy, I sold the original privately to a Japanese collector, on the strict understanding it would never be publicly exhibited.' Henry looked up again, his eyes pleading for understanding. 'I didn't want to admit what I'd done, because the Monet is one of the main visitor attractions at the house. People come here to see the Monet because they're interested in his work, people who otherwise wouldn't cross the threshold. And no one ever noticed, you know. All those so-called experts never spotted the swap.' He perked up as he pointed out his one-upmanship.

'And then when the thieves took the copy, you couldn't own up because that would mean admitting to the insurers that you'd been lying all along,' I said, feeling depressed at the thought of the risks I'd taken over a fake.

'I've been feeling terrible about taking their money under false pretences,' he admitted. 'But what else can I do? If I tell the truth now, they'll never reinsure me, and I'll never get cover anywhere else. I've painted myself into a corner.'

'You're not kidding,' I said bitterly. 'Not to mention putting my life at risk.'

Henry sighed. 'I know. I'm sorry about that. I simply didn't know how to tell you the truth. You've no idea what a weight off my mind it is to have told someone at last.'

'Yeah, well, the Catholics wouldn't have stuck

with confession all these years if it didn't have some therapeutic effect. The thing is, Henry, now I know for sure what I already suspected, I can't sit back and watch you defraud Fortissimus to the tune of seven figures. I've done some hooky things for clients over the years, but this is a few noughts too far,' I said, the iron in my voice matching the anger inside me.

He met my stare at last, panic sparking in his blue eyes. 'You said this came under client confidentiality,' he accused. 'You can't betray that confidence now!'

My first inclination was to say, 'Watch me,' and walk. But I'd got to like Henry. And I believed him when he said he was sorry about the shit I'd been through. Besides, it doesn't do in my business to get a name for selling your clients down the river. 'Henry, this isn't about betrayal. You're making me party to a million-pound fraud,' I said instead.

'But even if it does come out, there will be no suggestion that you knew about it. After all, if you'd known the painting was only a copy, you wouldn't have made such strenuous efforts to recover it,' he argued persuasively.

'But I'd know that I knew,' I said. 'That's the bottom line for me.'

Henry ran a hand through his gleaming hair. 'So what did you come back here for this morning, Kate? To get the truth and then throw me to the wolves?'

His words stung. 'No, Henry,' I told him sternly.

'I hoped you'd tell me the truth, that's true. But I don't want to shaft you. What I think we can do is stitch up a deal.'

He frowned. 'You want a cut, is that it?' Luckily for Henry, he sounded incredulous. If he'd seriously offered me a bribe, all bets would have been off.

'No, Henry,' I said, exasperated. 'What I mean is that I think I can do a deal with the insurance company.'

'You're going to *tell* them I was trying to defraud them?'

'I'm going to tell them what an honest man you are, Henry. Trust me.'

An hour later, I was waiting to see Michael Haroun. I'd taken the time to get suited up in my best business outfit, a drop-dead gorgeous, lightweight woollen tailored jacket and trousers in moss green and grey. This was going to be such a difficult stunt to pull off that I was going to need all the help I could get. Call me manipulative, but this was one occasion where I was willing to exploit testosterone to the full.

I only had to hang on for ten minutes, even though the claims receptionist had warned me he was in a meeting that could take another half-hour. That's the power of hormones for you. Michael grinned delightedly at me, plonking himself down next to me on the sofa. 'What a great surprise,' he said. 'I hope you've not come to call off our dinner date tonight?'

'No way. This is strictly a business meeting,' I told him. I didn't let that stop me brushing my knee against his.

'Right. Well, what can I do for you, Ms Brannigan?' he said teasingly.

'This is all a bit embarrassing, really,' I said.

He raised one eyebrow. Sexy, or what? 'Better get it over with, then.'

I pulled a wry face and tried to look innocent. 'I've just come from our mutual client, Henry Naismith. He's finally got round to clearing out some boxes of papers that were lurking in a dark corner of the cellar at Birchfield Place. And he found something rather disturbing.' I paused for effect.

'Not the Monet, I hope,' Michael joked.

'Not the Monet. What he did find was a bill of sale, and a note accompanying it in his father's writing.' I took a deep breath. 'Michael, the Monet was a fake. Henry's father had it copied a couple of years before he died. He secretly sold the original to a private collector on the understanding it would never be displayed publicly, and the fake's been hanging on the wall ever since.'

I'd never believed the cliché about people's jaws dropping till then. But there was no other way to describe what had happened to Michael's face. 'A fake?' he finally echoed.

'That's about the size of it.'

'It can't be,' he protested. 'We had an expert go over all those paintings when we first insured

Birchfield for Naismith. He authenticated all of them.'

I shrugged. 'Experts can be wrong. Maybe he was misled by the paperwork. I'm told the Monet had an immaculate provenance.'

'I don't believe this,' he exploded. 'We used the leading expert. Shit!' He turned away for a moment. Then, slowly, he swung round to face me. 'Unless we're really talking about your client, not his father.'

He was smart. I like that in a man, except when I'm up against him. I opened my eyes wide, aiming for the injured innocent look. 'What is this, Michael? I come here telling you your company's just saved itself a million quid payout and you're giving me a bad time? For Christ's sake, look at the bottom line here!'

His eyes narrowed. 'You're telling me he's dropping the claim?'

'As far as the painting is concerned, of course he is. He now knows the painting was a fake, he sent me to tell you the painting was a fake. If he was as dishonest as you're trying to make out, he could just have kept his mouth shut and pocketed the readies. Come to that, would he be paying to send me schlepping halfway across Europe in a head-to-head with the Mafia over something he knew was a copy? All Henry wants to do is set the record straight and sort out the reinsurance on what's left of his art collection.'

By now, Michael was scowling. 'And how do

we know the rest of the collection aren't fakes too?'

'They're not. Henry is willing to let you do any tests you want to on the other paintings. Experts, X-rays, whatever. He'll stand by the results. Michael, you owe us a bit of leeway here,' I continued, building up a head of righteous anger. 'If it hadn't been for the investigation Henry instigated, this bunch of robbers would still be emptying your clients' stately homes more regularly than the phases of the moon. Thanks to Henry, that problem has gone away. And now his honesty is saving you a sizeable hole in your balance sheet. Can't you just be grateful for that?'

I watched his eyes as he calculated his way through what I'd just told him. After a few moments, the clouds cleared and he smiled. 'I have to hand it to you, Kate,' he said. 'You are one smart operator. We have a deal. We don't pursue your client for fraud, and we reinsure, subject to more than the usual checks. In exchange for which, your client withdraws his claim in respect of his stolen Monet. Get him to put that in writing, will you?'

I held out my hand. 'Deal.'

Michael shook my hand, holding on to it rather longer than was necessary. 'I do realize I've been listening to *Jackanory*, but this is an outcome I can live with,' he said, needing to end the negotiation in the driving seat.

I let him. I'd got what I wanted. I stood up. 'See you tonight.'

'Half past seven, the Market Restaurant. I'll be there.'

By the time I'd walked back to the office, my brain felt like a bombsite. For once, Shelley took pity on me, leaving me alone to work my way through the pile of paperwork that had accumulated while I'd been roaming the mean streets. After my recent adventures, I was longing to get back to the relative peace of a tasty bit of computer fraud or even some routine process serving.

Alexis rang just before lunch, demanding to know what part I'd played in the dramatic arrest of Gail Morton and Desmond Halloran. Her own researches had come up with how the couple had met. Apparently, Halloran had been doing a portrait of one of Gail's friends and she'd gone along for the session to keep her mate company. It had seemingly been lust at first sight. There was a warning, if I'd needed one, about the consequences of letting physical attraction cloud one's judgement.

In exchange for that nugget, I gave Alexis the lowdown as deep background, and promised her the full story on the drugs-for-art scam just as soon as the various police forces had coordinated their efforts and done their sweep-up of the villains.

When I came off the phone, Shelley wandered into my office with a memo. 'New client,' she said. 'He's got a chain of record shops in the Northwest and his stock seems to be shrinking rather more than it should be. I've set up a meeting for you in the main lounge of the Charterhouse at half past three. OK?'

'Fine,' I sighed. 'Make that the last business of the day, would you? I need some quality time with my bathroom.'

'No problem,' Shelley said. Nothing ever is to her. Sometimes, I hate her.

I walked through the impressive doors of the Charterhouse Hotel at twenty-five past three. The huge red bullshit Gothic building, complete with looming tower, is one of Manchester's landmarks. It used to be the headquarters of Refuge Insurance and occupies a vast block on the corner of Oxford Road and Whitworth Street, bordered on a third side by the brown and sluggish River Medlock. Inside, the decorative glories of Victorian tiling and wood panelling have been left miraculously intact, a monument to a time when labour and materials were cheap enough to make every public building a cathedral to commerce.

I checked at the reception desk, but no one had been asking for me, so I settled down in a chair where I could comfortably see both entrances and where anyone coming in would be bound to see me.

At 3.32, Richard walked in. I breathed in sharply, while my stomach contracted in a cramp. At first, he didn't see me, since he was heading single-mindedly for the reception desk. I had a moment or two to study him. He looked satisfyingly hollow-cheeked, the shadows under his eyes visible even at ten yards. I reminded myself sternly that he probably hadn't been pining, merely enjoying too many late nights on the razz with the rockers. He was wearing Levis and a baggy Joe Bloggs T-shirt under the leather jacket I'd bought him in Florence. As I watched him talk to the receptionist, I felt a pain in my chest.

I saw the receptionist shake her head. He looked around then, and saw me for the first time. I tried to keep my face frozen as our eyes locked. He took an uncertain step in my direction, then stopped.

I stood up and moved a couple of steps away from my chair. It was a Mexican standoff. Shackled by pride and stubbornness, we remained firm, neither willing to be the one to back down. Before the deadlock could set in stone, a familiar voice from behind my shoulder boomed out, 'This isn't *High Noon*, you know. You're supposed to use your gobs.'

I swung round to see Alexis emerge from behind a pillar. 'You bastard,' I said.

'I didn't set this up just to watch the pair of you imitating Easter Island statues,' she complained, walking over to stand midway between us. 'Now, one step at a time, approach.'

By this time, both Richard and I were clearly fighting not to smile. In sync, we moved towards each other. God knows what the receptionists were making of the scene. When only Alexis stood between us, she stepped back and said, 'I'm out of here. Get it sorted, will you? The pair of you are doing everybody's heads in.'

343

I suppose she left then. I wasn't paying attention. I was too busy staring at Richard and remembering all the reasons I felt bound me to this man. Thinking too how right he'd been to resent people's perception of him as a wimp, when actually he's the strongest man I know. He's strong enough to step back and let me get on with my own life, strong enough never to make demands he knows I can't meet, strong enough to understand that our relationship gives both of us what we need without all the crap neither of us wants.

Somebody had to speak first, and I reckoned it might as well be me. 'I missed you,' I said.

'Me too. I'm sorry,' he added, his voice cracking.

'Me too.' I reached out a hand across the space between us. He linked his fingers with mine. 'We need to talk,' I said.

Then he smiled, that cute smile that cut me off at the knees the first time I encountered him in a sweaty nightclub, minutes before he reversed straight into my car. 'Later,' he said. 'Let's book a room.'

Richard was pouring the last of the vodka from the mini-bar into a glass for me when I noticed the time. I hoped Michael Haroun wouldn't still be waiting in the restaurant two hours after we'd arranged to meet. Deep down, I knew I didn't really care if he was. Sure, picking up some business from Fortissimus would have been nice. But being grown-up means recognizing that some prices are way too high to pay.